GHOSTLY KYOTO

87 SUPERNATURAL TALES FROM JAPAN

ÉRIC FAURE

SHAMBHALA

Shambhala Publications, Inc.
2129 13th Street
Boulder, Colorado 80302
www.shambhala.com

For information on the cover art, see page 254.
Interior design: Kate E. White

9 8 7 6 5 4 3 2 1

First Edition
Printed in the United States of America

Shambhala Publications makes every effort to print on acid-free, recycled paper.
Shambhala Publications is distributed worldwide by Penguin Random House, Inc., and its subsidiaries.

LIBRARY OF CONGRESS CATALOGING-IN-PUBLICATION DATA
Names: Faure, Éric author
Title: Ghostly Kyoto: 87 supernatural tales from Japan / Éric Faure.
Description: First edition. | Boulder, Colorado: Shambhala Publications, [2026] | Includes bibliographical references.
Identifiers: LCCN 2025040673 | ISBN 9781645474975 trade paperback
Subjects: LCSH: Ghosts—Japan—Kyoto | Haunted places—Japan—Kyoto
Classification: LCC BF1472.J3 F387 2026
LC record available at https://lccn.loc.gov/2025040673

The authorized representative in the EU for product safety and compliance is eucomply OÜ, Pärnu mnt 139b-14, 11317 Tallinn, Estonia, hello@eucompliancepartner.com.

GHOSTLY KYOTO

To Lydia

CONTENTS

INTRODUCTION

Japan is renowned for many fascinating things, including its ghost stories, which have been told for centuries through novels, paintings, plays, films, manga, and anime. These works contribute to the perception that the Japanese have always been deeply intrigued by death and the supernatural.

This impression is not entirely false. On the eve of the Obon Festival of the Dead, people once indulged in a form of entertainment known as the "Hundred Stories." They would gather in a room illuminated by one hundred lanterns, each taking turns to tell a fantastic story. After each story, a lantern was extinguished, the goal being to summon a supernatural creature when the final lantern went out.

However, the Japanese interest in the supernatural is more than mere fascination. Even if they sometimes deny it, the supernatural is deeply woven into their daily lives.

Ask a Japanese person about ghosts, and they will likely tell you, with utmost seriousness, that they have seen ghosts roaming the streets, or know someone who has.

Ask them about the Obon Festival of the Dead, and they will explain how they celebrate it by placing white dishes laden with offerings on their ancestors' altars, believing their ancestors have briefly returned to the Realm of Human Beings. They will describe how they build small bonfires in front of their homes to guide the deceased back to their dimension on trails of smoke.

Inquire about the house they have just built. Even though such traditions are fading, they might tell you about performing a rite to appease the earth gods before construction began. They will likely mention ensuring the front door does not face the northeast—the Demon's Gate, from which ghosts and monsters are believed to emerge. They might also recount how they called a Shinto priest or a yin-yang master to purify the house and expel any lingering spirits.

Ask locals in Kyoto about the city's history. They will tell you that Emperor Kanmu abandoned two capitals—Heijo-kyo (present-day Nara) and Nagaoka-kyo (present-day Muko and Nagaoka)—because of his fear of Angry Spirits. They will explain that when he founded Heian-kyo (modern Kyoto) in 794, he built Enryakuji Temple in the northeast and instructed its monks to ensure no ghosts or monsters could infiltrate the city.

Marvel at the number of temples and shrines in Kyoto, and locals will likely say, "It's not surprising, considering how many Angry Spirits we've had to placate!"

Ask about their children's education. They might tell you their children will pass their exams because they prayed at Kitano Tenmangu Shrine or another place dedicated to Sugawara no Michizane (845–903), a ninth-century poet who became Japan's most terrifying Angry Spirit after his death, only to be deified as the God of Studies.

Visit Kyoto yourself. You will notice the city is surrounded by mountains, on whose slopes traces of enormous pyres can be seen, shaped like Chinese characters or objects such as doors and boats. These pyres are lit on the night of August 16, marking the end of the Obon festival, to guide the spirits of the dead back to their realms.

Wander the streets of Kyoto, and you will see steles marking the locations of haunted residences. You may visit temples safeguarding cursed artifacts entrusted to monks by their owners for protection. You might find wells said to lead to Hell, and bells whose sounds can supposedly be heard in its depths. You will encounter countless places with histories steeped in ghostly tales.

When you grow tired of exploring the city on foot, ask locals about transportation. They will tell you that Kyoto cab drivers often refuse to take passengers to certain places after dark, such as Midoro Pond. They will warn you to avoid passing through the haunted Kiyotaki Tunnel.

Some may caution you about dangerous bridges. They might say you should not cross Uji Bridge if you are about to marry, as it is haunted by the ghost of a jealous woman. They may also warn you against the bridge on Kyoto's First Avenue, nicknamed the "Bridge of Return," which is strictly avoided for wedding or funeral processions. Wedding agencies and funeral parlors still honor this superstition today, refusing to cross the Bridge of Return to prevent engagements from breaking or ancestors from rising again.

After hearing all this, you will agree that in Japan—and in Kyoto, in particular—ghosts are more than just protagonists of fictional tales. While Japan is indeed renowned for its works of art featuring ghosts, these are not the kind of spirits I wish to introduce. Instead, I want to talk about "real" ghosts—the ones people truly believe in and that are at the heart of rituals and customs still practiced today.

I became fascinated by these ghosts shortly after arriving in Kyoto almost thirty years ago. If you start looking for them, you will find them everywhere! Let me give you some examples. I live at the foot of Mount Daimonji, where every August 16, bonfires are lit to guide the spirits of the dead back to their realm after they temporarily return to earth for the Obon festival. My daughter's kindergarten is located near two temples, Toboku-in and Shinnyodo. At Toboku-in, the ghost of the poetess Izumi Shikibu is said to appear. At Shinnyodo, monks sell "safe-conducts to Paradise" which they make using a seal granted by the King of Hell. Above the front doors of my neighbors' houses, you can spot small clay dolls depicting a Chinese ghost, said to ward off all forms of evil.

The stories behind these traditions can be found in a wide variety of sources: official chronicles, old collections of tales, tourist guides, travel journals, temple and shrine foundation stories, and Noh and Kabuki plays. Because these stories are sometimes told in a fragmentary way—since people in the past knew them well and didn't require detailed explanations—I often had to consult multiple sources to piece them together. This reconstruction sometimes required extensive fieldwork as well.

I have drawn from this rich body of literature to compile these ghost stories. After years of painstaking research, I present them here in a rewritten format that is easier to read and free of footnotes. I felt justified in using this approach because many of these stories were originally transmitted orally, and because guidebook writers and playwrights of the past often adapted them in similar ways.

So here, for your enjoyment, is a unique collection of tales about ghosts, spirits, and all manner of supernatural beings—something rare even in the Japanese language!

PART ONE

THE SIX REALMS

Japan's two great traditional religions have very different views of the afterlife. Shinto (Japan's indigenous religion) teaches that all the dead reside in the same afterlife, without distinction. Buddhism, however, offers a more complex perspective. It asserts that, upon death, individuals either enter Heaven (the Pure Land) or are reborn into one of the Six Realms of Reincarnation, depending on their deeds in life: the Realm of Hell, the Realm of Hungry Ghosts, the Realm of Beasts, the Realm of Fighting Demigods, the Realm of Human Beings, and the Realm of Celestial Beings. The stories in this part focus on ghosts who belong to the second category—the departed souls from the Six Realms. These tales recount how they fell into the Six Realms, became beasts or monsters, and ultimately found a way to be reborn in Heaven.

1 KANCHO'S SPECTACULAR ENTRY INTO THE PURE LAND

Japan's two great traditional religions have very different visions of the afterlife. Shinto (Japan's indigenous religion) asserts that the dead all go to the same place in the afterlife, the Land of the Yellow Springs. Buddhism, on the other hand, distinguishes between the dead and teaches that the celestial cohorts of Amida Buddha descend to earth to welcome the souls of his devotees and escort them to Buddhist Heaven, the Pure Land. Some legends tell that exceptional beings need no such welcoming committee and can reach the Pure Land on their own. Such is the case in the legend of Henjoji Temple, which tells how a monk named Kancho (916–998) entered the Pure Land on his own, under the astonished and awestruck gaze of his young disciple. According to the story, the child witnessed the scene while sitting on a stone he often used as a seat. Since that day, the "disciple's stone" has been believed to grant long life to those who come and sit upon it.

Long ago, there lived a monk named Kancho.

One day in the third year of Eien (989), Kancho built a temple outside the capital, on the edge of a pond called Hirosawa. There, he worshipped the merciful goddess Kannon (Avalokiteshvara in Sanskrit) and taught Buddhism to an ever-growing number of disciples.

Among these disciples was a young boy who was particularly fond of Kancho and followed him everywhere. Each time the old master went to pray on the banks of Hirosawa Pond, this disciple would leave the temple with him, sit on a stone beside him, and watch him with devotion. As a result, the young boy forged a special bond with Kancho and became able to see things usually hidden to ordinary mortals.

On the twelfth day of the sixth month of the fourth year of Chotoku (998), Kancho left his temple and went to pray as usual by the pond. The disciple followed him, sat on his stone as usual, and waited for his master to finish his prayers. But that day, things did not go as usual! The old monk sat down to pray and, quite literally, gave up his soul. The little disciple saw everything. He saw his master's soul leave his body, rise into the air, and perch on the branch of the pine tree that stood on the edge of the pond. The soul rested there for a few moments before transforming itself into a magnificent dragon and continuing its journey to the Pure Land before the disciple's stunned eyes.

"Master!" cried the boy. "Don't leave me!"

The dragon continued its ascent and finally disappeared into the clouds. The little disciple was all alone. Unable to bear it, he walked to the pond and threw himself in. His body was never found.

2 BONFIRES TO SEE OFF THE SOULS OF DEAD ANCESTORS

Buddhism teaches that the souls of dead ancestors return to earth during the month of August. At this time, people celebrate a festival called Obon and prepare to welcome back their dead ancestors. They erect an altar for them and, for the duration of the festival, place offerings of food on it. The Obon festival ends on August 16, and in Kyoto it concludes with the lighting of enormous fires on five surrounding mountains. The pyres are arranged to form shapes such as gates or boats, serving as guides to send the souls back.

Once upon a time, more than twelve hundred years ago, there lived an emperor called Kanmu who was very afraid of those known as the Angry Spirits.

He was so afraid of them that he changed his capital city twice to escape them. Finally, in the thirteenth year of Enryaku (794), Kanmu had a new capital built, which he named Heian-kyo ("Capital of Peace and Safety"). Shortly after settling into his new capital, Kanmu called a meeting of his ministers and told them a tale.

"One day," he began, "the god of Kasuga sculpted a statue representing the Buddha Amida and offered it to men. They asked him why he was giving them this statue. The god of Kasuga replied, 'If you pray to him at the hour of your death, Amida will come and take your soul to the Pure Land!'"

The ministers listened to the emperor, but they didn't understand why he was telling them such a tale. Kanmu went on, "I want a temple to be built at the foot of Mount Niyoigatake. I want the statue of Amida, the one I told you about, to be installed in this temple. In doing so, Amida will protect my capital and ensure that no Angry Spirit or wandering ghost roams its avenues."

Hearing Kanmu speak in such a way, the ministers praised his great wisdom and immediately gave orders. They had a temple built at the foot of Mount Niyoigatake and named it Jodoji, or "Temple of the Pure Land." The temple seemed to have fulfilled its purpose, for in the months and years that followed, there were no reports of any Angry Spirit in the capital.

Alas, one night, a fire broke out in the temple. The flames rose so high into the sky that, wherever they were, the inhabitants of the capital could see them. They all cried out in despair. Suddenly, as they stood lamenting, a miracle happened: The statue of Amida, the one installed in the temple, rose above the blaze, climbed higher and higher into the sky, and disappeared into the clouds!

The next morning, the current emperor, who had inherited Kanmu's throne and his fear of Angry Spirits, summoned his ministers and held a crisis meeting.

"It is a catastrophe!" exclaimed the emperor. "The statue of Amida has disappeared! There is no one left to look after the dead!"

"What about our dead ancestors who return to earth during Obon festival?" added one minister, equally panicked. "Who will show them the way back? If we don't act, the capital will be swarming with Angry Spirits and wandering ghosts!"

"Your Majesty," said another minister, "I may have an idea. I have heard that a monk, a certain Kukai, has just returned from China and learned many astonishing things."

"Fetch me this Kukai!" exclaimed the emperor.

The ministers hurried to fetch the monk and brought him to the palace. Once in the emperor's presence, Kukai was informed of the situation and asked if he had any ideas to solve the problem.

"By rising into the air above the blaze, Amida showed us how to ensure the departure of the dead," Kukai replied. "We must build a huge fire at the top of Mount Niyoigatake. The flames will rise to the heavens and show the dead the way back."

The emperor was overjoyed to hear such words and ordered Kukai to take charge of the operation. On the last day of the Festival of the Dead that year, Kukai and his disciples carried logs to the slope of Mount Niyoigatake facing the capital and arranged them to form the Chinese character meaning "great," 大. At nightfall, Kukai gave the signal, and the monks lit the pyres.

The emperor and the people of the capital saw a huge character appear on the slopes of Mount Niyoigatake. The dead also saw it. Guided by this providential fire, they rose into the air and returned to their realms. Kukai's idea had worked!

Seeing this, the emperor decided to transform these "Fires of Return" into an annual ceremony. This tradition still exists and is celebrated every year on August 16 at the end of the Obon festival.

3 THE DANCE OF THE DEAD

Enryakuji Temple is a Buddhist temple complex located on Mount Hiei, northeast of Kyoto. It was founded in 788 by Saicho (767–822), who later established the Buddhist sect known as Tendai. The temple grounds include 150 halls grouped in three areas: Todo ("East Pagoda"), Saito ("West Pagoda"), and Yokawa. In the latter area stands the Yokawa Chudo Hall, a center of faith devoted to the worship of the bodhisattva Kannon. It is said that one year, the statue of Kannon revered in this prestigious edifice came to life and rescued hordes of dead souls who had gathered in the temple courtyard.

In the summer of a certain year, monks of Yokawa Chudo, one of the halls of Enryakuji Temple, gathered to prepare for Obon, the Festival of the Dead. They cleaned the hall; wiped soot from its walls; and set up offerings before the statue of Kannon, the bodhisattva of compassion. They carried on with their tasks as usual. But that year, one monk made an observation that led his comrades to celebrate Obon in a completely new and unforgettable way.

"We must hurry," he remarked as he polished the ceremonial objects on the altar. "In a few hours, Great King Enma will open the doors to the Six Realms of Rebirth and allow the dead to return to earth."

"In doing so, they will be able to visit their homes," another monk replied. "There, their loved ones will welcome them, say prayers in their memory, and allow them to escape their condition and enter the Pure Land!"

"That's true," added a third monk, "but have you ever thought about the other dead, those who no longer have living relatives on earth? They, too, descend to earth, but they have nowhere to go and no one to intercede with the Buddhas on their behalf to grant them entry into the Pure Land."

These words sent shockwaves through the monks. They had never considered the plight of these wandering dead who had no descendants to welcome them.

"We must do something to help them!" exclaimed the monk who had started the conversation. "Let's invite them to our hall, pray for them, and ask Kannon to take them to the Pure Land."

Moved by their comrade's initiative, the monks quickly gathered before the statue of Kannon and recited prayers to the glory of the goddess.

At that same moment, Great King Enma opened the doors to the Six Realms and allowed their inhabitants to return to earth. Those with living relatives returned to their homes. The others, who had no descendants, also headed for earth but wandered aimlessly, as no one awaited them. Halfway there, however, they heard a gentle, harmonious voice calling out to them and directing them to a mountain.

At Yokawa Chudo, the monks continued to pray. Suddenly, they saw the statue of Kannon open its eyes. Yes, the statue had awakened! It climbed down from its pedestal, left the hall, and stopped in the courtyard. There, it made strange gestures with its hands and muttered incantations whose meaning the monks couldn't understand.

The next moment, the earth trembled and opened, allowing hordes of dead to emerge. Leading the way were the dead condemned to rebirth in the Realm of Hell, followed by the inhabitants of the Realm of Hungry Ghosts, the Realm of Beasts, the Realm of Fighting Demigods, and finally the Realm of Celestial Beings.

A crowd of souls from these realms gathered around the goddess, thanking her profusely, offering flowers, burning incense in her honor, and performing dances symbolizing their respective conditions. The inhabitants of Hell depicted their abominable tortures. The Hungry

Ghosts mimed their eternal quest for sustenance. The Beasts performed a dance of burden and prey. The Fighting Demigods portrayed their endless battles, and the Celestial Beings, despite their enviable state, evoked the inevitable degeneration of their divine forms.

As dawn broke and sunlight touched the courtyard, each soul was enveloped in light and gradually disappeared. For the monks who witnessed this miracle, there was no doubt: These lost souls had not returned to their realms. Kannon had led them to the Pure Land.

4 THE STONE THAT BLOCKS THE ENTRANCE TO THE NETHERWORLD

Tradition holds that the dead return to earth during the Obon festival in August. Legends, however, speak of passages that connect the worlds and allow the dead to return to earth at any time of the year. One such passage is said to lie in the clearing behind Hiyoshi Jinja Shrine. Fortunately, this gateway is now blocked by a stone, whose precise location is not known, and which is called the Stone of Hell. Here's how people came to know of this passage.

A very long time ago, there lived a monk named Shingen (1064–1136), who resided in Shoyobo, one of the halls of Enryakuji Temple.

One warm spring day in a certain year, Shingen descended from the mountain where his temple stood to go on a pilgrimage to Hiyoshi Jinja Shrine. There, he prayed to the god San-o Myojin. After finishing his devotions, he began his return journey. Just as he was about to cross the shrine's great gate, he stopped, amazed. He had just caught sight of a man who looked exactly like his old master Itsuke.

"It can't be my master!" exclaimed Shingen while staring at the man. "My master died three years ago. Still, the resemblance is so striking that I must approach this stranger."

Before he could think further, the man approached him with a big smile and said, "Aren't you my pupil, Shingen? It has been a long time! Don't you recognize me? I'm your old master Itsuke!"

"But that's not possible," stammered Shingen. "You can't be my master. You died!"

"That's true," replied the man. "I died, but I have come back to life. You may not know this, but the god San-o Myojin rescues from Hell all those who have prayed at least once at his shrine. If you don't believe me, follow me."

With these words, Master Itsuke turned and walked toward a clearing called Hachioji, located just behind Hiyoshi Jinja Shrine. Shingen followed him and witnessed the most astonishing sight. He saw dozens of dead people praying to the Buddhas and asking for permission to enter the Pure Land.

"How is this possible?" the monk asked his late master.

"The entrance to Hell is very close to here," Itsuke explained, pointing to a gaping hole in the ground. "The dead use this passage to return to earth and pray to the Buddhas."

This revelation both moved and terrified Shingen. Who wouldn't be frightened to learn that a gateway to Hell lay so close to their home? Shingen wasn't the only one troubled by this. Someone, whose name has not been recorded, was so worried that they placed a large stone over the hole to block the passage forever. It is said, however, that if you press your ear against this stone on the evening of Obon (August 16), you can hear the cries of the unfortunate inhabitants of Hell.

5 THE MONK POSSESSED BY HUNGRY GHOSTS

Buddhism teaches that individuals who were jealous or greedy in a previous life may be condemned to rebirth in the Realm of Hungry Ghosts. In this state, they become human-like creatures with swollen bellies and narrow throats, tormented by an unending hunger for a specific substance or object they can never truly consume. A legend from Kyoto speaks of such hungry spirits. Surprisingly, the story takes place in what is now Nishikikoji Street—a well-known shopping street where one can buy cooking utensils, vegetables, fish, meat, and all the ingredients needed to prepare traditional Japanese cuisine.

A very long time ago, there was a holy man who went by the name of Kiyotoku and lived in the capital with his elderly mother.

One day, Kiyotoku's mother died. He carried her lifeless body to the top of Mount Atago, sat down beside it, and prayed to the Buddhas, asking them to ensure that her soul could be reborn in the Pure Land. He was so devoted to this cause that he forgot to eat and prayed continuously for three years.

One night, he had the strangest dream. In the dream, his mother appeared beside him and spoke to him. "Kiyotoku!" she said. "You can return to the capital now. Thanks to your prayers, I have been able to enter the Pure Land."

Overjoyed, Kiyotoku descended Mount Atago and headed back to the capital. Along the way, he passed a field of onions. Seeing food for the first time in years, he couldn't resist the temptation. He entered the field, pulled up an onion, and ate it. It was delicious! He immediately pulled up another onion, then another, and another.

The field's owner suddenly appeared. "What are you doing in my field?" he demanded.

"I haven't eaten in three years," replied Kiyotoku.

The man, who had a kind heart, thought Kiyotoku must be very poor and said, "If that is the case, help yourself! My field is large."

Kiyotoku didn't need to be told twice. He ate and ate until he devoured every onion in the field! Yet his hunger was not satisfied. Kiyotoku looked around for another field, but there was none.

"Poor wretch!" exclaimed the kind owner, realizing the depth of Kiyotoku's despair. "Come and stay with me. I will give you something to eat."

The man brought Kiyotoku into his house, cooked large quantities of rice, and served him a thousand bowls filled to the brim. Kiyotoku devoured them all in no time!

The owner marveled at this and told his neighbors, who in turn spread the story. Eventually, word of Kiyotoku's insatiable hunger reached the chancellor, Fujiwara no Morosuke, who didn't believe it. Wanting to verify the tale, he invited Kiyotoku to his residence and served him a grand feast. Once again, Kiyotoku devoured every dish placed before him.

Morosuke, astonished, suspected a supernatural cause. It must be noted that Morosuke had an unusual gift—he could see what was hidden from ordinary mortals. As he observed Kiyotoku, he was horrified to see millions of dead spirits from the lower realms of Rebirth—those of Hungry Ghosts and Beasts—clinging to Kiyotoku's back. They were the ones consuming all the food!

"These creatures must have taken advantage of Kiyotoku's weakened state while he was praying for his mother's salvation," thought Morosuke.

After the feast, Kiyotoku wandered the streets of the capital. While walking down a street parallel to Fourth Avenue, he was suddenly seized by an irresistible urge to relieve himself. Though the dead spirits clinging to him consumed the food, it was Kiyotoku who suffered the consequences. Unable to hold back, he expelled an enormous quantity of excrement, splashing the entire area and literally painting the street brown!

Some time later, the emperor passed through this street on a stroll. The stench was so overwhelming that he asked its name.

"Since a recent incident, people have been calling it Kuso Koji, 'the Street of Shit,'" a minister explained.

The emperor was appalled.

"I cannot tolerate such a name in my capital!" he declared. "From now on, this street shall be called Nishiki Koji, 'Street of the Brocade Print.'"

And so, the street was renamed, beginning its transformation into the vibrant culinary center we know today.

6 THE POET WHO BECAME A SPARROW

Buddhism teaches that the deceased may be condemned to reincarnation in the Realm of Beasts, particularly those whose lives were marked by the killing of animals, such as fishermen or butchers. While Fujiwara no Sanekata (d. 998) was not engaged in such professions, it is said that upon his death in exile, he was reborn as a sparrow to find his way back to the capital. His final resting place lies within a temple named Kyoshakuji, or "Temple of the Return in the Form of a Sparrow," a poignant tribute to this extraordinary tale of rebirth and longing.

A long time ago, there lived a famous poet named Fujiwara no Sanekata. One day, Sanekata attended a banquet at the imperial palace. The guests discussed various pleasant topics, but Sanekata remained uninterested until the conversation turned to poetry. Passionate about literature, he joined the discussion and, in his enthusiasm, argued with another guest, Fujiwara no Yukinari, a protégé of the emperor. Disappointed by Yukinari's lack of poetic sensitivity, Sanekata grabbed his headdress and threw it to the ground, shocking the guests.

"Lord Sanekata!" exclaimed the emperor. "You are a poet and should know that poetry often references distant places, such as those in the province of Mutsu. Go and see those places!"

Although elegantly phrased, everyone understood the emperor's true meaning: Sanekata was being exiled to the farthest province from the capital. Sanekata understood too. Stoically, he packed his belongings and departed for Mutsu Province (modern Miyazaki Prefecture). He endured his punishment, convinced the emperor would soon recall him. But days turned into weeks, and weeks into months, with no pardon in sight.

One morning, Sanekata saddled his horse for a ride in a part of the region he had yet to explore. Distracted by dark thoughts, he reached an intersection without noticing a statue of a local god. Failing to pray to the statue, he offended the god, who spooked his horse. Sanekata fell and died instantly.

On the same day, back in the capital, the emperor and his ministers gathered at the Hall of Purity and Freshness to discuss state affairs. Suddenly, a sparrow flew into the room. It circled the astonished ministers, landed on a tray of food, and pecked at it before flying away. The next day, the sparrow returned and did the same thing. This happened every day thereafter.

"This bird visits us daily," the emperor remarked. "It is most unusual. Surely, it is trying to tell us something!"

The emperor was correct—the sparrow was indeed sending a message. But when no one understood it, the bird ceased its visits and found another way to communicate. It appeared in the dream of a monk named Kanchi, known for his ability to decipher hidden meanings. That night, Kanchi dreamed of a sparrow landing beside his bed* and speaking in human language.

"Master Kanchi," the sparrow said, "I am the reincarnation of Fujiwara no Sanekata. Because I was eager to return to the capital, I was reborn as a sparrow. Please pray for the salvation of my soul!"

The next morning, Kanchi awoke to find a small sparrow dead in his temple courtyard. Recalling his dream, he was convinced the sparrow was indeed Sanekata. He buried it and renamed his temple Kyoshakuji, or "Temple of the Return in the Form of a Sparrow," to preserve the poet's story.

* During the Heian period (794–1185), people used to sleep on piles of straw or tatami mats or directly on the ground. For simplicity's sake, we will use the word *bed* to designate the place on which the ancient Japanese slept.

7 THE MAN WHO BECAME AN OX

Seiryoji is a Buddhist temple located in western Kyoto, dedicated to the Buddha—who is known in Japanese as Shaka Nyorai. The temple houses numerous treasures of exceptional significance. Among them is its western gate, the Seimon. Some claim that its nickname, Yotsuashi-mon, derives from the fact that it is supported by four pillars. Others argue that the name should be rendered as "Four-Legged Gate," as it refers to a story about a man who was reincarnated into the Realm of Beasts.

Once upon a time, a very long time ago, there was a boy who lived in the capital with his elderly father.

One day, the boy's father suddenly passed away. Being a devoted son, the boy organized a proper funeral. However, terrified that his father might not enter the Pure Land, he decided to pray fervently to the Buddhas. He went to Seiryoji Temple, located in the west of the capital and dedicated to Amida, guardian of the Pure Land.

At the time, the temple was being rebuilt. To reach the Buddha hall, the boy had to navigate through oxen pulling carts of timber and scaffolding. Once inside, he begged Amida to ensure his father could escape the cycle of reincarnation and enter the Pure Land. He returned to the temple every day, repeating his prayers for seventeen days. At the end of the seventeenth day, the boy returned home and fell asleep. That night, he had the strangest dream. He dreamed that the statue of Amida from Seiryoji Temple appeared in his room, walked to his bedside, and spoke to him.

"Your father," Amida explained in the dream, "was reincarnated in the Realm of Beasts due to the sins he committed in life. He became an ox. In fact, you've seen him every day for the past seventeen days. He is one of the oxen working at my temple. To save him, perform a good deed in his name."

The next morning, the boy woke up, determined to act. Convinced that he had been visited by Amida, he hurried to Seiryoji Temple. There, he carefully observed the oxen working on the site. Finally, he recognized his father in one of the oxen carrying beams for the West Gate's restoration.

"Excuse me, sir," he said to the man guiding the ox. "This animal is my father. Could you sell him to me?"

The man, surprised but touched by the boy's determination, agreed to sell him the ox. Overjoyed, the boy took the ox home, where it rested and regained its strength. Then, without warning, the animal suddenly collapsed and died.

The boy cremated the ox, collected its ashes, and buried them beneath the West Gate of Seiryoji Temple. Once this was done, he returned to the Buddha hall and prayed to the statue of Amida.

"O Amida!" he said. "My father helped build the West Gate of your temple in his reincarnated form as an ox. He performed a good deed and deserves salvation!"

The monks present at the temple were deeply moved by the boy's prayer. They praised his filial piety and reassured him that Amida would surely take his father to the Pure Land. To honor the boy's devotion, they decided to name the West Gate *Yotsu-ashi no Mon*, or "Four-legged Gate." The gate still bears this name today.

8 THE BUDDHIST PAINTING ON A COWHIDE

*According to tradition, the monk Ninkai (952–1046) took great care of a cow, believing it to be the reincarnated form of his mother. When the cow died, Ninkai preserved its hide and painted a Buddhist representation of the universe (*gohi mandala*) on it. He then built a temple to house the painting, naming it Gyuhi-zan Mandaraji, or "Temple of the Mandala and Mountain of the Cowhide." Although Ninkai's original painting has not survived, his temple, now known as Zuishi-in, houses another painting on leather attributed to him.*

A long time ago, there lived a monk named Ninkai, nicknamed "Rain-maker Abbot" for successfully performing nine rain-calling rituals.

One night, Ninkai had the strangest dream. In it, his mother appeared beside his bed and spoke to him.

"My son," said the old woman, "I have just died. As punishment for the sins I committed in life, I've been condemned to the Realm of Beasts. I've been reincarnated as a cow!"

The next morning, Ninkai set out to find his mother's reincarnated form. After examining dozens of cows, he finally found her. He purchased the animal and took it back to his temple, where he cared for it lovingly.

That night, Ninkai had another dream. His mother appeared again and said, "My son, thank you for looking after me in this form. But that is not enough. I need to enter the Pure Land, and to do so, I must accomplish a good deed. Take me to a peasant and ask him to work me like a real cow."

The following morning, Ninkai sought out local peasants and asked them to take the cow and have it work in their fields. Although puzzled by his request, they agreed. The cow labored diligently for years. When it finally passed away, it was filled with a sense of accomplishment.

Shortly after its death, Ninkai had a final dream of his mother.

"My son," she said, "I am infinitely grateful for your efforts. Thanks to you, I've escaped the Realm of Beasts and entered the Pure Land!"

Overwhelmed, Ninkai buried the cow on a nearby mountain, later called Ushio, or "Mount of the Cow's Tail." He preserved its hide and painted a Buddhist depiction of the universe upon it. To honor the cow, he built a temple and named it Gyuhizan Mandaraji, or "Temple of the Mandala and Mountain of the Cowhide."

THE RED SHADOW ON THE TEMPLE WALL

The human beings reincarnated as oxen in the two previous stories find salvation through the efforts of their sons. These stories reveal a key aspect of the Japanese vision of the afterlife: A dead person's stay in one realm is not definitive. It is possible to escape, either by serving one's sentence or receiving outside help. The legend of another temple, Chishaku-in, provides yet another example of this belief.

Once upon a time, a very long time ago, there was a man who lived in the capital and worked as a hauler.

One summer day, a customer hired him to transport merchandise to a certain house. Delighted by the opportunity, the hauler quickly harnessed his ox, loaded the goods onto his cart, and set off. The blazing sun beat down on the city, driving passersby to seek shade. The ox, struggling under the heavy load, suffered in the intense heat. Still, the devoted animal pulled its master's cart tirelessly. As the day wore on and the sun climbed higher in the sky, the ox grew weaker. First, it slowed its pace. Then, as it passed a temple called Chishaku-in, it collapsed, unable to go any farther.

"This is no time to rest!" cried the hauler angrily.

Determined to finish his delivery and escape the heat, he struck the ox with his whip. The exhausted animal tried to rise but failed. Furious, the hauler struck it again, harder this time. Blood spurted from the ox's back, splattering the white wall of the temple. The poor creature let out a human-like moan and died. Hearing this haunting sound, the monks of Chishaku-in Temple rushed outside. They were horrified to find the lifeless ox and bloodstains marring their pristine wall.

"Let's fetch water and clean up these stains!" the monks exclaimed.

They scrubbed the wall, but the bloodstains reappeared. They tried again, but no matter how hard they cleaned, the stains would not disappear.

"Let's repaint the wall," they decided.

The monks brought brushes and white paint, carefully covering the stains. Yet again, the blood reappeared. This time, it formed the shape of an ox. Terrified by this phenomenon, the monks called their abbot. Observing the mysterious stains, the abbot said, "The bloodstains are a message. This ox is the reincarnation of a human being, and it wants us to pray for its salvation. We must ask the Buddhas to help its soul escape its current condition and be reborn in the Pure Land."

The monks, moved to tears, gathered in the prayer hall. Together, they chanted prayers, asking the Buddhas to save the soul of the unfortunate ox. In the end, they decided to preserve the bloodstain on the temple wall as a reminder of their mission to save all beings. They named it Aka-ushi no Kage, or "Red Shadow of the Ox."

To this day, the Red Shadow is said to remain on the temple wall, a silent witness to the compassion of the monks and the salvation of the ox's soul.

10 THE CAT AND THE PAINTING OF THE BUDDHA ENTERING NIRVANA

*Buddhism teaches that animals can be the reincarnated forms of humans and that, with outside help, they can succeed in reaching the Pure Land. One species, however, seems to be an exception: cats. It is said that cats are denied access to Heaven because, when Buddha Sakyamuni was preparing to enter Nirvana and all beings gathered to mourn him, cats remained indifferent, continuing their daily activities. This is why cats are not depicted in traditional paintings of the Reclining Buddha (*nehan-e*), exhibited annually in temples during March. There is one exception: The painting at Tofukuji Temple includes a cat among the gathered beings. Here is the story behind this unique depiction.*

Once upon a time, a very long time ago, there lived a monk named Mincho, who served at Tofukuji Temple.

One day, the shogun, Japan's military leader, visited the temple to pray before the Buddha statues. Mincho guided him to the prayer hall, where the shogun offered his prayers. Impressed by his visit, the shogun donated a large sum of money to the temple before returning to his palace.

"What should I do with this money?" Mincho pondered. After much thought, he decided to commission a painting of the Reclining Buddha. He bought a large silk canvas and began his work, carefully painting the Reclining Buddha surrounded by mourning beings.

Days turned into weeks as Mincho worked. One day, a cat wandered into the room, sat beside him, and watched him paint. Mincho, absorbed in his work, did not chase it away. That night, Mincho had a strange dream. The cat appeared in his room, trotted to his bedside, and spoke in the language of humans.

"When Buddha Sakyamuni lay on his deathbed, all beings gathered to mourn him—except cats," the feline explained. "Because of this, and because my fellow cats sometimes eat Buddhas reincarnated as mice, we are excluded from paintings of the Reclining Buddha. I wish to change that. Please include me in your painting. If you agree, I will help you complete it."

The cat then ran off and returned moments later, carrying a box of paint in its mouth. It placed the box beside Mincho's pillow and vanished. When Mincho awoke, he found the box of paint exactly as it had appeared in his dream.

"If this box is real," he thought, "then the dream must be real too. The cat truly wishes to atone for its species' sins!"

Moved, Mincho approached the temple abbot to explain the situation. "This cat seeks to repent," Mincho concluded. "It wants me to include its image in the painting."

"You know that is not possible," the abbot replied. "No cat has ever been depicted in a painting of the Reclining Buddha."

Mincho pleaded, and eventually, the abbot relented. Delighted, Mincho returned to his work and added the cat to a corner of the painting. As he painted, the real cat returned, watching intently. Stroke by stroke, the feline took shape on the canvas. When Mincho painted the final line, the cat sitting beside him vanished. Alarmed, he ran to inform the abbot of this extraordinary event.

"A miracle of such magnitude deserves to be commemorated," the abbot said. "We will call your work *The Painting of the Buddha Entering Nirvana with a Cat*. Furthermore, we will rename the valley behind our temple Enogu-tani, or 'Valley of the Painting Box.'"

This is how Tofukuji Temple came to possess a unique treasure: A painting of the Reclining Buddha featuring a cat, a symbol of repentance and redemption.

11 THE MONK WHO BECAME A MONSTER

Over time, many halls of Enryakuji Temple were destroyed and never rebuilt. Their existence is commemorated by stone markers scattered across the temple grounds. One such hall, known as Kyokusenbo, or "Pavilion of the Jade Spring," was said to have been outrageously magnificent. Its story features a man condemned to be reincarnated as a yokai.

Once upon a time, a very long time ago, there lived a monk whose name has been deliberately forgotten.

This monk arrived at Enryakuji Temple and constructed a hall for himself. Being fond of luxury, he built it with opulence that contrasted starkly with the temple's traditional simplicity. He named the hall Kyokusenbo, or "Pavilion of the Jade Spring." The other monks were deeply shocked by the extravagance but said nothing. The monk continued to live in his splendid hall until his death. After his passing, no one wanted to live in the hall. It wasn't just its indecent luxury that deterred them. Strange noises and shadows began to emanate from the empty building, convincing the monks that it was haunted by a supernatural entity.

One day, however, a brave and curious monk decided to investigate. He stepped into the abandoned hall and, standing in the grandiose space, recited an improvised poem:

Master of the Pavilion of the Jade Spring! You can
no longer live in this place!
The moon that floats in the night sky has taken
possession of it!
玉の泉も / との主は / 住まずして /
浮の空なる / 月ぞやどれる

No sooner had the monk finished speaking than the ground trembled. It wasn't an earthquake, but a shudder that heralded the arrival of the hall's master. Before the monk's horrified eyes, a creature with a grotesquely elongated neck appeared.

"Do not be afraid!" the creature exclaimed. "I will not harm you. I am the former master of this hall. Because of my unbridled love for luxury, I have been condemned to be reincarnated as a monster. However, your poem has awakened me to the gravity of my sins, and I have now been allowed to enter the Pure Land. I will leave now, but I ask you, Monk, to take good care of this hall. Do not let it fall into ruin."

With those words, the long-necked monster vanished as if by magic. Convinced that the place was no longer haunted, the curious monk moved into the Pavilion of the Jade Spring. He maintained it with great care, fulfilling the final request of its former master.

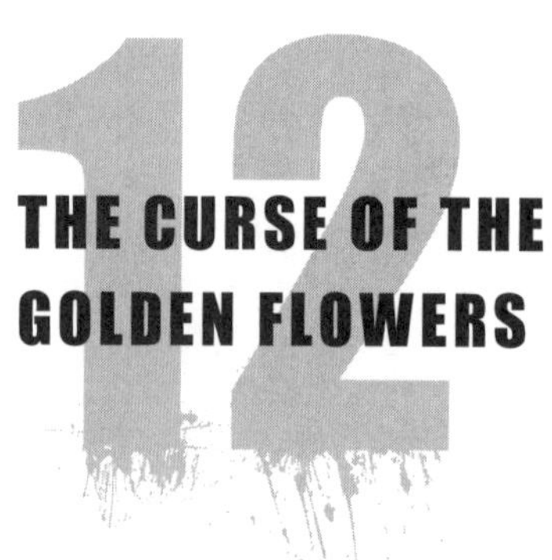

12 THE CURSE OF THE GOLDEN FLOWERS

Some schools of Buddhism teach that "insentient beings"—such as plants, trees, stones, and human-made artifacts—are part of the cycle of rebirth and that people can be reincarnated in the form of a plant. These schools also hold that these so-called insentient beings possess the quality of Buddhahood or Buddha-nature and are therefore capable of attaining enlightenment. The story of two graves near Yawata Municipal Library illustrates this belief. These graves belong to a ninth-century aristocrat and his young mistress. One of them is known as the "Golden Lace Grave" (Ominaeshi-zuka), and here is why.

Once upon a time, a very long time ago, there lived an imperial official named Ono no Yorikaze, who resided near the capital in the village of Yawata.

One day, Yorikaze traveled to the capital, where he caught sight of a beautiful young girl. Captivated by her charm, he approached her gallantly, courting her with elegant manners and words. Seeing that the girl responded favorably, he made her numerous promises and swore to visit her often. Yorikaze kept his word, returning regularly and treating her with great attention. Seduced by his kindness, the young girl began to dream of a future together, hoping he would one day ask her to marry him.

However, Yorikaze suddenly stopped visiting her. Naively, she concluded that he must have fallen ill. Worried for his health, she resolved to visit him at his home in Yawata. When she arrived, she knocked on the door of Yorikaze's house. A woman answered.

"I would like to speak with Lord Yorikaze," said the young girl.

"My husband is not here," replied the woman curtly. She was not naive and, upon seeing the young beauty at her doorstep, immediately understood the situation.

"That cannot be true!" exclaimed the young girl. "If he were married, Lord Yorikaze would never have promised me his love! He would never have sworn to stay by my side forever!"

Hearing these words, the mistress of the house became furious. She ordered the girl to leave immediately and slammed the door in her face. Heartbroken and distraught, the young girl wandered aimlessly along the road back to the capital. Along the way, she came upon a river. Filled with despair, she walked to its bank, undressed, carefully folded her kimono—adorned with delicate patterns of golden lace flowers—with great care, and threw herself into the water.

News of her disappearance reached Yorikaze some time later, and he was overcome with regret. He summoned monks and paid them generously to pray for her salvation, but their efforts were in vain. Still tormented by guilt, Yorikaze decided to visit the place where his young mistress had left her kimono before ending her life. When he arrived, he did not find the kimono—it had long since disappeared. In its place, however, golden lace flowers had sprung up.

"This cannot be!" exclaimed Yorikaze, astonished by the sight of the flowers.

He crouched down and picked a few. To his amazement, other flowers immediately sprang up to replace those he had just taken.

"You've been reborn as a flower, and you do not want me to forget you, is that it?" he stammered, terrified.

Convinced that the girl would never leave him alone, Yorikaze walked to the riverbank and threw himself into the water. Sometime later, a reed sprouted in the spot where he had drowned. Strangely, the reed grew and spread its branches toward the golden lace bush. The sight was both fascinating and unsettling. It was believed that Yorikaze had become a reed to remain eternally close to the reincarnated form of his mistress, fulfilling the promise he had failed to keep during his lifetime.

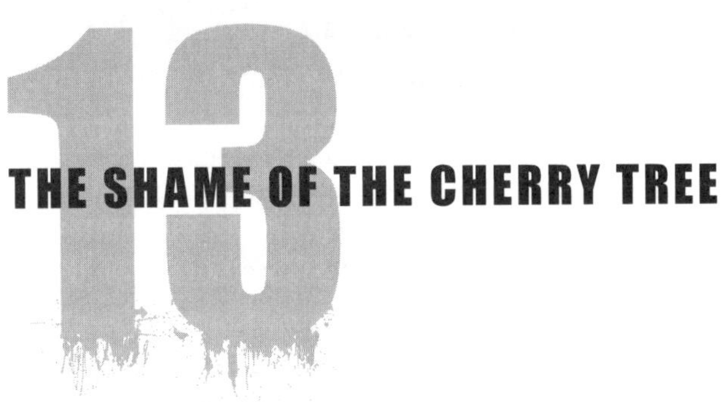

THE SHAME OF THE CHERRY TREE

The legend of Joganji Temple offers yet another example of the belief that plants possess Buddha-nature. This temple is located in a district called Sumizone (literally "Dyed Black") and is known by the nickname "Bokuzenji" ("Temple of the Ink-Black Cherry Trees"). These names stem from a legend about a cherry tree that, reprimanded by a poet for blooming during a time of mourning, produced blossoms as black as ink the following spring.

Once upon a time, long ago, there was a regent named Fujiwara no Mototsune. When he passed away in the spring of a certain year, all the inhabitants of Kyoto mourned his death.

No one grieved more than his old friend, the poet Kamutsuke no Mineo. With a heavy heart, Mineo joined the funeral procession, accompanying Mototsune to his final resting place, a grave a few kilometers south of the capital. After the ceremony, Mineo made his way home. Passing through the small village of Fukakusa, he noticed a temple called Joganji. The doors were open, so he took a casual look inside. There, in the courtyard, stood a cherry tree in full bloom, its blossoms celebrating the arrival of spring with magnificent beauty.

"What insolence!" exclaimed Mineo upon seeing the tree. "Does this tree have no shame, adorning itself in its most splendid finery on a day of mourning?"

Overcome with anger, he composed a poem on the spot:

If the wild cherry tree of Fukakusa has a heart,
let its petals be tinged with black next spring!
深草の / 野辺の桜し / 心あらば /
今年ばかりは / 墨染めに咲け

In the spring of the following year, cherry trees across the capital blossomed gloriously, welcoming the warmer weather—except for the one at Joganji Temple. Its blossoms were black as ink. When the monks awoke at dawn to find their cherry tree blooming in black, they were moved to tears. "Who wouldn't be touched," they thought, "realizing that even trees have hearts?" To commemorate this miracle, they named the tree Sumizome-zakura, or "Ink-Black Cherry Tree."

News of the miraculous tree spread quickly. Curious citizens from Kyoto flocked to Fukakusa to see the Ink-Black Cherry Tree. Among them was the warlord Toyotomi Hideyoshi. After admiring the tree, Hideyoshi called the temple monks and, with a displeased expression, said, "You only commemorated this miracle by naming the tree? Such an extraordinary event deserves more! From this day forward, your temple shall be called Bokusenji, the 'Temple of the Ink-Black Cherry Tree.' Furthermore, you must treat this cherry tree with the utmost respect. Neglect it, and I will punish you!"

Terrified, the monks vowed to care for the tree diligently. Thanks to Hideyoshi's decree, the Ink-Black Cherry Tree has been preserved for centuries and can still be admired today.

14 THE STORY OF ORYU, THE WILLOW SPIRIT

Sanjusangendo Temple houses 1,001 statues of Kannon, the bodhisattva who can assume thirty-three different forms to help sentient beings and guide them toward salvation. Legend holds that if one can find a statue resembling a deceased relative among the 1,001 statues, it signifies that the departed soul has entered the Pure Land. It is said that this temple, built in 1164, used as its main beam a willow tree whose Buddha-nature had been awakened by the actions of a man.

A long time ago, in a remote village in the mountains of Kii Province (modern-day Wakayama Prefecture), there lived a young man named Miura Yoshikatsu. One day, Yoshikatsu went for a walk that led him to the shrine of Mount Kumano. There, he witnessed a curious scene. A wealthy lord stood gesturing angrily at a massive willow tree that towered over the shrine's entrance.

"Fools!" the lord shouted at his retinue. "If none of you can climb this tree to retrieve my falcon, then cut it down!"

Yoshikatsu looked up and saw the cause of the commotion: The lord's falcon had flown into the tree, and its leash was tangled on the highest branch. The lord's retainers, unfazed by the sacred location, prepared their axes to chop down the tree.

"Wait!" cried Yoshikatsu, stepping forward for the first time. "You mustn't cut down this tree—it grows on holy ground. Allow me to retrieve your falcon instead."

The lord glared at Yoshikatsu but allowed him to proceed. Borrowing a bow, Yoshikatsu aimed carefully and fired an arrow, cutting the falcon's leash. The bird flew down and landed on the lord's gloved hand. Without a word of thanks, the lord barked more orders, gathered his retainers, and departed. That evening, Yoshikatsu returned home, content that he had saved the magnificent willow tree. As night fell, he went to bed, only to be awakened by a knock at his door. Curious who would visit so late, he opened it to find a beautiful young woman standing before him.

"My name is Oryu, meaning 'willow,'" she said softly. "If you allow me to stay, I will look after you."

Struck by her beauty, Yoshikatsu eagerly welcomed her into his home. She proved to be an excellent cook and caretaker. Over time, Yoshikatsu developed feelings for her and eventually made her his wife. Nine months later, Oryu gave birth to a son, whom they named Midorimaru ("Greenery").

Meanwhile, in the capital, Emperor Goshirakawa decided to build a temple dedicated to the goddess Kannon. Summoning a group of woodcutters, he gave them an important directive: "I have heard of an enormous willow tree at the entrance to Mount Kumano Shrine. Go and cut it down. Bring it back to the capital, and use it as the central beam of my temple."

The woodcutters acknowledged the order and set off for Kumano. When they arrived, they began chopping down the giant willow tree. Back at Yoshikatsu's home, something strange occurred. Every time the woodcutters swung their axes, Oryu winced and clutched her head in pain. Alarmed, Yoshikatsu asked her what was wrong. At first, she dismissed it as a headache, but as the pain worsened, she finally revealed the truth.

"My dear husband," she said, "do you remember the giant willow tree you saved years ago at Mount Kumano Shrine? That tree is me. I took human form to thank you for your kindness. But now, the emperor has ordered me to be cut down, and no one can oppose his will. I must leave you now. Please take care of our son. Farewell!"

With those words, Oryu rushed out of the house and disappeared before Yoshikatsu's eyes. At the very same moment, the woodcutters finished chopping down the giant willow tree. They pruned its branches, secured it with thick ropes, and prepared to move it. Despite their efforts, they found the tree immovable.

"Evil forces are at work!" one of the woodcutters exclaimed.

Hearing this, Yoshikatsu realized that his wife's spirit was resisting. He hurried to the tree, placed his hand on its trunk, and said gently:

"Do not worry. I will go with you to the capital."

To everyone's amazement, the woodcutters were then able to lift and transport the tree with ease. The journey to Kyoto went smoothly. Once there, the willow was fashioned into the ridge beam of the temple that Emperor Goshirakawa had commissioned. Yoshikatsu stayed in Kyoto, overseeing the construction. When the temple was complete, he sought and received permission to become a monk. In doing so, he remained near the temple and dedicated his prayers to the salvation of his wife's soul.

15 THE FORMER SKULL OF EMPEROR GOSHIRAKAWA

Buddhism teaches that living beings can be reborn into the Realm of Human Beings, granting them the opportunity to perform virtuous deeds and progress toward entry into the Pure Land. Like many other religions, it emphasizes that our actions in this life bear consequences in the next. A story associated with Sanjusangendo Temple offers a vivid illustration of this principle. Every year, on the second Sunday in January, the monks of Sanjusangendo perform a ritual known as the "Blessing of the Willow." During this ritual, they touch worshippers' heads with a willow branch to cure them of their ailments. This custom is said to have originated from an incident that inspired Emperor Goshirakawa to build this temple. It also illustrates an essential point of Buddhist teaching: Actions in this life have consequences—good or bad—in the next.

Once upon a time, a very long time ago, there lived an emperor named Goshirakawa.

One day, in the second year of Eiryaku (1161), Emperor Goshirakawa awoke as usual, attended to his duties, and suddenly suffered a violent headache. At first, he tried to endure the pain, but as it intensified, he summoned his physician. The doctor arrived immediately. He examined him but, to his shame, could not determine the source of the pain. Frustrated, the emperor then summoned yin-yang masters, monks, and healers. All efforts proved futile.

"Since men cannot help me, I must turn to the gods," Goshirakawa declared to his court. "Tomorrow, I will make a pilgrimage to Mount Kumano Shrine and ask the gods to cure me!"

That night, the emperor had an extraordinary dream. Kannon, the bodhisattva of compassion, appeared in his room, approached his bed, and said, "To cure your headaches, you must go to Byodoji Temple, a place dedicated to the Buddha of Medicine."

The next morning, Goshirakawa remembered his dream and announced to his astonished ministers that he would visit Byodoji Temple instead of Mount Kumano Shrine. At the temple, he prayed fervently to the Buddha of Medicine for many hours. Exhausted, he fell asleep. In his sleep, he had another strange dream. This time, an old monk appeared and spoke to him:

"Let me explain the cause of your suffering. In your previous life, you were a monk named Renge who served at Mount Kumano Shrine. You performed many meritorious deeds, which is why the Buddhas granted you rebirth in the Realm of Human Beings as an emperor. However, your earthly remains from that life were not properly buried. Your skull rolled into the waters of the Iwata River, where a willow tree grew through its eye sockets. When the wind blows, the movement of this tree shakes your old skull, causing your current headaches. If you retrieve your former skull and honor it with proper rites, your pain will vanish."

Upon waking, Goshirakawa remembered the monk's words. Convinced of the dream's authenticity, he summoned his most trusted men, explained the situation, and sent them to search for a willow tree growing from a human skull in the Iwata River. After an extensive search, they found the tree, cut its roots, and retrieved the skull. Delighted, the emperor commissioned a sculptor to carve a statue of Kannon and place the skull inside it. The moment this was done, Goshirakawa's headaches disappeared.

Grateful, he ordered the construction of a temple to house the statue. Upon its completion, he named it Zutsu-san Heiyuji Rengeo-in, or "Imperial Hermitage of the Lotus, Temple of Pain Easing, and Mountain of Headache Healing." To commemorate this event, the temple's monks introduced a ritual in which worshippers' heads are touched with a willow branch to cure ailments. This ritual continues today, attracting many who seek healing.

16 THE NAIL-PULLING JIZO

In the previous tale, a monk was reborn as an emperor thanks to the virtuous deeds he had performed in his former life. By contrast, the tale you are about to read features a man who suffers as a result of misdeeds committed in a previous incarnation. His wrongdoing consisted of performing a ritual of black magic, driving nails into a doll made in the likeness of a rival. Fortunately for him, Jizo (Ksitigarbha)—the compassionate guardian of travelers across the Six Realms of Rebirth—intervened and nullified the karmic consequences of the crime committed in his past life. The statue of Jizo responsible for this miracle is the one enshrined in a temple officially named Shakuzoji ("The Stone Statue Temple"), but which, due to the terrible events we are about to recount, is more widely known by its nickname: Kuginuki Jizo, or "Jizo Who Pulls Out Nails."

A long time ago, there lived a wealthy merchant named Kinokuniya Dorin. He owned a large house overlooking Aburanokoji Avenue and several successful shops, allowing him to live comfortably.

Dorin seemed destined for happiness, but everything changed on his fortieth birthday. Though he suffered no accident or illness, his hands began to ache terribly. Despite seeking help from doctors and healers, no remedy worked. His condition worsened to the point where he could no longer work. Dorin's neighbors and customers, moved by his kindness and generosity, frequently visited him to console him. One day, a neighbor offered more than sympathy.

"If human remedies have failed," the neighbor said, "you should turn to the Buddhas. It is said that the Jizo statue at Shakuzoji Temple performs miracles and cures ailments. You should pray there!"

Desperate, Dorin followed the advice. He visited Shakuzoji Temple, prayed earnestly to Jizo, and begged for healing. Exhausted, he returned home and fell into a deep sleep. That night, Dorin dreamt that Jizo appeared beside his bed and spoke:

"You are suffering in your hands as punishment for a terrible deed you committed at the age of forty in your previous life! Driven by hatred for someone, you crafted a straw doll in their likeness and went to Kifune Jinja Shrine at night. There, you placed the doll on a tree and hammered nails into it while uttering the person's name. Because of your actions, the gods misunderstood the true culprit desecrating their sacred tree and instead caused the death of the person whose name they heard. Your hands ache in this life because they are the very hands that committed this heinous act in your previous existence! It is only right that you should bear the consequences of this crime. However, since you came to pray to me, I have chosen to help you. I traveled across space and time to remove the nails you drove into the doll in your previous life. Behold!"

Dorin awoke and immediately returned to Shakuzoji Temple. He told the monks about his dream, recounting every detail of how Jizo had appeared to him, spoken of his past life, and described the removal of the nails. The monks listened intently, their curiosity piqued. To everyone's astonishment, when they approached the statue of Jizo, they discovered two rusty nails lying at its base.

"You weren't dreaming," the abbot said, holding up the nails with reverence. "These are the very nails you drove into the straw doll during your past life. Jizo has traveled through space and time to retrieve them, absolving you of your sin and healing your pain."

As the weight of the abbot's words sank in, Dorin realized that the pain in his hands had completely vanished. His relief was overwhelming, and tears streamed down his face as he knelt before the statue to give thanks. From that moment onward, Dorin's devotion to Jizo was unwavering. He became a regular visitor to the temple, sharing the story of his miraculous healing with anyone who would listen.

Inspired by his tale, neighbors and customers alike began flocking to Shakuzoji Temple to pray to the Jizo Who Pulls Out Nails, seeking healing and redemption for their own ailments and burdens. Over time, the temple's fame grew, and the walls of its halls became covered with ex-votos left by the faithful, each bearing a symbolic representation of the nails and pincers that Jizo had used to help Dorin.

17 MASTER KUYA AND THE THIEVES

To keep them from making the same mistake as the merchant in the previous story, Buddhism teaches people to refrain from committing evil deeds and to take advantage of their rebirth in the Realm of Human Beings to pray to the Buddhas. By doing so, they can ensure entry into the Pure Land and escape the Six Realms of Reincarnation. Throughout the centuries, many monks have dedicated their lives to spreading this message. One such monk was Kuya (903–972), who built a temple called Rokuharamitsuji. Kuya urged his followers to pray to Amida, the guardian of the Pure Land, so they might escape the cycle of suffering and achieve salvation. A famous statue of Kuya, now housed in Rokuharamitsuji's treasure hall, symbolizes this teaching. It depicts the monk with six tiny Buddhas emerging from his mouth, representing the nembutsu chant: Namu Amida Butsu *("I take refuge in Amida Buddha").*

Once, during the time of Kuya, many believed that civilization was nearing its end. Despite these grim circumstances, Kuya tirelessly encouraged people to turn to the Buddhas, particularly Amida, and pray for salvation. The residents of Kyoto adored and respected him, affectionately calling him "the Ascetic of the Markets" for his willingness to preach even in the bustling marketplaces of the capital.

One evening, Kuya returned to Rokuharamitsuji Temple later than expected. By then, the streets of Kyoto were shrouded in darkness, making them unsafe for travelers. Fully aware of the risks, Kuya quickened his pace. As he rounded a corner, a gang of thieves appeared, blocking his path. Armed with weapons, they approached him menacingly.

"Good sirs," Kuya said calmly, "you don't intend to harm me, do you? I am but a poor monk."

His words did not deter the thieves, who drew closer, brandishing their weapons. Faced with their hostility, Kuya began to cry loudly. This unexpected reaction startled the thieves.

"What's the matter, monk?" one of them asked. "Why are you crying like that?"

Kuya wiped his tears and replied, "Since you ask, I will tell you. You were born into the Realm of Human Beings, which is a rare and precious opportunity. Instead of using this chance to pray to the Buddhas and secure rebirth in the Pure Land, you are squandering it by committing evil deeds. I weep at the thought of the suffering that awaits you after death."

The thieves were struck by his words. They suddenly realized who stood before them and felt ashamed of their actions. The leader of the gang dropped his weapon, knelt before Kuya, and pleaded, "Master Kuya, help us! Take us as your disciples and guide us to the Pure Land."

Moved by their unexpected repentance, Kuya agreed. He led the thieves back to Rokuharamitsuji Temple, where he taught them how to pray to Amida and live virtuous lives. Thanks to Kuya's guidance, these men transformed their lives and worked toward earning rebirth in the Pure Land.

18 THE GIRL AND THE BUCKET OF WATER POURED ON JIZO'S STATUE

We have already spoken of Kyoshakuji Temple and noted how it earned its name, "Temple of the Return in the Form of a Sparrow," from the presence of the grave of a nobleman from long ago who was said to have been reborn as a sparrow. The temple is also renowned for its statue of Jizo, the Buddhist guardian of paths and travelers, who is venerated here under the name Oke-tori Jizo, or "Jizo of the Received Bucket." This nickname originates from a well-known story that serves as a cautionary tale about the consequences of one's actions. The story has inspired a famous play that is part of the repertory of Mibu Nenbutsu Kyogen—a form of traditional comic theater conceived by the monk Engaku in the early fourteenth century as a way to communicate Buddhist teachings to the common people. Performances of this play are held annually at Mibu-dera, another prestigious temple dedicated to the worship of Jizo.

Once upon a time, a very long time ago, there lived a young woman named Teruko. She was beautiful and longed for marriage, but she faced a heartbreaking obstacle: She had only three fingers on her left hand, a physical disability that prevented her from finding a husband. Resigned to her fate, Teruko abandoned her hopes of marrying in this life and placed her faith in the next. Each day, when she fetched water from the neighborhood pond, she made a detour to Kyoshakuji Temple. There, she poured a little water on the head of the Jizo statue, hoping to attract its attention, and repeated the same heartfelt prayer: "Jizo, I will never find a husband in this life. I beg you to ensure that in my next life, I am born without a handicap and can marry!"

One morning, as Teruko followed her usual routine, she arrived at the temple and was surprised to find a young man praying fervently before the Jizo statue. She recognized him as Wake Toshikiyo, a local craftsman who lived in the neighborhood with his wife. What she didn't know was that Toshikiyo, like her, was a devout worshipper of Jizo and prayed at the temple every day. Their eyes met, and in that instant, they fell deeply in love. Without hesitation, they exchanged promises of eternal devotion. Overcome by their connection, Toshikiyo returned home and told his wife that he was leaving her to be with Teruko.

The two lovers were overjoyed by their newfound love, but Toshikiyo's abandoned wife was devastated. Heartbroken and humiliated, she fell gravely ill and eventually died of grief. When news of her death reached them, Teruko and Toshikiyo were overcome with remorse for their selfish actions. Seeking atonement, they decided to renounce their worldly desires. Toshikiyo became a monk in a temple, and Teruko became a nun in a convent. They spent the rest of their lives praying for the repose of the soul of the woman they had wronged and never saw each other again.

What became of Teruko afterward remains unknown. Perhaps, through her devotion as a nun, she accumulated enough merit to be reborn as a woman free of disability, allowing her to fulfill her dream of marriage in her next life.

PART TWO

SPIRITS

Old beliefs hold that a person's spirit can leave the body to carry out various acts, often terrible ones. This idea is not particularly surprising, as similar concepts exist in Western traditions. However, in Japan, ancient beliefs go further, asserting that a spirit can emanate not only from the body of a deceased person but also from that of someone still alive. It is said that intense emotions, such as jealousy, can give rise to what is known as an *ikiryo*, or "spirit of a living person." In contrast to ikiryo, there are *shiryo*, or "spirits of the dead." These spirits are often found in places significant to them during their lifetimes or near their former residences. To remain in our realm, they may attach themselves to an object: a piece of cloth, a house pillar, a door, a bell, or even a grave. The stories in this part introduce these two fascinating categories of ghosts and recount how humans have managed to appease them.

19

THE STONE ON WHICH STOOD A WRATHFUL SPIRIT

*From the eighth century onward, the Japanese began attributing their misfortunes to the curse of Wrathful Spirits (*onryo*), high-ranking officials who had suffered unjust deaths and sought revenge by causing natural disasters or epidemics. They believed that the higher the rank of the wrathful spirit in life, the more devastating the curse. To appease these spirits, emperors had prayers recited in their memory, awarded them posthumous promotions, deified them, and constructed shrines for their worship. The most infamous of these Wrathful Spirits was Sugawara no Michizane (845–903), a brilliant scholar and statesman who had been falsely accused of treason. Banished to Kyushu, Michizane died in exile, embittered and unavenged. Following his death, a series of catastrophic storms, plagues, and fires swept through Japan, which many attributed to his vengeful ghost. In an attempt to appease him, Michizane was posthumously deified under the name Tenjin (Heavenly Diety), and shrines were built across Japan to honor him, including the famous Kitano Tenmangu Shrine. One such shrine, Suika Tenmangu ("Shrine of the Celestial God of Water and Fire"), features a peculiar rock in its courtyard, known as the "Stone of Rising into the Sky." It is said that Michizane's spirit once appeared atop this stone, in full view of terrified witnesses.*

More than a thousand years ago, there lived a renowned minister named Sugawara no Michizane, a man of great intellect and integrity. Despite his loyal service, Michizane became the victim of a malicious conspiracy. Falsely accused of a crime he did not commit, he was stripped of his position and exiled to the distant island of Kyushu.

There, in the solitude of exile, Michizane clung to hope. He believed that justice would prevail, and that the emperor would eventually forgive him and restore his honor. But this forgiveness never came. Isolated and disheartened, Michizane died far from the court, his heart heavy with unfulfilled aspirations. At the exact moment of his passing, an ominous darkness fell over the land, as though nature itself was mourning his death. The skies, shrouded in thick clouds, unleashed their fury. For seven days and nights, Japan was battered by relentless wind, torrential rain, and ferocious lightning.

The reigning emperor, Daigo, was deeply unsettled. He feared that these unprecedented calamities were no mere coincidence but rather a manifestation of something far more sinister. Troubled by this possibility, he resolved to uncover the truth. To this end, he summoned a learned monk named Son-i to the palace. Known for his spiritual prowess and deep understanding of the unseen forces that governed the world, Son-i was tasked with identifying the source of these disturbances and determining whether they were indeed linked to the tragic demise of the exiled minister.

Upon receiving the emperor's urgent summons, Son-i wasted no time. He quickly climbed into his cart, taking with him all the ceremonial tools he would need, including a magical sword, and set off for the capital. The storm raged around him, but he pressed forward, determined to fulfill his mission. As they approached the Kamo River, which flowed to the east of the capital, his servants abruptly stopped the chariot. Alarmed, they exclaimed, "The flood has washed away all the bridges! We cannot cross the river!"

The path to the imperial palace was blocked, and it seemed impossible to proceed. Son-i, however, remained undeterred. Resolute, he grasped his magical sword and addressed his servants: "Move the chariot toward the river! I will take care of the rest!"

The servants, though hesitant, obeyed. They guided the ox pulling the cart toward the raging river. Son-i began to recite powerful incantations, swinging his sword through the air with precise, deliberate movements. As his chants echoed, the waters of the Kamo River began to shift and part, creating a clear path through the torrent. With great urgency, the servants pushed the cart across this miraculous passage. But just as they reached the far bank, a deafening voice, like a roar of thunder, resounded from the heavens: "Monk, know that the gods have granted me the right to take my revenge!"

The voice's source became clear as the storm clouds above split open. A spectral figure descended and landed on a rock by the riverbank. Son-i and his servants froze in astonishment. It was none other than Minister Sugawara—his ghost, fierce and imposing, now fully visible in human form. The ghost's presence was as unmistakable as his anger. He fixed his gaze on Son-i and spoke with a voice that seemed to shake the very earth.

"Monk, I caused the Kamo River to flood its banks to prevent you from reaching the palace. But your magic has bested my efforts. Today, I bow to the strength of your power, but do not think my vengeance has ended!"

With those ominous words, the ghost of Sugawara no Michizane ascended once more into the sky and disappeared into the clouds. Instantly, the raging winds, driving rain, and flashes of lightning ceased. Calm returned to the land. The servants, still trembling from the encounter, turned to Son-i with expressions of gratitude and relief: "Master, you've saved the country!"

But Son-i shook his head, his expression somber. "Only for now," he replied. "Minister Sugawara's ghost will return. His anger is unrelenting. I must find a way to appease his Wrathful Spirit and bring him peace."

Son-i spent the following days in deep contemplation, pondering how to put an end to the Wrathful Spirit's rage. Finally, inspiration struck. He decided to build a shrine on the very spot where Michizane's ghost had stood by the riverbank. This shrine, a gesture of reverence and atonement, would honor the minister's memory and acknowledge his suffering. The shrine was completed and given the name Suika Tenmangu, or "Shrine of the Celestial God of Water and Fire," commemorating the elemental forces unleashed by the Wrathful Spirit. This act of devotion appeared to touch Michizane's ghost, for from that day forward, the natural disasters ceased. Peace returned to Japan, and the Wrathful Spirit of Sugawara no Michizane was at last placated.

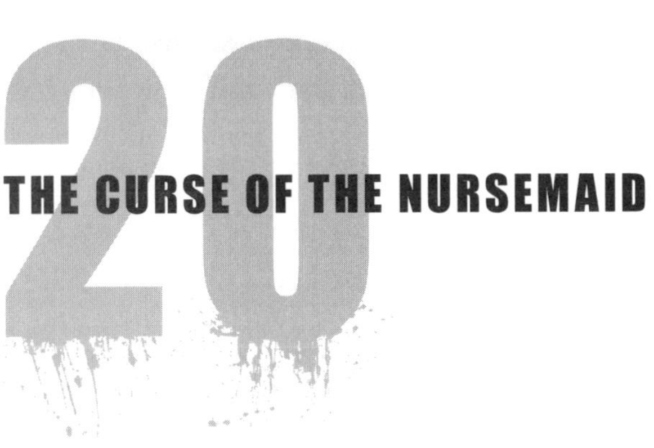

20 THE CURSE OF THE NURSEMAID

The curse of Sugawara no Michizane's Wrathful Spirit was placated in 947 with his deification and the construction of Kitano Tenmangu Shrine in his honor. The people of Kyoto rejoiced, grateful that the disasters wrought by his wrath had finally ceased. Remembering Michizane as not only a great minister but also a renowned poet, they began worshipping him as the God of Study and Calligraphy. But not everyone shared their joy. One woman was so enraged by Michizane's deification that she literally died of anger. Her spirit, it is said, left her body, took refuge in a boulder on a street leading to Kitano Tenmangu, and cursed all who visited the shrine. Much like Michizane, however, her spirit was eventually placated and elevated to divinity, becoming known as the Goddess of the Rock.

Almost eleven hundred years ago, there lived a brave and devoted nursemaid who worked for the powerful Fujiwara family. When the master of the house had a son—the boy who would later become known as Tokihira—this nursemaid was entrusted with his care. She loved him deeply, showering him with affection and raising him with great diligence. Yet, despite her efforts, Tokihira grew up to be a man as cold as he was cunning, consumed by jealousy and malice.

Tokihira's true nature came to light in the first year of Engi (901), when he orchestrated a vile plot against Minister Sugawara no Michizane. Fabricating false accusations, he succeeded in having Michizane dismissed from his position and sentenced to exile. The unfortunate minister, betrayed and disgraced, died in exile, his heart filled with sorrow and bitterness. Upon his death, Michizane's anger transcended the mortal realm. His spirit transformed into an *onryo*, a Wrathful Spirit, unleashing his fury upon the land. First, he claimed the life of Lord Tokihira, then he brought forth a series of disasters—storms, fires, and plagues—on the capital of Kyoto. The terrified populace, desperate to appease him, built a shrine in his honor. This shrine, Kitano Tenmangu, was dedicated to Michizane as the Celestial God of the Kitano Plain.

When the nursemaid learned of this, she was overcome with rage: "You deify a man condemned to exile, yet you neglect the memory of a son of the illustrious House of Fujiwara! How unjust!"

Her fury burned so hot that she literally choked with rage and died on the spot. Her soul, now untethered, rose from her lifeless body and drifted through the air. As she floated, her gaze fell upon a large boulder on the roadside leading to Kitano Tenmangu. She saw her opportunity. Her spirit plunged into the rock, fusing with it, and from that day forward, the boulder became cursed. She cast a spell on all who dared visit Michizane's shrine, hoping to deter worshippers from honoring the man she blamed for her untimely death.

But her efforts backfired. Instead of scaring people away, the rumors of the curse only attracted more worshippers, who flocked to the shrine in ever greater numbers to seek Michizane's protection. The nursemaid's anger deepened. Determined to exact revenge, she devised a new plan. When night fell, she took on the form of a child. In this guise, she wandered the dark streets of the neighborhood, waiting for unsuspecting travelers. At a bend in the road, the ghost-child spotted her first victim: a pilgrim returning from Kitano Tenmangu. She ran after him, leapt onto his back, and terrified him so completely that he died on the spot. Satisfied, she moved on in search of her next target. Night after night, she repeated this horrific act, claiming more victims.

Over time, the nursemaid's spirit became so consumed by her vengeful mission that she forgot the original source of her anger. She began indiscriminately attacking anyone who crossed her path after dark. The people of the district were paralyzed with fear. They refused to leave their homes at night, terrified of encountering the ghostly child. Eventually, their desperation drove them to action. They gathered in a house to discuss how they might rid themselves of the nursemaid's curse.

"It's tragic," one of them sighed. "When she was alive, she was a good woman—a loving nurse who cared for children and raised them with tenderness."

"But now she's a bloodthirsty monster," another replied. "What can we do to stop her?"

"Perhaps," someone suggested, "we should do as we did with Minister Sugawara—build a shrine in her honor and worship her as a goddess. Maybe that will calm her spirit."

The neighbors agreed that this was an excellent idea. Without delay, they set to work. First, they constructed a roof over the cursed boulder, transforming it into a shrine. Then, they began worshipping the nursemaid as a deity, giving her the titles Goddess of the Rock and Goddess of Breastfeeding. Moved by this unexpected reverence, the nursemaid's spirit softened. She abandoned her vengeful ways and embraced her new role as a protector. Devoted to the people who now prayed to her, she took her divine responsibilities seriously, ensuring the safety and well-being of the district's children. It is said that she continues to watch over them to this day.

21 THE FLYING HEAD OF A GREAT WARRIOR

In a room of a modest house in central Kyoto stands a small shrine called Kanda Jingu, or the "Shrine of the Divine Rice Field." At first glance, it may appear unremarkable, but this shrine marks a site with a chilling past: Over a thousand years ago, the severed head of one of Japan's most infamous Wrathful Spirits, Taira no Masakado (d. 940), was displayed here.

Almost twelve hundred years ago, there lived a formidable warrior named Taira no Masakado. Bold and ambitious, he seized control of eight provinces in eastern Japan and declared himself emperor. His reign, however, was short-lived. Forces loyal to the emperor of Kyoto launched a campaign against him, and Masakado was decisively defeated in battle. His severed head was brought back to Kyoto, mounted on a pike, and displayed at a crossroads as a grim warning to anyone who might dare to rebel.

While Masakado's soldiers were captured and thrown into prison to await execution, their plight did not go unnoticed. A compassionate monk named Kuya was moved by their suffering and made an impassioned plea to the emperor to spare their lives. To everyone's astonishment, the emperor agreed and released the prisoners into Kuya's custody. The monk took them to his temple, where he taught them the ways of Buddhism. Under Kuya's guidance, these once-feared warriors became devout followers of Amida Buddha, using their helmets as gongs and chanting, "Namu Amida Butsu" (I take refuge in Amida Buddha), as they marched through Kyoto's streets.

Meanwhile, Masakado's head remained fixed to its pike at the crossroads. Strangely, days passed, yet it showed no signs of decomposition. Even more unsettling, the head would open its eyes and bare its teeth whenever someone mocked or insulted it.

One fateful night, the head, driven by an unyielding desire to reunite with its body, broke free from the pike and soared into the air. It intended to return to the battlefield where its body lay, so that it might reassemble itself and continue its rebellion. However, overestimating its strength, the head soon grew weary. Losing altitude, it plummeted into a rice field in what is now Tokyo's Otemachi district. The local villagers, awed and terrified, recovered the head and buried it in a grave. Out of reverence—and perhaps fear—they built a shrine nearby, naming it Kanda Jingu, or the "Shrine of the Divine Rice Field."

Back in Kyoto, the people initially rejoiced at the news, believing Masakado's Wrathful Spirit had been laid to rest. Their relief was short-lived. The site where his severed head had been displayed seemed to have absorbed its anger and malevolence. One by one, the residents of the district began to suffer strange misfortunes: unexplained illnesses, accidents, and business failures. Family relationships deteriorated, and the neighborhood fell into despair. Desperate for help, they turned to Kuya.

"You performed a miracle by transforming Masakado's soldiers into pious monks," they implored. "Please, do the same for their leader. Appease his curse and restore peace to this district!"

Kuya promised to do what he could. Gathering his disciples, he went to the site where Masakado's head had been displayed. There, he built a small shrine, naming it Kanda Jingu in homage to the one erected in Tokyo. Day and night, he and his disciples prayed fervently for the salvation of Masakado's soul.

Masakado, even in his disembodied state, was deeply moved. First, Kuya had worked to save his loyal soldiers, and now the monk was working tirelessly to save him as well. Overcome with remorse, Masakado repented for the suffering he had caused the people of Kyoto and put an end to his curse. The residents of the district, grateful for the return of peace, began offering prayers at Masakado's shrine whenever they passed by. This tradition continues to this day, ensuring that the once-feared warrior is remembered not with hatred, but with reverence.

22 THE GHOST OF THE WISTERIA PAVILION

It is often said that Sugawara no Michizane, Taira no Masakado, and Emperor Sutoku (1119–1164) are the Three Great Wrathful Spirits of Japan. The latter's curse from beyond the grave was particularly feared, as he was a former emperor and thus a highly potent Wrathful Spirit, who had vowed to plunge the country into chaos and prevent any emperor from regaining power. Legend holds that Sutoku's Wrathful Spirit was partially placated when his former residence was converted into a shrine. Today, this place is known as Yasui Konpiragu Shrine. Due to its unique history, it has become a symbol of severing or forging bonds. Visitors come to pray either for the creation of positive relationships—such as marriage or career success—or for the breaking of harmful ties, such as addiction or toxic relationships. The rituals are performed in a curious manner: Worshippers pass through a hole in a sacred rock. Entering the hole from the front symbolizes forming a new bond, while exiting from the back signifies breaking an old one.

One thousand years ago, there lived a wandering monk named Daien. Hoping to visit Kyoto's renowned temples, Daien left his rural home and journeyed to the capital. By the time he arrived, night had fallen, and he found himself without a place to stay. Exhausted, he wandered through the deserted streets, searching in vain for shelter. Eventually, Daien came upon a grand but abandoned mansion. Weeds had overtaken its once-beautiful garden, and the house stood in a state of ruin. Without questioning why such a fine residence had been deserted,

Daien pushed his way through the overgrowth, entered the house, and settled into one of its rooms. As he was weary from his travels, he quickly fell asleep. A few hours later, he awoke with a start. Standing before him was a ghostly figure.

"Monk, do not be afraid!" the apparition said. "Stay where you are and listen to my story. I am Emperor Sutoku."

At the mention of Sutoku's name, Daien froze in terror. Who would not tremble when confronted by the ghost of a fallen emperor whose anger had shaken the heavens? Yet, fearing the consequences of disrespect, the monk remained still and listened.

"When I was alive," Sutoku began, "I often came to this mansion with my mistress, Lady Awa no Naishi. Here, we withdrew from the world, spending our days admiring the wisteria blossoms in the garden. But my brother betrayed me, usurped my throne, and exiled me to Shikoku. After my death, my spirit became consumed by rage. I sought vengeance against my brother and caused great suffering. Yet, from time to time, I return to this house. Here, among the wisterias, I remember the days of my happiness and feel my anger fade."

With that, Sutoku's ghost disappeared. At dawn, Daien hurried to the imperial court to report what he had seen. He recounted Sutoku's tale to Emperor Goshirakawa and concluded, "The flames of anger in your brother's soul diminish when he visits his old home. If you convert the mansion into a temple and station monks there to pray for his salvation, you may sever the bond of hatred that ties him to this world and put an end to his curse."

Goshirakawa agreed and immediately ordered the Wisteria Pavilion to be transformed into a temple. Monks were installed there, and they prayed ceaselessly for Sutoku's soul. The prayers were apparently effective, for Sutoku's vengeful activities ceased, and peace was restored. Over time, the people of Kyoto began to associate the temple with breaking negative bonds. To this day, Yasui Konpiragu Shrine is visited by those seeking to sever harmful connections or forge positive new ones, continuing the legacy of the Wisteria Pavilion.

THE STATUE THAT EATS PEOPLE

Over the centuries, many efforts were made to placate the Wrathful Spirit of Emperor Sutoku. To calm his wrath, posthumous honors were bestowed upon him, his remains were repatriated to Kyoto and reburied in a new grave, shrines were erected in his honor, and statues were carved to commemorate him. One of these statues, however, has gained a particularly fearsome reputation. Located in the courtyard of Sekizen-in Temple, it depicts Jizo, the compassionate bodhisattva who roams the Six Realms of Rebirth, guiding souls to the Pure Land. Yet this Jizo statue is known as Hito-kui Jizo, or "Jizo That Eats People," and is feared throughout Kyoto.

Nearly 850 years ago, Emperor Sutoku's life took a dramatic and tragic turn. In the first year of Hogen (1156), he was overthrown by his own brother and exiled to the remote island of Shikoku. Enraged by his betrayal and consumed by hatred, Sutoku began transforming himself into a living demon.

He let his hair and nails grow long and unkempt until he resembled a terrifying yokai. Finally, Sutoku cut out his tongue and, using his own blood, inscribed powerful curses and incantations on a scroll. Once his grim task was complete, Sutoku died, his soul filled with vengeance.

Sutoku's Wrathful Spirit quickly began exacting its revenge. First, it claimed the lives of the conspirators who had plotted against him. Then, the spirit unleashed two devastating fires that reduced much of Kyoto to ash. As if that were not enough, an epidemic followed, decimating the population of the capital. The scale of the destruction left the emperor at the time, Goshirakawa, desperate for answers. He convened a group of monks and sought their advice.

"Your Majesty," the monks explained, "these disasters are undoubtedly caused by the Wrathful Spirit of your late brother, Sutoku. His soul has strayed from the path of righteousness and has plunged into the darkness of vengeance. You must guide him back. Build a temple in his honor, carve a statue of Jizo, and ask this compassionate deity to lead Sutoku's spirit to salvation."

Goshirakawa was moved by this counsel and acted swiftly. He ordered the construction of a temple and the creation of a Jizo statue, which was named Sutoku-in Jizo, or "Jizo of Retired Emperor Sutoku." During the temple's inauguration ceremony, prayers were offered, imploring Jizo to lead Sutoku's soul away from anger and toward enlightenment. But things did not go as planned. In the weeks and months following the installation of the statue, new disasters began to strike Kyoto. These misfortunes were even more mysterious and destructive than before. Frustrated and fearful, Goshirakawa summoned a renowned wizard to the palace and asked him to divine the cause of the continuing calamities.

"The problem lies in the name of the statue," the wizard declared. "The name Sutoku-in Jizo sounds too much like Hitokui Jizo—'Jizo That Eats People.' Because of this unfortunate phonetic resemblance, the bodhisattva has misunderstood your prayers. He believes you are asking for more deaths, and so he is inadvertently granting your request!"

Horrified by the revelation, Goshirakawa realized that the curse of Sutoku had not been lifted. Before he could take further action to rectify the situation, however, he passed away. His successors, too, attempted various measures to appease Sutoku's Wrathful Spirit, but it was not until the Meiji era, nearly seven hundred years later, that the curse was finally pacified. In the late nineteenth century, Emperor Meiji had a shrine called Shiramine Jingu constructed and dedicated to the deified soul of

Sutoku. This act, combined with the centuries of accumulated prayers and rituals, finally brought peace to Sutoku's restless spirit.

And what of the infamous statue of Hitokui Jizo, the "Jizo That Eats People"? After Kyoto Medical University was established, the statue was moved to make way for the hospital. It was entrusted to the care of the monks at Sekizen-in Temple, where it remains to this day. Despite its tranquil surroundings, the statue continues to inspire unease among the people of Kyoto. Whispers of its dark reputation persist, and few are brave enough to stand near it for long.

24 THE ANGRY SPIRIT AND PRINCE GENJI'S MISTRESS

Ancient Japanese beliefs held that emotions such as anger or jealousy could give rise to a supernatural entity known as an ikiryo, *or "spirit of a living person," which would torment—sometimes fatally—the individual who had provoked those intense feelings. One of the most well-known examples of an ikiryo appears in the eleventh-century novel* The Tale of Genji, *written by Murasaki Shikibu, in which a woman's jealousy manifests as an ikiryo that ultimately causes the death of her romantic rival. Although this rival is a fictional character, her grave is said to exist and can be found in the inner garden of a house in downtown Kyoto. It is even said that the residents of this house hold an annual memorial service for this unfortunate victim of an ikiryo.*

Once upon a time, very long ago, there lived a prince from the house of Genji, known as Hikaru, "the Flamboyant." He was a contented man who split his time between his wife, Lady Aoi, and his mistress, the "Lady of Sixth Avenue."

One day, Genji decided to pay a visit to his old nurse. He had his servants prepare his cart and harness an ox, for in those days, it was customary for nobles to travel in oxcarts. Once the preparations were complete, the prince climbed into the cart, and they set off for his destination.

Upon arriving, Genji stepped out and looked around. His attention was immediately drawn to the magnificent flowers growing in the garden of the house across from his nurse's. They were moonflowers (*yugao*). Genji also noticed a beautiful young girl in the garden, likely no older than fifteen. The moment he saw her, he fell passionately in love. He nicknamed her "Yugao" and became obsessed with winning her affection.

Genji neglected his wife and mistress, devoting all his time to writing poems for Yugao. Through his persistence, he finally persuaded her to meet him at an abandoned house on Fifth Avenue. On the evening of their meeting, Genji climbed into his cart and was driven to the house. Upon arrival, he instructed his servants to unhitch the ox and wait for him in the garden. Meanwhile, Yugao arrived, and Genji, overjoyed, let her in. They sat together, chatting happily, exchanging promises of eternal love, and eventually fell asleep side by side.

Hours passed . . .

In the middle of the night, Genji suddenly woke up, startled by strange noises. He opened his eyes and was shocked to see a woman standing at the foot of his bed, gazing at him.

"So, this is it!" the apparition said reproachfully. "You no longer visit me because you have a new mistress!"

With those words, the woman vanished before Genji's eyes. Realizing he had witnessed a supernatural event, the prince quickly shook his young companion, still asleep beside him.

"Wake up!" he urged. "We must flee! This place is cursed!"

The girl did not respond. She was dead. Genji then remembered the apparition he had just seen. The woman who had appeared—he knew her! It was his mistress, the Lady of Sixth Avenue!

"She must have suspected I was abandoning her for someone else, and her jealousy must have taken form," thought the prince. "It became an ikiryo, a 'spirit of a living person,' and came to kill her rival in love."

With this realization, Genji called for help. His servants rushed over, and upon seeing Yugao's lifeless body, they understood that a terrible tragedy had occurred.

"Master," they said, "you are a married man. You cannot stay here. Go home quickly! We will take care of everything."

Convinced, the prince left, and his servants wrapped Yugao's body in a carpet and took it to Toribeno, a moor where, at the time, it was customary to leave the dead. They then informed Yugao's parents.

To ensure their daughter's salvation, the family erected a grave in the garden of their house. On the anniversary of her death, they began a tradition of summoning a monk to recite prayers. Over the centuries, successive owners of the house continued to honor Yugao's memory, and this tradition persists to this day.

25

THE CURSED FIELD OF THE LADY OF GION

The dead can appear in the same form as when they were alive (which will be discussed in the next part), but their spirit (called shiryo, or "spirit of a dead person") can also take up residence inside a place or object (cloth, pillar, door, bell, grave) and remain there, for better or for worse. This was the case of an eleventh-century noblewoman who became legendary as the "Lady of Gion." It is said that upon her death, her spirit lingered on the site of her former residence, and even after her house vanished, her vengeful spirit continued to cast a terrible curse on anyone who dared to take possession of the field. It is also said that the nearby Amida-do Temple and the stone marker beside it were constructed to appease her wrathful spirit.

Once upon a time, a very long time ago, there lived a noble lady whom everyone called the Lady of Gion because she lived near Gion Shrine (now Yasaka Jinja Shrine).

One day, the retired emperor Shirakawa (1053–1129) made a pilgrimage to Gion Shrine, and by chance, he caught sight of the Lady of Gion. As soon as he laid eyes on her beauty, he fell madly in love with her, and from that moment on, he regularly visited her. The Lady of Gion attributed her happiness to the gods, and to show her gratitude, she built a chapel in her garden and placed a statue of Amida Buddha there.

When she died, the locals remembered how joyful she had been in her home. In homage to her, they decided to bury her in the garden of her estate. Time passed, and with no one to take up residence, the house of the Lady of Gion gradually fell into ruin and finally disappeared from the landscape. All that remained was a piece of land, which the locals called "the lady's field."

People sought to take over the field to either build homes or cultivate it. However, those who attempted to do so mysteriously fell ill and suffered terribly until they abandoned their plans. There was no doubt in anyone's mind: The field was cursed, haunted by the spirit of the Lady of Gion, who would not allow anyone to settle on the site of her house.

Not far from this cursed spot stood a temple called Sorinji. One day, a young boy from outside Kyoto entered the temple to study and become a monk. In his spare time, the boy developed a habit of walking around the neighborhood. During one of these walks, he stumbled upon "the lady's field." There, he spotted a stone that caught his eye with its beauty, both in shape and color. The boy reached out, picked up the stone, slipped it into his pocket, and returned to the temple.

That night, the young monk fell ill. He developed a fever that worsened as time passed. He cried out in distress, waking the other monks who rushed to his bedside. They found him in a pitiable condition. Hours turned into days, and his health continued to deteriorate. Ultimately, he teetered between life and death.

"What is happening to you?" his friends asked. "What have you been doing?"

"I don't know," the young monk replied. "It all started when I returned from my walk. First, I felt unwell, then the fever began."

The monks pressed him further, asking where he had been walking. The boy described the streets and places he had passed through. When he mentioned "the lady's field," his friends grew alarmed.

"Did you do anything there?"

"No . . . Well, I just picked up a stone and put it in my pocket."

"It is the curse of the Lady of Gion! She has made you sick because you took a stone from her!"

Upon hearing this, the young monk became terrified.

"If I don't return her property immediately," he exclaimed, "she will kill me!"

To the astonishment of his friends, he got up, left the temple, and walked toward the cursed field. There, he returned the stone and begged the Lady of Gion to end his curse. The moment the stone touched the ground, the young monk's fever vanished as if by magic!

26 THE CURSE OF MASTER KUKAI'S CALLIGRAPHY

To convey the idea that to err is human, the Japanese might say, "Even the monk Kukai makes mistakes with his paintbrush." This expression is rooted in an incident that occurred over twelve hundred years ago, when Kukai (774–835), a revered monk, was commissioned to repaint the tablet of Otenmon (the "Gate of Obedience to Heaven"), the main entrance of the imperial palace. It is said that some impudent individuals dared to criticize Kukai's calligraphy, and as a result, they paid a steep price—victims of the curse of his vengeful spirit. The gate where this tale is set has long since vanished, but a replica, built in 1895, still stands today as the entrance to Heian Jingu Shrine.

Long ago, during the reign of Emperor Saga, an incident occurred in the tenth year of Konin (810) that greatly distressed the sovereign. While strolling along the wall of his palace, he noticed that the inscriptions on the tablets of the four southern gates had faded almost beyond recognition. Time and the elements had worn away the once-pristine calligraphy.

Deeply displeased, Emperor Saga returned to the palace and convened his ministers, issuing them the following command: "The inscriptions on the southern gate tablets are no longer legible. These gates hold great symbolic significance, and only the finest artist will suffice to restore their dignity. I have decided that the monk Kukai shall undertake this task."

The ministers, well aware of Kukai's reputation, readily agreed. Renowned for his mastery of calligraphy, Kukai had studied the art in China and was celebrated for his extraordinary skill. Tales of his remarkable abilities abounded, with some claiming he could paint on water or compose poetry while simultaneously wielding five brushes—one in each hand, each foot, and even his mouth.

Kukai was summoned to the palace without delay and entrusted with repainting the inscriptions. He first restored the tablets of the three smaller gates, demonstrating his unmatched precision and artistry. Finally, he ascended a ladder to repaint the characters *O-ten-mon* (応天門)—"Gate of Obedience to Heaven"—on the tablet of the main gate. When his work was complete, the ladder was removed, and all present marveled at the beauty and perfection of his calligraphy. At that moment, an aristocrat began to laugh derisively, pointing at the calligraphy. His peers, taken aback by his rude behavior, asked what the matter was.

"It's just that," the aristocrat replied with a smug grin, "your virtuoso has forgotten a stroke in the character *o* (応)!"

The ministers looked up in alarm and, to their dismay, saw that he was indeed correct: The character was missing a stroke. Ordering the ladder to be brought back, they prepared to correct the mistake.

"No need for the ladder!" exclaimed Kukai, dipping his brush back into the ink. With a flick of his wrist, he tossed the brush into the air. It landed precisely on the tablet, completing the character with the missing stroke. The mocking aristocrat's laughter stopped, and he too began to praise Kukai's talents.

From that point forward, Emperor Saga and his successors took great care to protect the inscriptions painted by Kukai. Yet, despite their best efforts, the weather gradually took its toll, and over time the calligraphy faded and disappeared. Concerned, Emperor Murakami summoned the greatest calligrapher of his time, Ono no Michikaze, to restore the inscriptions.

Upon examining Kukai's faded calligraphy, Michikaze, with a haughty air, pointed at one of the gates and exclaimed, "This gate is called Suzakumon, the 'Gate of the Red Bird,' but I can barely recognize its name in this dreadful scribble! The character for 'red' (朱) looks more like 'rice' (米). It seems Master Kukai meant to write 'Rice Bird Gate'!"

After making this disparaging remark, Michikaze climbed the ladder and repainted the characters on the gate's tablet. Once finished, he descended and announced that he would return another day to finish the other gates. He then went home. That night, Michikaze experienced a strange dream: A giant appeared before him, towering so high that its head seemed to vanish into the clouds. The giant placed a foot on Michikaze's head and pressed down.

"Who are you? What have I done to offend you?" cried Michikaze in terror.

"I am a servant of Master Kukai," the giant intoned.

Michikaze awoke with a start, realizing it had been a dream. The next morning, he returned to the palace to repaint the remaining tablets. Afterward, he confided in a palace acquaintance about his unsettling dream.

"You have brought upon yourself the wrath of Master Kukai's spirit by mocking his calligraphy," his friend said. "Kukai's anger has reached beyond the grave, and one of his servants has come to teach you a lesson!"

Terrified, Michikaze lived in constant fear of Kukai's curse. As he aged, he suffered from painful hands that rendered him unable to hold a brush. At court, it was widely believed that his illness was a consequence of Kukai's curse. Many years later, a calligrapher named Fujiwara no Yukinari was commissioned to repaint the southern gates of the palace. Unlike Michikaze, Yukinari was careful never to speak ill of Kukai and even laid flowers at his statue, hoping to stay in the good graces of the master calligrapher.

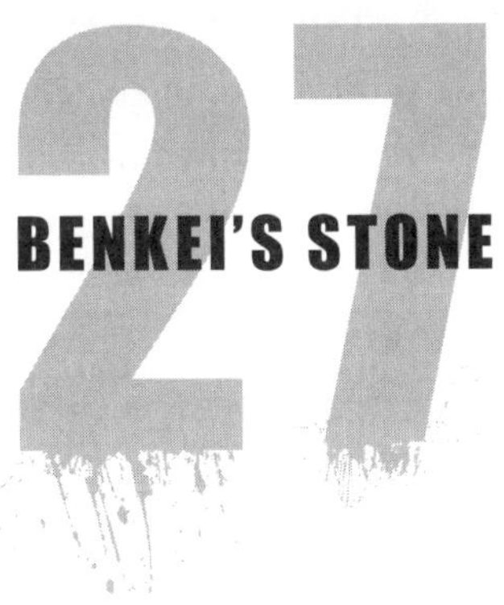

27 BENKEI'S STONE

As many stories show, when a person dies, their spirit can sometimes leave their body and take refuge in an object. Often, this is to cause harm, but not always. One notable exception is the stone that stands by the roadside on Kyoto's Third Avenue, which, according to tradition, shelters the spirit of the legendary warrior Musashibo Benkei. Far from being feared, this stone has long been revered by locals. Until recent times, parents would bring their sons to the stone, asking Benkei's spirit to bless them with the strength and courage for which he was famed.

More than eight hundred years ago, there lived a boy named Benkei, who spent his early years studying at Enryakuji, the great temple on Mount Hiei. Benkei, however, was not an ideal student. Instead of dedicating himself to the sacred scriptures, he preferred to roam the forest during the day, playing pranks on his classmates. At night, he would sneak out of the temple and head into the bustling city of Kyoto to amuse himself in its lively streets. Before setting off on his nightly adventures, Benkei would often sit for a while on a particular stone by the side of the road. Over time, he developed a fondness for this stone, thinking of it as "his" stone. It became a part of his routine, and he grew attached to it.

One day, torrential rains struck Kyoto, causing the Kamo River to overflow its banks. The raging waters swept away homes, temples—and Benkei's beloved stone. The following evening, when Benkei went into the city, he was dismayed to find the stone missing. Distraught, he set out in search of it. After much effort, he discovered it four kilometers from its original location, near the entrance to a temple called Kyogoku-dera. Relieved to have found it, Benkei was, however, delayed in returning to Mount Hiei.

His absence did not go unnoticed. When he finally made it back to the temple, the abbot reprimanded him harshly for his tardiness and expelled him from Enryakuji. Banished, Benkei sought a new purpose in life and eventually entered the service of Minamoto no Yoshitsune, one of Japan's greatest warriors. He fought alongside Yoshitsune with unwavering loyalty. When fortune turned against them, the two men fled and sought refuge with Fujiwara no Hidehira, lord of Hiraizumi Province. But their peace was short-lived. After resuming their journey, they were ambushed, and both perished.

When Lord Hidehira learned of their deaths, he was filled with regret for not having protected them. Seeking to honor their memory, he called a meeting of his vassals to discuss how best to pay tribute to the two fallen warriors.

"I wish to commemorate these great men," Hidehira said. "What can we do to honor them?"

"My lord," one vassal suggested, "I have heard of a stone in Kyoto that Benkei cherished. We could bring this stone to Hiraizumi and pay tribute to him through it."

Hidehira found the idea excellent and sent his most loyal retainers to Kyoto to retrieve Benkei's stone. After a long journey, they returned with it, and Hidehira placed it in his garden. Every day, he prayed before the stone, asking it to protect his province. Remarkably, during Hidehira's lifetime, Hiraizumi was spared from both natural and human disasters. However, trouble began after Hidehira's death, when the stone was neglected. No one came to pray to it anymore, and the stone grew sad. Eventually, its sadness turned to resentment. In the first year of Kyoroku (1528), the stone began to moan.

"I want to go back to Kyoto!" it cried.

The people of Hiraizumi ignored the stone's pleas. Frustrated by their indifference, the stone decided to teach them a lesson. Shortly afterward, a terrible epidemic swept through the region, claiming countless lives. The survivors, bewildered by the devastation, began to wonder what had caused such suffering.

"I know the cause!" exclaimed an elderly man who remembered the old ways. "It is not the gods who are punishing us. It is Benkei's stone! It has brought this plague upon us because we neglected it and refused to heed its wishes."

Horrified by this revelation, the people resolved to set things right. They decided to return the stone to Kyoto as it had asked. The bravest among them undertook the task of transporting it.

Legend has it that the moment the stone was reinstalled at the entrance to Kyogoku-dera Temple, the epidemic came to an abrupt end. The people of Kyoto, delighted by the return of Benkei's stone, welcomed it with reverence. Remembering the tragedy that had struck Hiraizumi, they took great care to honor it. For generations, it became a cherished custom to bring male children to the stone and pray for Benkei's spirit to grant them strength and bravery. This practice continued well into recent times, keeping the legend of Benkei's stone alive.

28 THE GATES THAT WEEP AT NIGHT

The second object in Kyoto believed to be inhabited by the souls of the dead is a gate. This gate, known as Hyakutataki no mon ("Gate of a Hundred Blows"), now stands at the entrance of Kannonji Temple, but it originally belonged to the prison of Fushimi-Momoyama Castle. Legend holds that it shelters the spirits of prisoners who did not survive the traditional beating administered to new arrivals. It is also said that until a monk finally put an end to their torment, their moans could be heard every night.

Nearly four centuries ago, a chancellor named Toyotomi Hideyoshi maintained order and security with ruthless efficiency. He arrested troublemakers and imprisoned them in the Fushimi-Momoyama Castle dungeon. His zeal overwhelmed the prison guards, who eventually complained about their workload.

"My lord," they pleaded, "you send us more prisoners than we can hold! No matter how many we execute to make room, it's never enough!"

Hideyoshi listened carefully. "I understand," he replied. "Here is what you will do: For every new prisoner, tie him to the prison gate and beat him a hundred times with a cane. If he survives, release him."

The guards, relieved by this directive, carried it out eagerly. Each new captive was tied to the prison gate, subjected to a brutal beating, and released only if they survived. The gate soon gained infamy in the capital, where it was dubbed Hyaku-tataki no mon, the "Gate of a Hundred Blows."

The punishment continued until the dismantling of Fushimi-Momoyama Castle. Its stones, beams, and even its infamous gate were repurposed to repair Kyoto's war-damaged temples. The monks of Kannonji Temple received the gate as a gift to replace their own war-destroyed entrance. Grateful for this donation, they installed the gate, unaware of its dark history. Their relief was short-lived. Not long after, a parishioner approached the monks with an alarming tale.

"The other night," he began, "I passed by your temple and heard cries of pain. I looked around, but no one was there. Then I realized—the sounds were coming from your gate! It was weeping and groaning like a human being!"

The monks reassured him, dismissing the sounds as mere wind. But similar stories soon emerged from other visitors, filling the monks with unease.

"What if the cries are real?" they asked themselves. "What if the gate is truly haunted?"

The abbot, observing their growing fear, decided to act. "Do not worry," he declared. "I will keep watch tonight and uncover the truth."

That evening, the abbot stationed himself in the courtyard. As night fell, the gate creaked open, emitting sounds that froze him in his tracks. They were not mere creaks, but moans of agony—human cries of pain. Tears welled up in the abbot's eyes as he realized the gate was haunted by the tormented spirits of those who had perished under Hideyoshi's decree.

"These are the souls of the prisoners who died under the cane!" he exclaimed. "Their suffering binds them to this gate. We must release them!"

The abbot retreated to the temple's prayer hall, where he devoted a hundred days to intense prayers, beseeching the Buddhas to guide the lost souls to the Pure Land. On the final day, he approached the gate. This time, as night fell, the gate remained still and silent. The abbot knew then that his prayers had been answered—the souls had found peace, and the gate was freed from its spectral burden.

29 THE GHOST IN THE BELL OF HOKOJI TEMPLE

In the belfry of Hokoji Temple hangs a bell that stands 4.2 meters tall and weighs eighty-two tons—one of the three largest bells in Japan. Beyond its immense size, this bell is famous for a more unsettling reason: It is said to house the spirit of a woman whose likeness sometimes appears on its bronze surface.

Nearly four hundred years ago, a warlord named Toyotomi Hideyoshi, known for his extravagant tastes, decided to embark on a grand project. In the fourteenth year of Tensho (1586), he announced his intention to build a magnificent temple and erect a colossal statue of the Vairocana Buddha. Hundreds of workers were enlisted for the project, and, remarkably, the construction was completed in under three years. Pleased with this achievement, Hideyoshi personally presided over the inauguration ceremonies and named the temple Hokoji, meaning "Temple of Great Compassion."

But fortune is fickle. Not long after its completion, a devastating earthquake struck the region, reducing the temple to ruins. Undeterred, Hideyoshi immediately ordered the temple's reconstruction. However, he did not live to see it completed, as his life came to an end before the work was finished. His son, Hideyori, took over the task, overseeing the final stages of the temple's restoration. As part of the reconstruction, Hideyori commissioned the creation of a new bell for the temple. He instructed a monk to engrave auspicious phrases, meant to symbolize peace and prosperity, on its bronze surface. Among these phrases were four characters that read, "land and homes, peace and tranquility." The inscription expressed Hideyori's sincere wish for a future free of disaster.

Yet this seemingly benevolent gesture sparked an unexpected fury. Tokugawa Ieyasu, who had by then become Japan's supreme ruler, learned of the bell's inscription and reacted with outrage.

"What insolence!" he thundered upon hearing the report. "The characters for 'peace and tranquility' include my own name. This phrase could be interpreted to mean, 'Ieyasu dismembered, peace on the land.' This is an unforgivable insult!"

Fueled by anger, Ieyasu declared war on Hideyoshi's family. His forces stormed their castle, slaughtered its occupants, and drove Hideyoshi's widow, Lady Yodogimi, to commit suicide. Still not content, Ieyasu turned his ire toward Hokoji Temple itself. He ordered his soldiers to destroy the offending bell, determined to erase what he perceived as an affront to his authority. When the soldiers arrived at the temple, they were met by the frantic abbot and his monks. Terrified, the monks pleaded with the soldiers to turn back.

"Why are you so afraid?" asked the leader of the soldiers.

"Our temple is haunted!" the abbot replied. "Whenever anyone approaches the bell to ring it, the ghost of a woman appears. She stands beside the bell-ringer, watching his every move. It is as though she is guarding the bell and ensuring no harm comes to it."

The leader of the soldiers dismissed the story as a fabrication. Sensing his disbelief, the abbot urged him to inspect the bell for himself.

"Come with me," the abbot said. "I will show you what we have seen."

The abbot led the soldiers to the belfry and directed their attention to the surface of the bell.

"Look closely," the abbot instructed. "Examine the area near the four characters that have offended Lord Ieyasu."

The soldier approached the bell and noticed a faint white mark on its surface. Leaning in for a closer look, he realized with a start that the mark was not random—it was the image of a woman's face. To his astonishment, the face bore an uncanny resemblance to Lady Yodogimi.

"Do you see now?" the abbot asked. "Lady Yodogimi's spirit has come to guard this bell. She cannot allow it to be harmed, for this temple was built by her husband and restored by her son. To destroy the bell is to invite her wrath. Can you imagine the consequences?"

The soldier, shaken by the abbot's words and the sight of the ghostly image, hurried back to report to Ieyasu. After listening to the account, Ieyasu, too, grew uneasy.

"We cannot risk invoking the curse of this ghost," he concluded. "I rescind my order."

Thus, the bell and the temple were spared from destruction. To this day, the mysterious white mark resembling a long-haired woman remains visible on the bell's surface, a haunting reminder of the legend that saved Hokoji Temple.

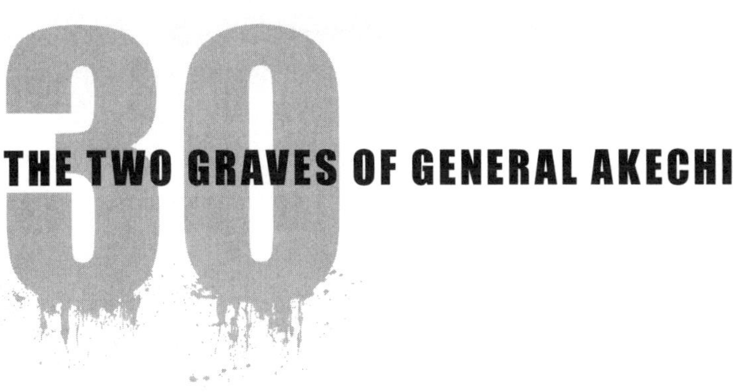

30 THE TWO GRAVES OF GENERAL AKECHI

*Graves, unsurprisingly, are places where the souls of the dead may appear—for better or for worse. Such is the lesson drawn from the legends surrounding the two burial sites of the traitorous general Akechi Mitsuhide (1526–1582). Located in the heart of Kyoto, the first grave holds his severed head and was, for many years, a popular site of prayer for those suffering from headaches (*Akechi Mitsuhide no tsuka*). The second grave contains his body and lies within a thicket known as the Akechi Grove (*Akechi no yabu*), a place that long inspired dread among local residents.*

Akechi Mitsuhide was a general who served Oda Nobunaga, one of Japan's most powerful warlords. On June 21, 1582, Mitsuhide betrayed Nobunaga by attacking Honnoji Temple, where his lord was residing. Forced to commit seppuku, Nobunaga died, leaving Mitsuhide as Japan's new leader. But Mitsuhide's triumph was short-lived.

Three days later, he was ousted and fled Kyoto with a small band of followers, attempting to reach his castle at Sakamoto in the neighboring Omi Province. On his way through a bamboo forest, villagers ambushed him, piercing his side with a spear. Blood sprayed onto the bamboo, staining it red—a color it is said to retain to this day.

Mortally wounded, Mitsuhide asked his soldiers to help him perform seppuku. They obeyed, and after his death, they severed his head to keep it from enemy hands. They hid it in the bamboo grove before retreating.

Later, villagers found the head and delivered it to the authorities, who displayed it on a spike at Awataguchi, a gateway to Kyoto. Eventually, a relative of Mitsuhide, a flute player living in the Umemiya district, retrieved the head and buried it in his garden. Initially, the neighbors feared the grave, avoiding it at all costs. But one day, a man plagued by chronic headaches approached it.

"I've suffered these headaches for years," he prayed aloud, "and no one can cure me. You, who have lost your head, might understand my pain. Please help me."

To his astonishment, the headache vanished immediately. Grateful, the man spread word of the grave's miraculous power. From then on, the locals viewed the grave not with fear, but as a place of healing.

Meanwhile, the owner of the bamboo grove where Mitsuhide had died faced his own ordeal. Night after night, he and his family were disturbed by ghostly sounds—the thunder of invisible horses galloping through the forest.

"They're the spirits of Akechi and his men," he concluded. "Their horses are still trying to carry them to Sakamoto Castle! "

Unable to endure the hauntings, the man turned to the village monks. "I'll give you my bamboo grove," he offered desperately, "but you must free these spirits!"

The monks accepted the grove and held a ceremony to pray for Akechi and his men. They begged the Buddhas to guide the restless spirits to the Pure Land. Their prayers seemed to work, for the ghostly gallops ceased. The grove became peaceful, and the owner's family was finally able to sleep soundly once more.

31 THE LANTERN OF THE TEA MASTER

Daitokuji, a temple of the Rinzai Zen school in Kyoto, is renowned for its tranquil sub-temples. Among these is Jukoin, celebrated for the beauty of its main hall, its tea pavilion, and a particular stone lantern in its garden. According to tradition, this lantern marks the grave of the legendary tea master Sen no Rikyu (1522–1591). It is said that Rikyu's spirit resides within the lantern, and by placing an ear against its stone, one may hear the faint sound of him practicing tea ceremony.

Nearly four centuries ago, there lived a boy named Sen no Yoshiro, the son of a merchant from the prosperous town of Sakai. Yoshiro did not follow in his father's footsteps. Instead, he entered Daitokuji Temple in Kyoto and became a monk, taking the name Sen no Rikyu. While studying sacred scriptures, Rikyu became fascinated by the art of tea ceremony, which was immensely popular at the time. His dedication to the craft elevated him to the status of a master, and he became the tea instructor to none other than Toyotomi Hideyoshi, the most powerful man in Japan.

Yet, Rikyu and Hideyoshi clashed over their differing philosophies of tea ceremony. Their first dispute occurred when Hideyoshi, seeking to display his wealth, built a gilded tearoom in his castle and asked Rikyu to host a ceremony there. Rikyu refused, declaring that such opulence was antithetical to the refined simplicity that defined his art.

After leaving Hideyoshi's castle, Rikyu sought solace on the slopes of Mount Funaoka, accompanied by his closest disciples. Though he concealed it well, Rikyu was deeply troubled. Defying Hideyoshi could have dire consequences, and he feared the repercussions. As he walked, lost in thought, his gaze fell upon a weathered stone lantern. Perhaps it had stood there for centuries, unnoticed amid the wilderness, waiting for this very moment. Struck by its presence, Rikyu admired the lantern for a long time before turning to his disciples and saying, "Look carefully at this lantern. Remember it well, for when I die, I want it to serve as my tombstone."

His disciples, alarmed by their master's ominous words, promised to honor his wishes. Little did they know how soon they would be called upon to fulfill that promise. Tragedy struck a few months later when the abbot of Daitokuji commissioned a statue of Rikyu and installed it above the temple gate to honor him. When Hideyoshi learned of this, he was outraged.

"The abbot knows I visit Daitokuji regularly!" Hideyoshi bellowed. "Does he expect me to pass beneath the statue of a man who is beneath me in rank? This is an insult! Rikyu must pay with his life!"

A messenger was dispatched to deliver the grim verdict. On the twenty-eighth day of the second month in the nineteenth year of Tensho (1591), Rikyu obeyed the order, performing the ritual suicide of seppuku. His severed head was displayed on the First Avenue Bridge, a chilling reminder of Hideyoshi's authority. Rikyu's body, however, was entrusted to his disciples, who buried him in the garden of Jukoin. Remembering their promise, the disciples retrieved the lantern from Mount Funaoka and placed it atop Rikyu's grave as his tombstone. It was then that they heard it:

Shaka, shaka.

Startled, they searched for the source of the sound but found nothing.

Shaka, shaka.

The faint noise continued. It resembled the sound of a whisk stirring matcha in a tea bowl.

Shaka, shaka.

"It's coming from the grave!" exclaimed one of the disciples.

Placing his ear against the stone, he confirmed it. The sound of Rikyu's tea whisk echoed faintly from within the lantern. Even in death, Sen no Rikyu continued to practice his beloved tea ceremony!

32 THE STATUE WITH GROWING HAIR

Because of their appearance, dolls are perhaps the objects most naturally associated with souls. This association can be forged for purposes of black magic by crafting a doll in the likeness of a romantic or political rival. Such was the case in the story of the merchant Kinokuniya Dorin, who suddenly began to suffer pain in his hands because, in a previous life, he had created a doll in the image of a rival. This kind of association could also be used for healing purposes, allowing one's ailments to be transferred onto a doll made in one's likeness. The practice is still observed in certain shrines, where worshippers write their names on paper dolls and blow upon them in hopes of transferring their afflictions and receiving healing. It is said that a monk named Danzei (1550–1613) formalized this logic of assimilation by carving a statue in his own image and embedding strands of his hair into it. The operation appears to have succeeded, for this unusual statue is now venerated under the name Uegami no Sonzo, or "The Venerable Statue with Growing Hair," and continues to draw worshippers to Kochidani Amidaji Temple, where it remains on display.

Almost six hundred years ago, a monk named Danzei established a temple in the mountains north of Kyoto. Known as Kochidani Amidaji, or "Amida Temple of Kochidani," the site became a haven for those seeking spiritual guidance. Danzei devoted himself to spreading the teachings of Amida Buddha, the guardian of the Pure Land. His sermons attracted large crowds, and many chose to study under his mentorship. One day, Danzei gathered his disciples and made an extraordinary announcement.

"I intend to become a Buddha with my actual body," he declared. "To achieve this, I will retreat to a cave and gradually stop eating."

His disciples were devastated.

"Master," they pleaded, "if you leave us, who will guide us along the path to enlightenment? Without you, how can we hope to reach the Pure Land?"

Moved by their anguish, Danzei paused to consider their concerns.

"You are right," he admitted. "Before I go, I must leave you with a guide—someone who can offer you the wisdom and comfort you need."

After much thought, Danzei found a solution. He sculpted a statue in his own likeness and attached two strands of his hair to its head, affixing them near its ears. The statue, he explained, would serve as their guide in his absence. Once the figure was installed in the main hall of Kochidani Amidaji, Danzei retreated to a cave, where he undertook the ascetic practices that would allow him to transcend this world and become a Buddha with his living body. Weeks passed, and the inevitable occurred: Danzei attained Buddhahood. Though saddened by their loss, his disciples found solace in the statue he had left behind. Then, something extraordinary happened.

The strands of hair that Danzei had attached to the statue began to grow. Slowly but unmistakably, the figure's head became covered with hair. Witnessing this miracle, the disciples were overcome with joy. To them, it was proof that their master's spirit remained among them, guiding them from beyond. They redoubled their prayers to the "Venerable Statue with Growing Hair," which they believed now embodied Danzei's enduring presence. To this day, the statue remains in Kochidani Amidaji's prayer hall, a symbol of faith and a testament to the extraordinary bond between Danzei and his disciples.

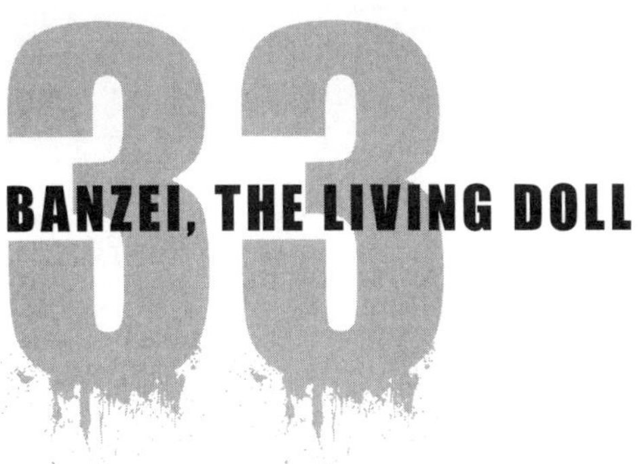

33 BANZEI, THE LIVING DOLL

The two stories we have just explored reveal that certain individuals, such as monks or yin-yang masters, possess the remarkable ability to infuse inanimate objects with a form of life. However, other legends suggest that a far simpler method can achieve the same result: showing deep affection toward an object. Through this consistent care and love, the object's latent Buddha-nature can awaken, granting it life. An extraordinary example of this phenomenon is on display at Hokyoji, a temple better known in Kyoto by its evocative nickname, Ningyo-dera, or "Doll Temple." This object is a doll named Banzei which, for reasons we are about to recount, came to life and continues to patrol the temple's corridors to this day.

Nearly four hundred years ago, there lived a princess who adored dolls. Among her many possessions, one doll held a special place in her heart. It was called Banzei and represented a little girl. The princess loved Banzei dearly, spending countless hours sewing clothes and crafting toys for her.

One day, the princess made a life-changing decision: She would leave the palace, renounce her worldly life, and become a nun at Hokyoji Temple. She abandoned her luxurious possessions, but one thing she could not leave behind was Banzei. Unable to part with her beloved doll, she brought it with her to the nunnery. Banzei, deeply moved by this act of devotion, came to life that very evening. She climbed down from the cushion where she had been placed, approached her mistress, and spoke in the voice of a child: "Princess! To thank you for your endless kindness, I will serve you. By day, I shall help you with your chores. By night, I will carry a lantern and patrol the corridors in your stead."

The princess, astonished but touched, gladly accepted Banzei's offer. The doll kept her promise and worked tirelessly, assisting her mistress during the day and patrolling the temple at night. Banzei faithfully served the princess until the day of her mistress's death.

Some time later, another princess arrived at Hokyoji to take vows as a nun. She moved into the same quarters once occupied by Banzei's beloved mistress. The doll, still seated on her cushion, observed the newcomer carefully. When she felt sure the young woman was kind and worthy, Banzei came to life once again.

"Good evening," Banzei said, startling the new nun. "My name is Banzei. If you wish, I can help you with your duties at the convent."

Although initially shocked, the nun quickly recovered and replied, "I would be greatly honored by your assistance."

Delighted, Banzei resumed her role. By day, she helped with chores, and at night, she took her lantern and patrolled the temple corridors. In time, Banzei met the other nuns and carefully explained her presence. Each time, she found the right words to reassure them. Eventually, every nun in the convent came to know of Banzei's existence and pledged to keep her secret.

However, one person remained unaware: the Mother Superior. One fateful evening, while Banzei was making her rounds, lantern in hand, the Mother Superior happened upon her in the corridor. Startled and outraged, she cried out, "What is this monstrosity? A doll walking the halls? An inanimate object must remain inanimate!"

Overcome with anger, the Mother Superior lunged at Banzei, seized her, and smashed her to the floor. The noise drew the other nuns from their rooms. They found Banzei's lifeless body in pieces. Distraught, they gathered the fragments, painstakingly glued them back together, and returned Banzei to her cushion.

"We have done all we can," one nun said sorrowfully. "But will it be enough?"

"Mistreated objects often harbor an angry spirit," another nun warned. "What if Banzei turns into a monster and seeks revenge on the Mother Superior?"

The nuns knew the danger was real. Stories of objects transforming into vengeful creatures to punish their tormentors were common in their traditions. They deliberated at length and finally decided on a solution.

"We should hold a special religious ceremony in Banzei's honor," one nun proposed.

The others agreed wholeheartedly. They assembled in the prayer hall and recited sutras for Banzei's peace and forgiveness. Their prayers seemed to work, for the Mother Superior was never haunted or harmed by supernatural forces. While Banzei refrained from seeking revenge, the experience left her wary of humans. She became more sensitive and, at times, displayed a willful streak. Even today, Banzei is known to show her displeasure by removing the kimono she has been dressed in or refusing to sit on her cushion. Thus, Banzei continues to dwell in the Doll Temple, a reminder of the mysterious bond between humans and the objects they hold dear.

34 KYOTO'S ALARM BELL

*The eastern edge of the city of Kyoto is bordered by a mountain range poetically known as the "Thirty-Six Peaks of Higashiyama" (*Higashiyama Sanjurokupo*). One of these peaks is Mount Kacho. At its summit stands a tomb called "The Mound of the General" (Shogun-zuka), because, according to tradition, it houses a statue modeled after a general from long ago—Sakanoue no Tamuramaro (758–811). For over a thousand years, this statue has been said to protect Kyoto. Unlike the animated doll Banzei, it does not move, but it makes its presence known in a way that is both remarkable and unsettling.*

Nearly twelve hundred years ago, Emperor Kanmu, plagued by a fear of so-called Angry Spirits, decided to relocate the imperial capital. In the thirteenth year of Enryaku (794), he abandoned the previous capital and established a new one on the site of what is now Kyoto. He named it Heian-kyo, meaning "Capital of Peace and Safety."

Once the city was built, Emperor Kanmu gathered his ministers, leading scholars, and experts from across the realm, addressing them as follows: "I want my new capital to live up to its name and truly embody peace and security. What do you propose we do to ensure its safety?"

The ministers deliberated for some time. Finally, one of them spoke up: "We should craft a statue of a mighty warrior, bury it atop a mountain overlooking the capital, and charge it with protecting the city."

Emperor Kanmu and his council agreed. They debated who should serve as the model for this protective figure and ultimately chose Sakanoue no Tamuramaro, a celebrated general. Having recently pacified the barbarian regions of the northeast, Tamuramaro was a symbol of strength and stability—perfect for the role of guardian of the capital. The finest craftsmen in the country were summoned to undertake the task. They sculpted a clay statue in Tamuramaro's likeness, outfitting it with armor, a metal helmet, a sword, a bow, and a quiver full of arrows.

When the statue was complete, a grand procession carried it to the summit of Mount Kacho, one of the peaks overlooking Heian-kyo from the east. The ceremony was attended by Emperor Kanmu, his ministers, and numerous monks. The statue was buried within a mound on the mountaintop, its gaze turned toward the city to watch for approaching enemies. The monks recited prayers, and Emperor Kanmu stepped forward to address the statue: "See to it that Heian-kyo is protected from disaster and remains eternally the capital of Japan!"

Years passed, and the statue remained silent, watching over the city. Then, on the morning of the eighth day of the seventh month in the first year of Hogen (1156), the General's Mound began to emit a strange rumbling noise. The sound grew louder throughout the day and persisted until sunset. The next morning, the retired emperor Sutoku gathered an army and launched a rebellion in an attempt to reclaim the throne, turning the streets of Kyoto into a battlefield. The people of the city connected the rumbling of the General's Mound to the rebellion and concluded that the statue had warned them of the impending crisis.

Years later, on the seventh day of the seventh month in the third year of Jisho (1179), the General's Mound rumbled again—in this instance, three distinct times. The first rumble was heard throughout Kyoto, the second across Yamashiro Province, and the third throughout the entire country. The next day, the Taira and Minamoto clans went to war, plunging the nation into the Genpei War. The conflict began in Kyoto, spread to Yamashiro Province, and eventually engulfed all of Japan. From that point on, the people of Kyoto became convinced that the General's Mound was a harbinger of catastrophe. Its ominous rumblings were believed to foretell impending disasters, and, tragically, the mound proved its reputation many times in the centuries that followed.

Today, the General's Mound remains a silent sentinel, a reminder of the ancient belief that Kyoto's safety was entrusted to the spirit of a great warrior, ever vigilant from his perch atop Mount Kacho.

35 SHOKI, "THE DEMON SWALLOWER"

If you descend from the heights of Mount Kacho and wander through the historic quarters of Kyoto, you will notice small tile figures above the front doors of many houses. These figures depict a bearded man with piercing, round eyes, wielding a scepter or sword, and sometimes trampling a snarling demon underfoot. This figure is known as Shoki, a representation of a seventh-century ghost who once saved the emperor of China from grave peril.

On a summer day in the second year of Bunka (1805), an apothecary on Third Avenue had what he thought was a brilliant idea. Believing he could ward off epidemics, he decided to install a tile shaped like a demon's head on the roof of his house.

"The hideous face of this monster will frighten the God of Epidemics away from my store," he told himself.

Without hesitation, he put his plan into action. A menacing demon tile was installed above the façade of his shop, staring out over the street. However, across the street from the apothecary's store lived a young couple. Soon after the installation of the demon tile, the wife's health began to decline. She grew progressively weaker until she fell seriously ill and was confined to her bed. Alarmed, her husband called for a doctor.

The doctor examined the woman thoroughly but found no physical signs of illness. After careful consideration, he concluded that the ailment had a supernatural origin. Searching for clues, he inspected the house, peered through the windows, and noticed the demon tile glaring from the apothecary's roof.

"I have found the cause of your wife's illness!" the doctor exclaimed. "That tile across the street, while protecting your neighbor's store, is deflecting harmful influences toward your home, much like a mirror reflects sunlight!"

The husband was relieved to have an explanation but grew despondent when he realized that the problem was not ordinary and could not be resolved with conventional medicine. Turning back to the doctor, he pleaded for a solution.

"The ailment is indeed no ordinary one," the doctor admitted. "Give me some time to think, and I'll devise a cure."

The doctor left the house deep in thought. A demon that invades a house and causes illness . . . The story felt familiar. Then it came to him. He remembered the tale of Zhong Kui, the "Demon Swallower," from seventh-century China. According to legend, Zhong Kui was a deceased official who returned to the mortal world as a ghost to protect Emperor Hsuan Tsung from the torment of a malicious demon. After being saved, the emperor commissioned a painting of Zhong Kui and encouraged his subjects to display reproductions of it on their doors to ward off evil spirits.

Inspired by this legend, the doctor hurried to a tile-maker in Kyoto's Fukakusa district. He shared the story of Zhong Kui and commissioned a tile depicting the fearsome ghost official. The craftsman set to work and created a tile in Zhong Kui's likeness, complete with his iconic stern expression and imposing stance. The doctor took the tile to the young couple's home and installed it on their façade, directly facing the apothecary's demon tile.

As soon as the two supernatural figures "met," a silent confrontation began. The demon tile seemed to glare menacingly, but it couldn't withstand Zhong Kui's intense gaze. Eventually, the demon looked away, its malevolent influence neutralized. Almost immediately, the young woman's health improved. She regained her strength and was soon back to her daily activities.

Word of the doctor's ingenious cure spread quickly throughout the city. Inspired by his success, Kyoto's residents began commissioning tiles depicting Shoki (the Japanese name of Zhong Kui) to protect their homes. These figures, representing the legendary demon swallower, were installed above doors to ward off illness and malevolent spirits. Even today, as you stroll through Kyoto's historic streets, you can spot these protective tiles—a testament to Zhong Kui's enduring legacy and the timeless belief in the power of guardian spirits.

THE CURSE OF THE GHOST STATUE

All these tales about statues underscore a crucial lesson: The creation of such objects should be entrusted to skilled professionals and undertaken for appropriate reasons. Crafting an object that portrays or embodies a person, even an imagined one, can be fraught with peril and lead to dreadful consequences. Those who recklessly create such items or fail to care for them often find themselves beset by misfortunes, swiftly seeking the assistance of monks to free themselves from these cursed objects. Some temples have even developed a specialization in safeguarding such items, with their monks performing rituals to pacify the alleged curses. For instance, Kyoto's Manshu-in Temple is known for sheltering ghostly paintings entrusted to the monks by parishioners claiming to be cursed. Similarly, the monks of Rokudo Chinnoji Temple are charged with appeasing the curse associated with a statue of Oiwa, Japan's most famous ghost.

About 120 years in the past, there lived a wealthy businessman whose name has been omitted for reasons that will soon become evident.

This businessman was a fervent admirer of Kabuki theater, especially plays that featured ghostly apparitions. Among these, his favorite was *Yotsuya Kaidan* [The Ghost Story of Yotsuya], which tells the tragic tale of a woman, disfigured and murdered by her husband, who returns as a vengeful ghost.

One day, driven by his fascination, the businessman visited a potter in the Kiyomizu district and commissioned a ceramic statue of Oiwa, the spectral heroine of his beloved play. The request deeply unsettled the potter.

"Are you certain you wish for a statue of Oiwa? Wouldn't it be unwise to create an image of a ghost?"

The businessman, unfazed by the warning, dismissed the potter's concerns and paid him handsomely to complete the task. Some time later, he returned to collect the finished statue and proudly displayed it in his home. But almost immediately, calamities began to strike. Misfortunes plagued his family, and his prosperous business started to collapse. In his despair, the businessman became convinced that he had fallen victim to the infamous curse of Oiwa. Desperate to escape his plight, he took the statue to a local shrine and implored the priests to take it into their care. However, the priests recoiled at the sight of the statue, its disfigured features a faithful likeness of Oiwa.

"We cannot take responsibility for such an object," they declared, visibly shaken. "You should take it to Rokudo Chinnoji Temple, where a statue of Enma, the King of Hell, resides."

Disheartened but determined, the businessman retrieved the statue and made his way to Rokudo Chinnoji Temple. He recounted his harrowing ordeal to the monks, pleading with them to accept the statue and free him from its malevolent curse. After some deliberation, the monks consented. They placed the statue of Oiwa in one of the temple's halls, positioning it beside the statue of Enma. However, their decision soon caused unrest among their parishioners.

"When we come to pray before the King of Hell," they complained, "our eyes are drawn to the statue of Oiwa. Its terrifying visage haunts us and robs us of sleep! Please find another way to neutralize its curse."

Faced with this delicate dilemma, the monks pondered their next move. Leaving Oiwa's statue beside Enma would drive away their parishioners. Yet relegating it to storage risked provoking the statue's wrath, inviting further vengeance. Finally, they devised a solution: They constructed a small chapel in the temple's courtyard and enshrined the statue of Oiwa within. This chapel, now known as Oiwa Myojin (the "Great Deity Oiwa"), remains standing to this day. However, its doors are kept perpetually closed, ensuring that no visitor is frightened by the ghostly image within.

PART THREE

GHOSTS AS WE USUALLY IMAGINED THEM

This part focuses on a type of ghost that is more familiar to us because it also exists in Western traditions: The spirit of a deceased person who assumes a form visible to the naked eye in order to appear on earth. In Japanese legends, people often turn into ghosts because they are unable to detach themselves from a specific place—typically the location where they lived or where they died, often under tragic circumstances. They may also become ghosts because they have an unresolved task: delivering an object to someone, exposing their murderer, or seeking justice for a wrong committed against them. Finally, some become ghosts because their bodies are incomplete, preventing them from resting peacefully.

37 THE GHOST OF THE WATERFRONT MANSION

Let us now delve into a type of ghost that feels more familiar, as it exists in Western traditions as well: spirits who manifest in visible forms, often appearing in the prime of their mortal lives or as they looked at the moment of death. Such ghosts are most often found in the places they cherished in life. Unable to part with their beloved homes, they refuse to pass on to the Pure Land, becoming a category of spirits known as jibakurei, *or "Earth-Bound Spirits." Kyoto's most renowned ghost of this kind was Prince Minamoto no Toru (822–895). He lingered in the human realm out of love for his splendid mansion. Today, nothing of the mansion remains, save for a stone marker that reads, "Site of Kawara-no-in, Mansion of Minamoto no Toru."*

More than eleven centuries ago, Prince Minamoto no Toru resided in an exquisite mansion on the banks of the Kamo River. Toru adored his residence with such fervor that, even after his death, he could not bear to leave it. Thus, he became what is called a jibakurei—an "Earth-Bound Spirit"—and continued to dwell there unseen.

At first, his family was unaware of his spectral presence. So, when they learned that Emperor Uda greatly admired the mansion, they offered it to him as a gift. Overjoyed, the emperor moved in. He toured the grand estate, exploring its rooms and admiring its gardens, before settling down to sleep. But a few hours later, Uda awoke with a start. He heard the unmistakable sound of footsteps echoing through the corridors of the deserted mansion, coming ever closer to his chamber. The sliding door opened slowly, and a figure stepped into the room, standing ominously before his bed. To the emperor's growing horror, it was a ghost—the ghost of the late Prince Toru!

"You cannot stay here," the ghost declared. "Leave now, before it is too late!"

An ordinary man might have fled in terror, but Uda was no ordinary man. As emperor of Japan, he maintained his composure and addressed the ghost with authority: "Toru, though you have become a ghost, do not forget your manners. In life, you were of lower rank than I. Even in death, you owe me respect!"

Realizing his breach of decorum, the ghost bowed his head humbly and withdrew.

Uda, undeterred, added, "This mansion is now mine, and I shall return tomorrow, accompanied by my favorite concubine."

True to his word, the emperor returned the following evening with Lady Fujiwara no Hoshi, his beloved consort. Together, they sat on the veranda, gazing at the moonlit sky before retiring for the night. But their slumber was once again disturbed by the sound of footsteps. The ghost of Toru reappeared, standing menacingly before them.

"You ignored my warning!" he bellowed. "This time, you shall pay the price!"

The ghost lunged toward Uda, who deftly dodged the attack. Enraged, Toru turned his fury on Lady Hoshi, terrifying her so profoundly that she collapsed and died on the spot. Uda seized the opportunity to escape the haunted mansion, fleeing into the night. At dawn, he returned to find his concubine's lifeless body. Overcome with grief, he summoned his servants and ordered, "Bring me Master Jozo at once!"

The monk was renowned for his spiritual prowess, having once prayed his own father back to life. Upon his arrival, the emperor explained the dire situation and pleaded, "Master Jozo, pray to the Buddhas and restore Lady Hoshi to life!"

The monk agreed. He erected an altar in the room and began his prayers. To everyone's astonishment, his fervent devotion succeeded: The imperial concubine was resurrected. The emperor expressed his profound gratitude and promptly left the cursed mansion, vowing never to return. From that day forward, the mansion stood abandoned. Without care or occupants, it fell into ruin, becoming uninhabitable—even for a ghost. Prince Toru's spirit eventually departed, and a blood-drinking monster later took up residence, only to be driven away when a flood from the Kamo River washed away the last remnants of the estate.

Today, nothing remains of Minamoto no Toru's grand mansion but a solitary stone marker, silently commemorating its history.

38 THE BELL OF THE CURSED TEMPLE

*Kenninji Temple is the oldest Zen temple in Kyoto. Among its many treasures is a beautiful bell tower that houses a bell known as the "Dharani Bell" (*Darani no kane*). The bell takes its name from an old ritual in which monks would strike it every evening during the Hour of the Boar (9:00–11:00 p.m.) while reciting the Dharani of Kannon's compassion in memory of Minamoto no Toru. This practice stems from the bell's origin: It is all that remains of a temple once built to soothe the Earth-Bound Spirit of Minamoto no Toru—a temple he himself destroyed by triggering a flood of the Kamo River.*

Long ago, Prince Minamoto no Toru lived in a splendid residence on the banks of the Kamo River. So attached was he to this home that, even in death, he refused to leave it. Transformed into a jibakurei—an Earth-Bound Spirit—Toru haunted his mansion, driving away any who dared to reside there. His spectral presence filled the locals with fear, but for a time, they tolerated it. One day, their patience wore thin. The townspeople gathered to discuss how to rid themselves of the ghost's curse.

"I have an idea," one man proposed after much debate. "We should build a temple on the grounds of his mansion, appoint monks to pray for his soul, and guide him to the Pure Land."

The plan was met with unanimous approval. Together, they erected a temple complete with a prayer hall, monks' quarters, and a bell tower. But soon after the temple was completed, a torrential downpour lashed the capital. The Kamo River overflowed, sweeping away homes and eventually the newly built temple.

"This cannot be mere coincidence," the locals lamented. "Surely, malevolent forces are at work, determined to prevent the temple's construction."

Indeed, even the great bell from the temple's belfry was carried off by the floodwaters, sinking near the Seventh Avenue Bridge. Determined, the townspeople resolved to recover the bell. They waited for the floodwaters to recede, then secured thick ropes around the submerged bell. Despite their best efforts, the bell refused to budge.

"We'll never succeed," some despaired. "Toru's ghost is determined to keep the bell beneath the river."

At that moment, a monk named Yosai appeared. Recently arrived in Kyoto, he had established a temple on the opposite bank of the river—what would later become Kenninji.

"Do not lose hope," Yosai reassured them. "Allow me to assist."

The monk set off through the city, recruiting strong men wherever he went. Before long, he had assembled an impressive team. Leading them back to the riverbank, Yosai instructed the men to grasp the ropes and pull. Yet even their combined strength failed to lift the bell.

"Master Yosai, we told you so," the locals said. "The ghost's curse is too powerful."

"Do not despair," Yosai replied. "I have a plan. Instead of shouting 'Heave ho!' as you pull, call out my name: 'Yosai!'"

Though skeptical, the men obeyed. At Yosai's signal, they shouted his name in unison and pulled with all their might. To everyone's astonishment, the bell emerged from the water. Overwhelmed by this miracle, the townspeople entrusted the bell to Yosai. He took it to his temple, hung it in a new belfry, and began ringing it 108 times a day—the number of human passions that hinder spiritual enlightenment. From that day forward, Toru's ghost was never seen again. And so, the legend endures: A bell once cursed now serves as a symbol of liberation, its tolling a reminder of the power of perseverance and prayer.

THE HORSE-RIDING GHOST

Nanzenji Temple was originally the mansion of a monk named Dochi. So deeply did he love this place that, when he passed away, his spirit lingered, unable to abandon it. Like Minamoto no Toru, Dochi became a ghost attached to a place. Yet his story held a dramatic twist: When an emperor decided to take up residence in his former retreat, Dochi sought to drive him away, appearing as a ghost riding a horse. To pacify the angry spirit, a shrine named the Grand Master on Horseback was constructed. This sanctuary still stands, hidden in the tranquil woods behind Nanzenji Temple.

Once upon a time, long ago, there was a monk named Dochi who served as the head of Miidera Temple in the province of Omi. He devoted many years to his sacred duties. But as he aged, the desire for solitude grew within him. Seeking peace and quiet for his final years, he resigned from his position and began wandering through the mountains that stretched between Omi and the capital.

It was during this journey that Dochi discovered an exquisite clearing. Nestled by a gentle waterfall and surrounded by the serene sounds of nature, it seemed like the perfect place for quiet contemplation. There, he built a modest hermitage and spent his days in prayer to the Buddhas. Dochi grew so attached to his hermitage that, when he passed away, he could not bear to leave it. His spirit lingered, becoming one with the place. For years, this attachment caused no trouble. But one day, Emperor Kameyama heard of the beautiful clearing.

"Master Dochi's hermitage is said to be located in an enchanting spot," declared the emperor. "I shall transform it into a grand mansion and make it my residence!"

Without hesitation, the emperor summoned carpenters and ordered them to renovate the hermitage as quickly as possible. The workers toiled day and night, and soon the emperor's vision was realized. Delighted, he moved into his new mansion, accompanied by his court. Dochi's spirit, however, did not take kindly to this intrusion. Enraged at the disturbance, he decided to frighten the emperor and his courtiers into leaving. He began by appearing in ghostly form, slamming doors, and making eerie noises at all hours. But his efforts were in vain—the emperor and his entourage refused to be driven out.

Frustrated, Dochi resorted to a more dramatic tactic. Taking the form of a monk on a white horse, he galloped to the top of the waterfall overlooking the clearing. The sound of the spectral horse's hooves echoed through the night, shaking the mansion and terrifying its inhabitants. At dawn, Emperor Kameyama, deeply alarmed, summoned his yin-yang master and demanded an explanation.

"Who is the ghost that haunts this place?"

The yin-yang master consulted the oracles and soon delivered his verdict.

"The ghost is none other than Master Dochi," he revealed. "He is angered because you have disturbed his sanctuary."

"What can be done to appease him?" the emperor asked.

"The Buddhas can calm his spirit," replied the yin-yang master, "but their intervention can only be secured by the prayers of a truly virtuous monk."

The emperor wasted no time. He summoned Mukanfumon, a revered monk known for his spiritual purity.

"Pray to the Buddhas," the emperor implored. "Ask them to guide Master Dochi to the Pure Land."

Mukanfumon agreed and prepared an altar at the mansion. He prayed with great fervor, his chants resonating through the clearing. His devotion moved the heavens. Amida Buddha and Celestial Beings descended, their radiance filling the forest. The Buddhas spoke gently to Dochi's spirit, urging him to release his earthly attachments. Touched by their words, Dochi relinquished his anger and allowed himself to be led to the Pure Land. Relieved, Emperor Kameyama expressed his gratitude by commissioning the construction of a chapel in the forest behind the mansion. This shrine, dedicated to the "Great Master on Horseback," became a place of worship and a lasting tribute to the monk whose spirit had finally found peace.

40 THE GHOST AND THE CHERRY BLOSSOMS

Ariwara no Narihira (825–880) was an aristocrat, a celebrated poet, and—according to tradition—an Earth-Bound Spirit. Unlike many spirits, his attachment was not born of tragedy or possessiveness for his former home, but rather of cherished memories. The site of his spectral presence is Oharano Jinja, a shrine nestled at the foot of Mount Oshio, the westernmost mountain in Kyoto's Nishinokyo district.

One spring, two residents of Shimogyo Ward decided to visit Mount Oshio to admire its famous cherry blossoms. They had heard of the mountain's breathtaking beauty and longed to witness it firsthand. Upon arriving, they were dismayed to find the summit already crowded with people. After some effort, they managed to secure a small spot for themselves and settled down to revel in the splendor of the blossoms.

As they sat in quiet contemplation, an old man in tattered clothing appeared. He held a delicate branch of cherry blossoms in his hand and moved slowly through the crowd. His shabby appearance drew disdainful glances from many visitors, who saw him as an affront to the refined beauty of the scene. But the two men from Shimogyo were intrigued. They beckoned the old man to join them. The stranger accepted their invitation and sat with them beneath the flowering trees. For a time, he simply gazed at the blossoms in silence. Then, unexpectedly, he spoke: "On this day, even Mount Oshio remembers the time of the old gods."

The two men were stunned. The old man's words were a direct quote from a famous poem by none other than Ariwara no Narihira. They could scarcely believe that someone of such ragged appearance could be so well versed in classical poetry. Their astonishment grew as the old man continued to speak, reciting verses from other renowned poets and waxing lyrical about the beauty of the cherry blossoms. Then, as suddenly as he had appeared, the old man vanished before their very eyes. A local man, seated nearby, had witnessed the entire scene. Seeing the bewilderment on the faces of the two men from Shimogyo, he leaned over and whispered, "I believe you've just encountered the ghost of Ariwara no Narihira. Many centuries ago, Narihira came to Mount Oshio to admire the cherry blossoms. It was here that he composed the very poem the old man recited. His spirit has been known to return to this place, drawn by his love for the blossoms. If you wish to witness more wonders, you should stay here tonight."

Grateful for the advice, the two men decided to follow it. They resolved to spend the night on Mount Oshio, hoping for further glimpses of the extraordinary. As the evening deepened, the men found themselves lulled by the tranquility of the mountain and soon began to doze. It was then that a resplendent chariot appeared, seemingly out of nowhere. Adorned with cherry branches, it rolled majestically to the summit.

A figure in elegant court attire stepped out of the chariot. To the amazement of the two men, the figure began to dance, performing an ancient courtly ritual beneath the cascading blossoms. His movements were graceful, his bearing noble. The two men knew at once that they were in the presence of Ariwara no Narihira himself, restored to his former glory. As the ghost danced, the petals of the cherry blossoms began to fall, creating a shimmering curtain that gradually obscured him from view. The two men could no longer see him, and soon they found themselves waking under the light of dawn.

Had they been dreaming? Or had they truly witnessed the ghost of Ariwara no Narihira? They would never know. But the memory of that magical night on Mount Oshio stayed with them for the rest of their lives, as vivid and ephemeral as the cherry blossoms themselves.

41

NARIHIRA'S GHOST AND THE ENAMORED VILLAGER

Ariwara no Narihira (825–880), a celebrated poet and an incorrigible seducer, found himself embroiled in a scandalous love affair that forced him to flee the capital. After his dalliance with an imperial concubine came to light, he sought refuge in a remote countryside village, where he spent the remainder of his days. According to tradition, his spirit became bound to that place, tormented by the unrequited love of a young village girl whose affections he had been completely oblivious of. This poignant tale endows Jurinji Temple, where Narihira's grave lies, with a special allure. Even today, as in centuries past, young single women make pilgrimages to this sacred site, fervently praying to find their destined soulmate.

More than twelve centuries ago, there lived an aristocrat named Ariwara no Narihira, famed for his poetic brilliance and legendary charm. One fateful year, Narihira succumbed to his desires and seduced a concubine of the imperial court. When their forbidden liaison was discovered, he was compelled to abandon the capital and retreat to an unassuming village in the countryside. There, the poet lived quietly, wandering the surrounding fields and hills each day. His presence did not go unnoticed. One day, a young village girl caught sight of him as he strolled past. His dignified bearing, noble features, and air of melancholy captivated her at once. She fell deeply in love.

Unable to resist the sight of him, she began to arrange her days so that their paths would cross. Each time she saw him, her heart swelled with unspoken longing. But Narihira, lost in his thoughts, paid her no mind. Determined to make herself known, the girl resolved to speak to him. Yet, every time she saw him, her courage failed her. The vast gulf between their stations in life seemed insurmountable, and she could not bring herself to confess her feelings. Her silent suffering did not escape the notice of the other villagers, who soon pieced together the cause of her despair.

As the days passed, her anguish deepened. Finally, consumed by her unrequited love and the hopelessness of her situation, the young girl threw herself into a pond near the village. Her lifeless body was discovered by the villagers just as Narihira was returning from one of his walks. Hearing the commotion, Narihira approached and inquired about what had happened. The villagers recounted the tragic story of the girl's love for him, a love to which he had been oblivious.

"But I didn't know she loved me!" he exclaimed, stricken with regret. "Ah, if only I had known!"

Guilt weighed heavily on Narihira's heart. The sorrow of the young girl's death haunted him, and the remorse he felt slowly consumed him. It wasn't long before his regret manifested as an illness that sapped his strength and eventually claimed his life. The villagers, deeply moved by the double tragedy, buried Narihira near the temple where he had lived. They erected a stupa over his grave and took it upon themselves to offer daily prayers and offerings in his memory.

One evening, as a villager approached Narihira's grave with an offering, he saw something extraordinary: A fireball suddenly emerged from the stupa, rose into the sky, and drifted toward the pond where the young girl had died. The next evening, and the evenings that followed, others witnessed the same phenomenon. They observed that the fireball always hovered over the pond, as if searching for something—or someone. Perplexed, the villagers turned to their elder for guidance.

"It's clear," the elder said after hearing their accounts. "That fireball is the spirit of Lord Narihira. Even in death, he is tormented by his regret over the girl's death. His soul cannot rest, and so it rises each night to seek her by the pond."

The villagers were deeply moved by the elder's words. They prayed that Narihira's restless spirit might one day find peace, perhaps by reuniting with the soul of the young girl he had unknowingly spurned. To this day, the story lingers. Local records note that as recently as 1932, villagers reported seeing a mysterious fireball rise from Ariwara no Narihira's grave and drift toward the pond. Whether the poet's soul ever found solace remains a mystery, but his tale endures—a poignant reminder of love, loss, and the weight of unspoken words.

THE GHOST'S GIFT

Legends often recount how the dead linger in the Realm of Human Beings due to unresolved grievances or unfinished tasks. Such was the case of the renowned poet Sugawara no Michizane (845–903), who is said to have returned as a ghost to deliver a statue of the god Daikoku to the monks of Honkokuji Temple. This statue, gifted by a restless spirit, has endured through the centuries and is still displayed today in the Daikoku hall of the temple.

Approximately 450 years ago, a monk named Nissei served as abbot of Honkokuji Temple.

One evening, as the sun dipped below the horizon, a knock echoed through the temple doors. Nissei opened them to find an old man standing before him, clutching an object wrapped in cloth.

"What brings you here at this hour?" Nissei asked politely.

"To tell the truth, I have come to sell a statue," the old man replied, his voice calm yet earnest.

With that, he unveiled the object in his hands. Beneath the cloth was a statue of Daikoku, one of the Seven Gods of Happiness. The carving radiated a presence both serene and powerful. Nissei studied it carefully and immediately recognized its value.

"I will gladly buy this statue," he said.

The old man's face brightened. "Excellent," he replied. "I shall leave it with you now and return tomorrow morning to collect my payment."

"As you wish," Nissei agreed. Then, handing the old man a sheet of paper and a brush, he added, "Please write down your name and address so I may know where to find you if needed."

The old man took the paper, scribbled something on it, folded it meticulously, and handed it back to Nissei. With a deep bow of gratitude, he departed into the night. Morning arrived, but the old man did not return. Perplexed, Nissei remembered the paper the man had left with him. Unfolding it, he anticipated finding a name and address. Instead, he discovered a poem:

I dwell beneath the pines of the distant
    Kitano Plain.
My abode lies within the shadowed Sedge Moor.
遥々と北野の松の下住居、 /
    宿は葎のかげの菅原

Nissei reflected deeply on the enigmatic words. Slowly, their meaning dawned upon him. "I initially interpreted the word 'Sugawara' as 'Sedge Moor,' but it can also signify a family name. Thus, the poem could be read as: 'I am from the house of Sugawara.' With its mention of the Kitano Plain, the message becomes unmistakable. My mysterious visitor was none other than Sugawara no Michizane, the renowned statesman of old, who is now venerated as the God of Scholarship in the Kitano Plain!"

Sugawara no Michizane, once a revered scholar and poet, had been unjustly accused of treason and exiled in disgrace. Upon his death, his anguished soul became an Angry Spirit, unleashing calamities upon the court that had wronged him. In time, a shrine was built in his honor on Kitano Plain to appease his wrath and secure peace. But why had Michizane's ghost come to Honkokuji Temple? Why had he entrusted Nissei with the statue of Daikoku? These questions remained unanswered.

Understanding the statue's extraordinary provenance, Nissei resolved to honor the sacred trust placed in him. He ordered the construction of a special chapel in the temple courtyard. There, he enshrined the statue, ensuring it would be safeguarded for generations to come. The statue of Daikoku, gifted by the ghost of Sugawara no Michizane, remains in Honkokuji Temple to this day, its presence a silent testament to a spirit's enduring legacy.

43 THE POET'S GHOST AND THE ITINERANT MONK

It is said that the poet-warrior Taira no Tadanori (1144–1184) lingered in the Realm of Human Beings as a ghost, bound by an unfulfilled task that prevented him from finding peace in the Pure Land. To complete this task, he appeared before the mansion of his former master, Fujiwara no Toshinari (1114–1204), a renowned poet of his time. Today, all that remains of Toshinari's mansion is a shrine he once built in his garden, dedicated to the Goddess of Poetry. Known as Niitamatsushima Jinja, this place has become a pilgrimage site for poets and artists, inspired by the strange events that transpired there.

Nearly a thousand years ago, Taira no Tadanori lived as a celebrated general, skilled in both the art of war and the world of letters. In 1183, when the Taira family was at war with the Minamoto clan, fate turned against them, forcing them to flee Kyoto. Amid the chaos of departure, Tadanori, driven by a poetic mission, left his fleeing relatives and rode to the mansion of his old mentor, Fujiwara no Toshinari. Knocking urgently at the gates, Tadanori called out, his voice heavy with urgency, "Master, open the door! I beg you, please. I have something of the utmost importance to entrust to you!"

Toshinari, hearing his former pupil's pleas, opened the door and let him in. Tadanori bowed deeply and spoke with fervor: "Master, I do not wish to be remembered merely as a fugitive or a warrior. I want to leave behind a legacy as a poet. Here, I have compiled one hundred of my poems in this scroll. Please, if you deem any of them worthy, include them in the imperial anthology you are preparing by the emperor's command."

Toshinari, moved by the sincerity of Tadanori's request, took the scroll and promised to examine its contents. Grateful, Tadanori thanked his master and departed to rejoin his family. His journey was tragically cut short when he perished in battle at Suma Bay, in the province of Arima (present-day Kobe).

Though his body found rest in a grave, Tadanori's soul remained restless. A burning question haunted him in the afterlife: Had Toshinari kept his promise? Had even one of his poems been included in the anthology?

Indeed, Toshinari was impressed by Tadanori's work, which overflowed with beauty and emotion. After much deliberation, he selected one poem for inclusion. Yet, fearing that the emperor would reject a poem penned by an enemy general, Toshinari attributed it to an anonymous author. Tadanori's spirit, aware of this omission, felt both pride and frustration. While his work was honored, his name was absent—a bittersweet recognition. Desperate to have his name restored, Tadanori searched for a way to communicate his wish.

Years passed until one fateful evening, a wandering monk passed by Suma Beach, seeking shelter for the night. Spotting a cherry tree, the monk rested beneath its branches and soon fell into a deep sleep. Seeing his chance, Tadanori's ghost entered the monk's dreams. In vivid detail, he recounted his story, from his poetic aspirations to his untimely demise. With heartfelt urgency, he made his request: "I implore you, Noble Monk, to journey to Fujiwara no Toshinari's mansion. Ask him to credit my name for the poem included in the anthology. It is my only wish before I can ascend to the Pure Land."

The monk awoke at dawn, the dream fresh in his mind. Convinced that he had been visited by Tadanori's spirit, he turned to the general's grave and made a solemn vow: "I shall do my utmost to fulfill your wish."

Before setting off for the capital, the monk built a small altar near Tadanori's resting place. He prayed to the Buddhas, asking them to guide

Tadanori to the Pure Land and grant him eternal peace. As for the monk's journey and whether he succeeded in restoring Tadanori's name to the poem, the records remain silent. But the tale endures, reminding all who hear it of the unyielding power of art and the desire for recognition that transcends even death.

44 THE ANGRY SPIRIT OF UJI BRIDGE

Japanese ghosts are also known to appear at the site of their death, whether it was violent or natural. They make their presence known by causing disasters, emitting eerie moans, or manifesting in forms visible to the naked eye. One such ghost haunts the bridge in the neighboring town of Uji. To gain her favor, the townspeople built a shrine in her honor: Hashi Hime Jinja, the "Shrine of the Lady of the Bridge." Yet even today, out of fear of awakening her jealousy, they avoid crossing the bridge during certain joyful occasions, such as weddings. There are several theories about what led the woman now revered as the Lady of the Bridge of Uji to become a ghost. Here are two of them.

Once, long ago, there lived a wealthy but deeply unhappy man named Okada Shikibu in the city of Uji. His misery stemmed from his wife's intense jealousy. If she deemed a servant girl too attractive, she would dismiss her immediately and replace her with someone less comely. If she overheard her servants discussing love, her fury would drive her to withhold their meals for days. Worst of all, whenever her husband stepped out for a walk, she would suspect infidelity and lock him in his room. For years, Shikibu endured his wife's tyranny. But eventually, his patience wore thin. He warned her that if her behavior continued, he would leave her. The threat, however, had the opposite effect. His wife, consumed by rage, declared, "If you abandon me, I will become an Angry Spirit and curse you to your death!"

Shikibu attempted to calm her, but jealousy had overtaken her reason.

"You're already planning to leave me, aren't you? It's because you have another woman, and you want to marry her! That's it, isn't it? You men are all the same! I'll make you pay!"

With those words, she stormed out of the house, ran to Uji River, and threw herself into the waters. Horrified, Shikibu begged local fishermen to recover her body. They searched tirelessly but found nothing. Seven days later, Shikibu had a disturbing dream. His wife appeared in his room, approached his bed, and said, "I shall curse every married man who crosses Uji Bridge, forcing them to part with their wives!"

The following day, Shikibu dismissed the dream as mere imagination. However, reports soon reached him: Friends who had crossed Uji Bridge with their wives argued and separated. Boaters carrying newlyweds across the river described strange disturbances in the water. Shikibu quickly realized his wife's ominous threat had come true—she had become an Angry Spirit. He gathered the villagers and proposed building a shrine at the bridge to appease her wrath. Eager to end the chaos, the townspeople agreed. Together, they constructed a shrine dedicated to "the Lady of the Bridge," where her spirit could be venerated and her anger pacified.

THE WOMAN WHO LOST HER HUSBAND TWICE

The Lady of Uji Bridge is a renowned figure whose tragic tale has inspired numerous variations. Here is another version of the story.

Long ago, a captain lived in Uji with two wives. Because of her proximity to the city's iconic bridge, his primary wife was affectionately called Hashi Hime, or "Lady of the Bridge." One day, the Lady of the Bridge discovered she was pregnant.

"Dear husband," she said, "I've heard that seaweed soup eases the discomfort of pregnancy. Could you go to the seaside and gather some for me?"

"Of course," the captain replied cheerfully. "I'll ride to Naniwa (Osaka) Bay and fetch the best seaweed for you!"

He mounted his horse and galloped to the bay. Whistling happily, he began collecting seaweed, unaware that his melody had awakened the Dragon King, who dwelled beneath the waves. Enraged by the disturbance, the Dragon King surfaced, seized the captain, and dragged him into the depths. Days passed, and the Lady of the Bridge grew increasingly anxious. Desperate, she set out for Naniwa in search of her husband. Along the coast, she discovered an abandoned house. Compelled to enter, she encountered her husband's ghost.

"Do not fear," the ghost said gently. "Though I am dead, I remain here because I cannot leave you. I use my robe as a blanket and sleep alone. Will my wife, the Lady of Uji Bridge, wait for my return tonight?"

After reciting this melancholic poem, the ghost vanished. Heartbroken, the Lady of the Bridge returned to Uji in tears. Seeing her distress, the captain's second wife inquired what had happened. Upon hearing the story, the second wife became incensed.

"What?" she exclaimed. "Our husband's ghost composes poems only for you? I'll teach him some manners! I'll demand he write one for me too!"

Determined, she traveled to the abandoned house and confronted the ghost. As before, he wandered aimlessly, repeating, "I use my robe as a blanket and sleep alone. Will my wife, the Lady of Uji Bridge, wait for my return tonight?"

Outraged, the second wife stormed at him, "Even in death, all you think about is your first wife! Ghost or not, I'll make you pay for ignoring me!"

She lunged at the apparition, but at that moment, a strange phenomenon occurred: The ghost, the house, and the second wife all disappeared, leaving no trace. The Lady of the Bridge lived out her days and, after her death, the people of Uji honored her memory by building a shrine at the site of her home. They dedicated it to the Lady of the Bridge, whose poignant story endures as part of the city's lore.

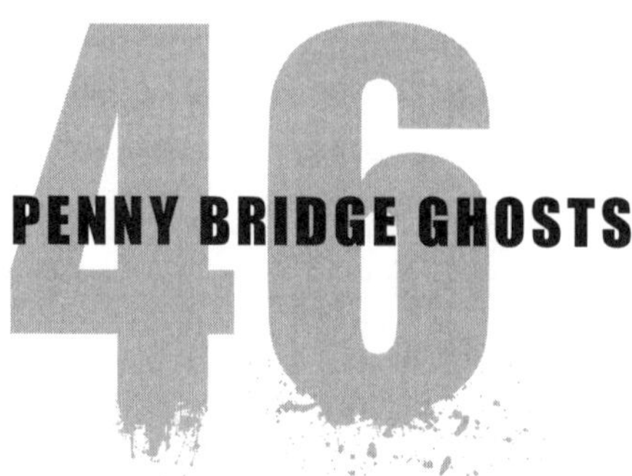

46 PENNY BRIDGE GHOSTS

The bridge connecting the cities of Nagaokakyo and Muko is called Ichi-mon-bashi, or "Penny Bridge," so named because it was Japan's first toll bridge. This ingenious initiative greatly enriched the coffers of the local lord but also brought tragedy, as those who dared to cross the bridge without paying the toll were mercilessly executed. It is said that their restless ghosts still haunt the bridge, their lamentations audible on summer evenings.

Long ago, torrential rains descended upon the province of Yamashiro (modern-day Kyoto Prefecture), causing rivers to swell and overflow. Among these rivers, the Obata burst its banks, washing away the bridge that spanned the Saigoku Kaido, the vital road connecting the capital to the western provinces. Upon learning of this disaster, the shogun summoned the local lord and commanded him to rebuild the bridge immediately, as the capital could not remain severed from the western provinces. The lord, bowing to the shogun's orders, returned to his domain and convened his counselors.

"The shogun has demanded the reconstruction of the bridge over the Saigoku Kaido," he declared grimly. "The cost will drain our treasury, leaving us nothing to address the other damage caused by the floods."

After lengthy deliberations, the lord and his counselors devised a solution.

"We shall rebuild the bridge," the lord proclaimed, "and introduce a toll for passage. The revenue collected will replenish our coffers and fund the restoration of our fiefdom!"

The counselors applauded the plan, and construction of the new bridge began. Once completed, a guard was stationed at the bridge entrance to collect the toll of one penny from each traveler. The guard, Hanpei, was a kind-hearted and generous man. One day, while on duty, he noticed a villager walking along the riverbank, casting furtive glances toward the bridge. Sensing something amiss, Hanpei watched closely as the man entered the river and swam across.

"I should stop him," Hanpei thought, "but he must be a poor man who cannot afford the toll. I'll pretend I didn't see anything."

And so, Hanpei averted his gaze, allowing the man to cross unnoticed. Unbeknownst to Hanpei, the scene was observed by other villagers, who quickly deduced that he was intentionally turning a blind eye. Soon, word spread: Whenever Hanpei was on duty, one could swim across the river without fear of reprisal.

The villagers grew bold, and many began crossing the river under Hanpei's watchful but lenient eye. As a result, the revenue from the toll declined steadily. Alarmed by the drop in income, the lord launched an investigation and soon discovered Hanpei's leniency. Enraged, he dismissed Hanpei and replaced him with a team of stricter guards, instructing them to execute anyone caught evading the toll.

The new guards, loyal and unyielding, carried out the lord's orders with brutal efficiency. Each time they caught a villager attempting to swim across the river, they beheaded the offender without hesitation. Before long, the banks of the Obata River were littered with corpses. But these tragic victims lost more than their lives. Consumed by frustration and grief over their failure to cross the river, they became ghosts, doomed to haunt the area around Penny Bridge. Their spectral forms wandered restlessly, still trying to achieve in death what they could not in life.

Centuries have passed, yet the legend endures. On certain summer evenings, it is said that their voices can still be heard. Between mournful sobs, they whisper the same desperate plea: "Let us cross!"

47 THE GHOST OF THE DISSECTED CORPSE

In the graveyard of Seiganji Temple stands a memorial stele upon which fourteen names are engraved. The tale behind this stele is both intriguing and poignant, illustrating a distinctive aspect of Japanese ghost lore: A person may linger in the Realm of Human Beings as a ghost if their body is not intact at the moment of death.

Nearly three centuries ago, there lived a doctor named Yamawaki Toyo. One day, Toyo dissected an otter and was horrified to discover that the information contained in the anatomy manuals of the time—texts that had been relied upon for centuries—was incorrect.

"These old textbooks fail to depict the placement of the viscera accurately!" he exclaimed upon making this revelation. "If they are erroneous about animals, they might also be wrong about human anatomy."

This unsettling thought consumed Toyo. Determined to uncover the truth, he resolved to dissect human corpses to verify the accuracy of these ancient texts. However, obtaining such specimens was far from straightforward. While acquiring otters was one matter, securing human cadavers was another entirely. After much deliberation, Toyo devised a plan. In the second month of the second year of Horeki (1754), he approached the governor, Sakai Tadamochi, and presented his case.

"For the advancement of science," Toyo explained, "I request access to the corpses of recently executed prisoners from Kyoto's prison for dissection."

Moved by the pursuit of knowledge, Tadamochi agreed. "I will ensure that arrangements are made," he said, drafting a letter to the director of the Kyoto prison. The letter granted Toyo permission to obtain the bodies of the recently executed. Armed with this official decree, Toyo visited the prison and secured fourteen cadavers. Returning to his laboratory, he decided to begin his work with the youngest among them. Methodically, he opened the corpse's torso and meticulously examined its organs. Exhausted by his labor, he retired to bed.

That night, Toyo experienced a vivid and unsettling dream. A young man appeared in his room and approached his bed. The clarity of the vision startled Toyo awake—only to find the figure still standing before him. Upon closer inspection, he recognized the young man as the very individual whose body he had dissected earlier that day. The realization struck him with terror: The young man was a ghost.

"Yes, I am a ghost," the apparition said, his tone filled with sorrow and reproach. "I became a ghost because of you. I was innocent of the crime for which I was condemned. Though men judged me harshly, the Buddhas acknowledged my innocence and sought to guide me to the Pure Land. Yet your actions—dismembering my body—have bound my spirit to this world, leaving me unable to ascend."

Toyo, deeply shaken, replied with genuine remorse. "I had not considered that the dead might require their bodies to pass into the next world. I am truly sorry for my ignorance and the suffering I have caused. I will do everything in my power to right this wrong and ensure that you and your companions find peace."

"Thank you," the ghost murmured, before vanishing as suddenly as he had appeared. Toyo was profoundly moved by this encounter. The following morning, he sought out an artisan skilled in creating religious sculptures.

"I need you to carve a statue of Amida Buddha, the guardian of the Pure Land," he instructed. "I also wish for replicas of human organs, crafted from cloth, to be placed inside the statue."

"Reproductions of human organs?" the craftsman asked, perplexed. "Why such an unusual request?"

"So that Amida may understand my plea," Toyo explained. "I wish for the Buddha to restore the bodies of those I dissected and guide them to the Pure Land."

The artisan agreed to undertake the task, and Toyo expressed his gratitude. He then visited a stonemason and handed him a sheet of paper.

"On this paper are fourteen names," Toyo said. "I would like you to engrave them upon a memorial stele."

The stonemason promised to fulfill the request, and Toyo returned home. Once the statue and the stele were completed, Toyo took them to Seiganji, a temple devoted to the worship of Amida Buddha. There, he recounted his story to the monks, who were moved by his earnest desire to bring peace to the spirits of the departed. The monks installed the statue within the temple and placed the stele in the graveyard. They then conducted a solemn ceremony to honor the fourteen individuals whose lives and deaths had become intertwined with Toyo's quest for knowledge.

From that day onward, Toyo was never again visited by the ghost of the young prisoner. He took this as a sign that the spirits of the fourteen had been restored and had entered the Pure Land. Freed from the weight of guilt, Toyo resumed his research and, in time, published *Zoshi* [Notes on Viscera], the first treatise on human anatomy in Japan.

48 THE PARADE OF GHOST SOLDIERS

During the thousand years it served as the capital of Japan, the city of Kyoto witnessed countless battles and became the resting place of innumerable warriors whose spirits, it is said, still linger, wandering the streets or even parading through them. Among these spectral figures, the most famous are the members of the Shinsengumi militia—a group infamous for its ruthless pursuit of those who supported Japan's opening to the outside world during the tumultuous closing years of the Edo period. Most of the Shinsengumi met their tragic end in 1868 at the Battle of Toba-Fushimi. Legend has it that their ghosts appeared when the municipality of the time sought to move their commemorative stele to make way for a racecourse.

In the mid-nineteenth century, American ships entered Edo Bay, and their commanding officer, Commodore Perry, demanded that Japan open its ports to foreign trade. The country found itself divided: Some Japanese welcomed the idea of opening their borders, while others vehemently opposed it. Among the latter was the shogun, the military ruler of Japan, who governed in the emperor's name. The shogun authorized the formation of the Shinsengumi, a militia tasked with suppressing supporters of foreign influence.

For years, the Shinsengumi relentlessly pursued the "pro-openers." However, as time passed, the latter gained strength. On the fifth day of the first month of the fourth year of Keio (1868), they engaged the shogunal forces and the Shinsengumi in a decisive battle at Toba-Fushimi, south of Kyoto. The pro-openers emerged victorious. The defeated Shinsengumi were massacred, their bodies abandoned to decay on the battlefield. The people of Toba-Fushimi were deeply moved by the gruesome sight.

"Even if they were our enemies, we cannot leave them like this," one resident said, appalled at the carnage.

"Indeed, we must do something for them," agreed another.

Defying official orders, the villagers collected the bodies of the fallen Shinsengumi and gave them a proper burial at a place called Senryomatsu. A few decades later, in 1907, they erected a memorial stele in honor of these warriors who had died for beliefs they did not share. The war between the supporters and opponents of Japan's opening to the world lasted a few more months before finally concluding. With the rise of Emperor Meiji's government, modernization swept across the nation. In Kyoto, one such development was the construction of a racecourse on the site of the Toba-Fushimi battlefield.

The racecourse quickly became a popular attraction, drawing large crowds. By 1967, to accommodate the growing number of spectators, the municipality decided to expand the parking lot and build a footbridge for easier access from Yodo Station. Workers arrived, armed with heavy machinery, and began excavating the area. During their work, they came upon the Senryomatsu stele. Unaware of its significance, the foreman dismissed it as an obstacle.

"This stele is in the middle of the construction site!" he declared. "Dig it up and dispose of it."

The workers obeyed. The stele was discarded, and work resumed. That night, the residents of the neighborhood were startled awake by eerie voices echoing across the old battlefield.

"Put it back! Put it back where it was!" the voices demanded.

Several brave locals ventured outside, only to witness a chilling sight: a ghostly procession of Shinsengumi warriors marching solemnly across the battlefield. Horrified, they rushed to inform the foreman the next morning, but he dismissed their accounts as superstitious nonsense.

However, strange accidents began to plague the construction site. Equipment malfunctioned, injuries occurred, and progress slowed to a crawl. Every night, the ghostly voices returned, accompanied by the spectral parade of Shinsengumi soldiers chanting, "Put it back where it was!"

The foreman, initially skeptical, grew uneasy. The frequency and severity of the accidents were too unusual to be mere coincidence. Recalling the locals' warnings, he began to wonder if the site was indeed cursed.

"Perhaps they were right," he thought with growing dread. "The ghosts of the Shinsengumi must be behind this!"

Convinced that his workers were victims of a supernatural curse, the foreman ordered the memorial stele to be reinstated at its original location. He also sought help from the monks at nearby Myokyoji Temple, imploring them to conduct a religious ceremony to appease the restless spirits. The monks, moved by the foreman's tale, organized a solemn service to honor the departed Shinsengumi warriors. They prayed for the ghosts' peace and performed rituals to lift the curse. According to local accounts, the nightly disturbances ceased after the ceremony. The construction site was free of further accidents, and the residents of Toba-Fushimi never again heard the spectral lament of the Shinsengumi.

PART FOUR

GHOSTS OF WOMEN

This part focuses on women who, according to tradition, are particularly prone to becoming ghosts. Why does Japanese tradition say this is so? Because women supposedly stir confusion in men's hearts and face great difficulties entering Heaven. Because, as abused women, they seek to expose their murderers. Because, as women who died in childbirth, they long to care for the child they left behind, even one born in the grave.

49

THE GHOST SHIP SAILING ON A SEA OF MIST

According to certain traditions, Enryakuji Temple was built on Mount Hiei to protect the North-East, known as the "Demons' Gate," and to prevent ghosts and monsters from invading Kyoto. The temple acts as a kind of invisible barrier before which, it is said, all manner of ghosts gather. Some of these ghosts wait for an opportunity to penetrate Kyoto and commit evil deeds, while others go to Enryakuji Temple in the hope of leaving the human realm and attaining enlightenment. Interestingly, most of these ghosts are women, as certain beliefs suggest that women face greater difficulty than men in detaching themselves from worldly things and reaching the Pure Land. These ghosts are said to roam one of the slopes leading to the top of Mount Hiei, curiously named Funa-saka, or "Boat Slope," despite the mountain being far from any sea.

Once upon a time, a monk from Enryakuji Temple—whose name remains unmentioned for reasons that will soon become apparent—left the temple one evening. He descended to the nearby village of Sakamoto, where he indulged himself at an inn, eating and drinking to his heart's content. Before dawn, he hurried back up the mountain. The slope was steep, and his steps were unsteady, so he kept his head down, focusing on his footing.

It was because of this that he didn't see the object in the middle of the path. He bumped into it head-on and fell backward. Sobering instantly, he stood up and saw . . . a boat! A boat sailing on a sea of mist, climbing the path toward the temple! The monk rubbed his eyes, pinched his skin, and slapped his cheeks. He wasn't dreaming—there really was a boat on the path, and it had passengers. But what passengers! Women clad in the white robes and triangular headdresses of the dead.

"Ghosts! They're ghosts!" shouted the monk at the top of his lungs. "That boat is full of ghosts! I recognize some of them—they're the mothers or wives of the monks from my temple!"

As the monk screamed in terror, the ghostly boat continued its ascent. It reached the summit of Mount Hiei and stopped. The passengers disembarked, formed a solemn line, and began walking around the temple halls, chanting prayers. The monk followed them as quietly as he could. Unfortunately for him, the last ghost in the line sensed his presence. It turned sharply, locked eyes with him, and then rejoined the others. Overwhelmed with fear, the monk fainted. When his fellow monks found him hours later, he recounted the extraordinary events he had witnessed.

"Our mothers and wives," his comrades explained, "were not allowed to enter the temple while alive. They died without seeing us again, which caused them great sadness. Unable to let go of this longing, some become ghosts, climbing the mountain to catch a glimpse of us."

This explanation did little to comfort the monk who had seen the ghost ship. Quite the contrary—when he realized he had truly witnessed a boat full of ghosts, he died of fright. His tragic story served as a cautionary tale for his fellow monks, who avoided the slope after dark. Yet, remembering that the ghosts were their loved ones, they honored their memory by naming the slope Funa-saka, or "Boat Slope," a name it still bears today.

50 THE GHOST OF THE FUNERARY TABLET

Kamedo Hall, a sub-temple of Enryakuji, stands on the former site of Gochi-in Temple. This now-vanished temple is remembered for a tale of a woman who returned as a ghost to perform virtuous deeds and attain the Pure Land.

Once upon a time, in an age long past, there lived a man whose name remains unspoken, for he possessed the somewhat extravagant trait of loving his wife with an intensity that bordered on madness.

One fateful day, in a year now forgotten, the man's beloved wife suddenly passed away. Her death plunged him into deep sorrow, but it also filled him with great concern, for he was acutely aware of the immense difficulty women faced in breaking free from the eternal cycle of reincarnation and achieving rebirth in the Pure Land. He became consumed by the thought that he must do something, anything, to ensure her salvation. After much contemplation, he resolved to seek the help of a craftsman skilled in the creation of religious objects. He went to him with a request.

"I would like you to make a funerary tablet," the man said, "and engrave the name of my dearly departed wife upon it."

The craftsman, moved by the man's earnestness, promised to give his utmost attention to the task. He labored diligently, and after some time, the tablet was completed. The man, with great reverence, wrapped the tablet in a cloth and set out for Enryakuji Temple. Upon his arrival, he spoke to the first monk he encountered—a monk who served at Gochi-in Temple.

"Excuse me," the man began, his voice filled with emotion. "I have here the funerary tablet of someone who meant the world to me. Might I ask you to place it in your temple and recite prayers so that the soul engraved upon it may find its way to the Pure Land?"

The monk, hearing the man's words, immediately recognized that the "person who meant so much" was likely a woman.

"I will take care of the funerary tablet," the monk assured him, his voice filled with compassion. "Please return to the capital, and rest assured that the tablet will be placed with the utmost respect."

The man, his heart slightly eased, turned and made his way back to the capital. Meanwhile, the monk returned to his temple and carefully placed the tablet on the Buddha's altar. He recited a prayer in memory of the deceased, and with that, he retired for the night. But a few hours later, he was abruptly awoken by strange sounds—suspicious noises emanating from the room where the Buddha's altar stood. Curious, he rose from his bed and ventured into the room but found no one there. However, upon further inspection, he noticed something most peculiar: The funerary tablet he had placed on the altar was shaking.

"Perhaps a mouse brushed against it as it scurried by," the monk thought, dismissing his unease and gently returning the tablet to its rightful position.

Yet, just as he settled back into bed, he heard another sound—this time from outside the temple. Intrigued, the monk followed the sound, which resembled splashing. But this was no ordinary splash; it was the sound of someone bathing, the kind of splashing that could only come from someone immersed in water. The monk's curiosity grew, and he allowed the strange noise to guide him to the edge of a pond. There, to his astonishment, he saw a beautiful woman bathing in the moonlit waters, her figure as radiant as the full moon above, and she was murmuring what seemed to be a prayer.

Shocked and horrified, the monk fled back to his temple, his heart racing. But he could not shake the image of what he had seen. The following evening, when he once again heard the strange sounds coming from the Buddha's altar room, he made up his mind to investigate further. He rushed to the pond once again and concealed himself behind a thicket, waiting and watching. Soon he saw the woman reappear, bathing in the pond, her beauty shimmering in the moonlight as if she were some celestial being.

"How heavenly!" the monk whispered, overcome by awe.

The woman, hearing him, turned sharply and called out in anger. "Who are you?" she demanded. "Why do you disturb my sacred bathing ritual?"

The monk, caught off guard, stammered, "I . . . I . . . It is because you are a woman, and women have no right to enter our temple. But tell me, how did you even manage to enter in the first place?"

The woman's eyes darkened, and she replied, her voice cold yet full of sorrow, "You came here because you were disturbed by the sounds of the funerary tablet on your altar, did you not? Well, I am the woman whose name is inscribed upon that tablet. A few days ago, I listened to a sermon by your abbot, who spoke of how one could enter the Pure Land through ascetic practices, such as immersing oneself in a pond and reciting prayers. I decided to try it for myself. So, my spirit emerged from the tablet to perform these exercises in the pond and strive for my salvation."

The monk, deeply moved by her words, felt tears welling in his eyes. Unable to find the words to comfort her, he returned to his temple and vowed never to disturb the poor woman again in her ascetic practices. For many days, he continued to hear the faint sounds of the funerary tablet on the altar, accompanied by the gentle splashing of water. And then, one day, the sounds ceased altogether. The monk, after a long pause, came to the quiet conclusion that the woman had at last achieved her salvation and been reborn into the Pure Land.

51 THE GHOST WHO BRINGS GOOD NEWS

At the entrance to the Daikodo (Great Reading Hall) of Enryakuji Temple stands a monument called the Mound of the Holy Woman. According to tradition, this monument was erected to honor a woman who returned to the world of the living as a ghost to accomplish a virtuous act and gain entry to the Pure Land.

Long ago, in the fifth month of the fourth year of Encho (926), there lived a monk named Son-i, who served at Enryakuji Temple.

One night, Son-i had a strange and vivid dream. He dreamt that an ox-drawn carriage, the kind used by high-ranking court officials, appeared on top of Mount Hiei and made its way toward the Great Reading Hall. The monks in the dream rushed to greet the eminent guest they assumed would step out of the carriage. However, to their astonishment, the curtains parted to reveal not a nobleman but a lady of high rank. One of the monks, flustered, approached the carriage. "My lady," he said, "you must not leave the carriage! Women are strictly forbidden from entering the grounds of our temple."

The lady responded with calm dignity. "I am aware of your rule," she said, "but it applies only to the living. I am no longer of this world, and thus, it does not concern me."

The monks were taken aback. "You are a ghost! But why have you come here, to our temple?"

"I have come to deliver a message," she said. "I wish to congratulate Son-i on his appointment as the new abbot of Enryakuji Temple."

Having delivered her message, the noble lady climbed back into the carriage, which disappeared along with her attendants before the monks' astonished eyes. At that moment, Son-i awoke from his dream. Startled, he found it strange to have dreamed such a thing.

"It was just a dream," he thought, "and nothing more. After all, I am an unremarkable monk, entirely unsuited for the role of abbot. It is impossible."

Reassuring himself, he went about his daily tasks, determined to forget the incident. Later that day, however, the temple was abuzz with commotion. Monks rushed through the corridors, shouting, "A messenger from the emperor is approaching!" Son-i followed the excited crowd to the temple gates. There, they met the imperial emissary, who delivered an extraordinary proclamation.

"I bring an order from His Majesty the Emperor," the emissary announced solemnly. "Son-i is to be appointed the next abbot of Enryakuji Temple."

Son-i was stunned. The words echoed the declaration of the ghostly lady from his dream. Unable to deny what he had just heard, he humbly thanked the emissary and accepted the appointment, recognizing it as the emperor's will. As the monks celebrated the news, Son-i noticed that the emissary seemed troubled. Concerned, he approached him.

"You appear distressed, sir. Is something troubling you?"

The emissary hesitated before replying. "Forgive me, but I have just lost my wife. She passed away last night, and I am still in mourning."

Deeply moved, Son-i expressed his condolences. Then, struck by a sudden thought, he inquired, "May I ask the time of her passing?"

The emissary named a precise moment, and Son-i's heart raced. That was the exact time he had seen the noble lady in his dream. Intrigued and with some hesitation, he described the ghostly woman: her appearance, her noble bearing, and her clothing. The emissary's eyes widened.

"Everything you have said matches my late wife," he exclaimed. "But how could you know her?"

"I did not know her," Son-i replied, "but her spirit visited me last night to announce my appointment as abbot. She came to our temple, defying the rules that bar women, because she was no longer bound by earthly laws."

The monks and the emissary were awestruck by this revelation. It was clear that the deceased wife had chosen to perform one final act of virtue, delivering the good news to Son-i to ensure his appointment. After accepting his role as the thirteenth abbot of Enryakuji Temple, Son-i decided to honor the memory of the woman who had delivered the message. He commissioned the construction of a burial mound in front of the Great Reading Hall, the place where she had appeared to him in the dream. He named it the Mound of the Holy Woman. The mound became a sacred site, a testament to the extraordinary events that led to Son-i's appointment. Curiously, it has remained undamaged through the centuries, as if protected by the very spirit it commemorates.

52 THE GHOST WHO SOUNDED THE ALARM

Visitors to Enryakuji Temple rarely resist the temptation to ring its famous bell. Known as the "Bell That Brings Happiness," it is said to ensure immediate rebirth in the Pure Land for all who sound it. This custom traces its origins to a fateful encounter involving a ghost—a woman seeking redemption.

Long ago, there lived a monk named Tenkai, who served at Nankobo, one of the sub-temples of Enryakuji Temple.

One autumn night in the ninth month of the second year of Genki (1571), Tenkai was jolted awake by an insistent knock at his door. Rising in confusion, he opened it to a sight both eerie and heart-wrenching: Before him stood the ghost of an old woman. Her complexion, a peculiar shade of deep purple, resembled the skin of an eggplant.

"Master Tenkai," the ghost implored in a voice refined yet antiquated, "forgive my intrusion and listen to my plight. When I was alive, I served as a lady-in-waiting to the empress in the imperial palace. My fate took a tragic turn one fateful day some eight hundred years ago when I accidentally took a life. I evaded justice in life but faced it after death. Taken before the Great King Enma's court, I was sentenced to the lowest levels of Hell, where I endured unimaginable torment for what seemed an eternity."

Her spectral voice quavered as she continued, "One day, I overheard a whisper of hope. It was said that even a soul condemned to Hell might escape its torments and find rebirth in the Pure Land if they could accomplish a deed of merit. From that moment, I resolved to return as a wandering ghost, desperate for the chance to redeem myself."

Tenkai, moved by her harrowing tale, could not bear to turn her away. "Your desire for salvation is noble," he said solemnly. "You may remain within the temple grounds and await the opportunity to perform a meritorious act."

The ghost bowed deeply in gratitude before vanishing into the shadows. From that night onward, she wandered through the temple's alleys, awaiting her chance to make amends. Her moment came on the twelfth night of the ninth month. While patrolling the temple grounds as usual, the ghost spotted torches flickering in the distance and heard the ominous clamor of metal. Alarmed, she exclaimed, "Soldiers are ascending the mountain! They are coming to attack the temple!"

Unbeknownst to her, these were the troops of Lord Oda Nobunaga, who sought to crush the monks of Enryakuji and erase their influence. His orders were merciless: Burn the temple, destroy its treasures, and leave no survivors. Realizing the imminent danger, the ghost raced to the temple's belfry. Grasping the rope, she rang the bell with all her might, the sound echoing across Mount Hiei and rousing the monks from their slumber. Thanks to her warning, many monks managed to flee and avoid the massacre that would follow. When the soldiers' raid finally ended, Tenkai and the surviving monks returned to survey the ruins. They were astonished by the number of lives spared.

"It was the Eggplant-Skinned Ghost who saved us," Tenkai explained, recounting her tale of regret and redemption. His story brought tears to the eyes of those who heard it, and they fervently prayed that her act of merit had secured her rebirth in the Pure Land. Indeed, she was never seen again.

In time, the legend grew. People remembered how the ghost had sounded the temple's bell and escaped damnation. From this, a belief took root: Those who rang the bell of Enryakuji Temple could also hope to attain the Pure Land. And so, the Bell That Brings Happiness became a symbol of salvation, its chime forever linked to the story of a ghost redeemed.

53

THE EMPRESS WHO WANTED HER MORTAL REMAINS ABANDONED IN A BURIAL GROUND

In the decades following the establishment of the capital in what is now Kyoto, three nearby plains were designated as burial grounds where the dead were abandoned: Adashino to the west, Rentaino to the north, and Toribeno to the east. While these burial grounds have long since disappeared, their legacy endures in place names and legends of ghosts said to haunt their entrances. One such site is Katabira no Tsuji, or the "Intersection of the Shroud." This crossroads, which marked the entrance to the western burial ground, owes its name to a chilling incident that took place nearly twelve hundred years ago.

Long ago, there lived an empress named Danrin. Renowned for her beauty, she made courtiers' hearts flutter whenever she appeared at court. Her piety was equally striking, often leaving monks humbled by her devout prayers in the temples. Yet, far from taking pride in this adoration, Empress Danrin was deeply troubled by the transient nature of worldly admiration. She devoted her life to the principle of impermanence, and when she sensed her end approaching, she summoned her ministers and declared, "I do not wish for my body to be entombed in an imperial mausoleum after my death. Instead, I ask to be left on the plain of Adashino. Those who are enslaved by love will witness my decay and understand that nothing endures. The monks will see my body deteriorate and pray more fervently to the Buddhas. In this way, all will find rebirth in Heaven."

The ministers, profoundly moved by her words, promised to honor her wishes. When the inevitable day arrived—the fourth day of the fifth month in the third year of Kasho (850)—they kept their vow. Danrin's attendants prepared her body with the utmost care. They dressed her in the traditional white burial kimono and placed a ceremonial headdress on her head. Then they laid her upon a cart and set off for Adashino. As they approached the bleak plain, the wind began to howl. A sudden gust, fiercer than the others, swept across the moor and carried off the empress's headdress. It floated gracefully through the air before falling at a crossroads that marked the boundary between the capital and the burial ground.

"The empress is sending us a sign!" exclaimed the head of the attendants. "She wishes to be left where her headdress has fallen!"

Respecting this interpretation, the attendants unloaded her body at the crossroads and departed. No sooner had they turned their backs than stray dogs and crows descended upon the corpse, consuming the flesh until only bones remained, which the wind and rain gradually scattered.

Not long after this grim event, a man was crossing Adashino Plain one evening, attending to urgent business. As he neared the crossroads, he spotted the silhouette of a woman standing there. Surprised, for it was unusual to see women out after dark in such a dangerous area, he approached—and to his horror, realized it was the ghost of Empress Danrin. Her body, half-devoured by scavengers, stood before him in a ghastly state. Terrified, the man screamed and fled back to his home, abandoning his errand.

Soon other locals began to report sightings of Danrin's ghost at the entrance to Adashino. With each apparition, her body appeared more ravaged, evoking both pity and fear. Distressed, the villagers sought guidance from a monk at the local temple.

"Even in death," the monk explained, "Empress Danrin is imparting a profound lesson. Through the decay of her body, she reminds us that nothing in this world is permanent and urges us to meditate on the fleeting nature of existence."

The villagers, moved by the monk's wisdom, decided to honor the empress's sacrifice. As a tribute to her efforts to inspire meditation on life's impermanence, they named the crossroads at Adashino's entrance Intersection of the Shroud. Though the burial grounds themselves have vanished, the name endures to this day.

54 THE DEAD WOMAN WHO DIDN'T WANT TO GO TO THE BURIAL GROUND

While some female ghosts ask to be taken to the graveyard, others refuse to go and return home instead. The two stories that follow feature precisely this kind of ghostly woman. The first tells of an unmarried woman who refused to be taken to Toribeno, the eastern graveyard, and managed to have herself buried in the garden of her own house. Her grave still exists. It is known as the "Mound of the Civil Servant's Daughter" (Hannyo-zuka), and even today, it continues to inspire fear among the residents of Kyoto. To avoid provoking the wrath of this woman who never experienced the joys of marriage, couples refrain from passing by together and instead walk past her grave one at a time.

Long ago, there lived a governor with two daughters. The younger daughter was married and lived in the capital near the intersection of Takatsuji and Muromachi Streets. The elder daughter remained unmarried and resided with her sister, helping with the household chores.

One fateful day, the elder daughter passed away suddenly. Grief-stricken, her parents placed her body in a coffin and, with the help of neighbors, carried it to Toribeno, the burial ground east of the capital. Yet, as they journeyed, they noticed the coffin felt strangely light. Curiosity compelled them to stop and open it—only to find it empty!

"Could her body have fallen out along the way?" one pallbearer speculated.

Determined to find her remains, the group retraced their steps, scouring the road in vain. As dusk approached, they abandoned the search and returned home, only to discover the deceased lying on her deathbed as though she had never left.

"We must have forgotten to place her in the coffin," the father reasoned, relieved. "We'll ensure she is taken to Toribeno tomorrow morning."

The following day, the family and neighbors double-checked that her body was inside the coffin before resuming their journey. Yet again, midway to Toribeno, the coffin became inexplicably light, and once more the body vanished—only to reappear back in her room. On the third day, when they tried to lift the corpse, they found it impossibly heavy, resisting their efforts entirely.

"What sorcery is this?" one bearer exclaimed.

"This is no sorcery," replied an elderly neighbor. "It's her spirit sending a message—she doesn't want to be buried at Toribeno. She wishes to remain here."

Taking heed of this interpretation, her father declared, "If she wishes to stay, we shall respect her will. Let us dig a grave beneath the house and lay her to rest there."

The group did as he suggested, carefully burying her beneath the floorboards. This time, the body felt light and cooperative. Thereafter, her parents honored her memory with offerings and prayers at the family altar. As the years passed, the parents and close relatives died one by one, leaving no one to tend to the grave. The neighbors grew uneasy, fearing that the neglected spirit of the elder daughter might rise in anger. To appease her and prevent any vengeful curses, they built a burial mound over her grave and named it the Mound of the Civil Servant's Daughter.

Life carried on. But the spirit of the buried woman began observing the people walking by her grave. One day, she noticed a couple deeply in love. A wave of envy washed over her as she realized she had never experienced the joys of love. Bitterness turned to anger, and in her jealousy, she cursed the pair. Moments later, the couple quarreled and separated forever. Consumed by envy, the woman's spirit began casting spells on every couple who dared to pass her grave, causing heartbreak and discord. It wasn't long before the locals recognized the pattern. Concerned, they convened one evening to discuss the problem.

"I have a solution," proposed one neighbor. "Let us build a shrine in her honor and venerate her as the Civil Servant's Eldest Daughter."

"And since the word for 'civil servant's daughter' (*hannyo*) sounds nearly identical to the word for 'prosperity' (*hanjo*), we can revere her as a deity of commerce!" another chimed in.

The neighbors agreed wholeheartedly and pooled their resources to construct a small shrine next to her burial mound. The spirit, touched by this gesture, abandoned her vengeful ways. Embracing her new role as a goddess, she devoted herself to bringing prosperity to all who came to pray at her shrine. The townsfolk were overjoyed by her transformation, but they remained cautious. Couples continued to separate and walk past the mound individually, a custom observed to this very day.

55 THE GHOST WOMAN AND THE TAXI DRIVER

The motif of the dead woman returning home is a recurring theme in Japanese legends. It already appeared in the tale of the civil servant's daughter, which dates back to the thirteenth century. It resurfaces in more modern stories, where the ghostly woman is now driven home—this time by taxi! The phenomenon was first reported by the highly respected newspaper Asahi Shinbun, *which, in an article dated October 7, 1969, published the account of a taxi driver who had picked up a female passenger and discovered, during the ride, that she was a ghost. Below is the translated version of the original article.*

THE PASSENGER WHO VANISHED FROM A TAXI!

Police Break into a Cold Sweat Over a Peculiar Statement!

In the early hours of October 6, 1969, a female passenger mysteriously disappeared from a taxi as it drove through the streets of Kyoto. The driver was left questioning whether she had ever truly entered the cab—or if she had somehow fallen out during the journey. The Kamigamo precinct's police were baffled by the unsettling mystery. Here's the testimony of Mr. A, the driver involved:

"My name is A. I work as a driver for the Kyowa Taxi Company. On the night of October 6, around half-past one in the morning, I had just dropped off three passengers at the intersection of Konoe and Higashioji Streets in the Sakyo Ward, right in front of Kyoto University Hospital.

After writing the trip details in my logbook, I heard a knock on the half-open passenger-side window. Standing there was a woman, seemingly in her forties. Her shoulder-length hair was wet and disheveled. She asked in a faint voice, 'Can you take me in your cab?' I nodded, let her into the car, and started the engine. When I asked where she wanted to go, she replied in a weak, almost inaudible tone, 'To Midoro-ga-ike Pond.' I glanced at her through the rearview mirror. Her hollow cheeks and sickly appearance unsettled me. Feeling uneasy, I refrained from asking her any further questions during the ride. Still, I kept checking the mirror occasionally, especially before making turns. Each time, I saw her sitting quietly in the back seat. About ten minutes later, we approached the pond. I asked her where exactly she wanted to go, but there was no response. When I turned around to look, she was gone. The back seat on the left-hand side, where she had been sitting, was empty. All that remained was a strange brown liquid on the seat. Just moments earlier, I had clearly seen her in the mirror. Now she had vanished. For a second, I wondered if she could have fallen out along the way."

In his distress, Mr. A flagged down a passing car and asked the driver to contact the Kamigamo precinct police. Within minutes, no fewer than fourteen police cars arrived at the scene. The officers searched the area for an hour but found no trace of the woman matching Mr. A's description. However, they did discover a truck belonging to the dissection unit of Kyoto University Hospital, parked discreetly about fifty meters from the site of the incident. This odd detail raised further questions, especially since Mr. A had initially picked up his passenger right outside the hospital's dissection unit. The five-kilometer stretch that Mr. A drove with his mysterious client falls under the jurisdiction of the Kawabata, Shimogamo, and Kamigamo police precincts. Yet none of these stations reported any accidents or unusual incidents during the night of October 5/6. Mr. A concluded his statement with these words:

"I admit I was driving fast, but the doors of my taxi are automatic—they cannot be opened from the inside. I don't believe my passenger could have fallen out. I wasn't dreaming!"

56 STATUES FILLED WITH LOVE LETTERS

One of the traditionally believed reasons women face difficulty entering the Pure Land is their ability to stir confusion in men's hearts. Legend has it that the more beautiful a woman is, the harder it becomes for her to achieve salvation. This was true for Empress Danrin, who, as recounted in another tale, used her death to exemplify the fleeting nature of earthly existence, encouraging others to focus on the spiritual rather than the material. Similarly, the poetess Ono no Komachi, celebrated as one of the three most beautiful women in human history—alongside Cleopatra of Egypt and Empress Yang Guifei of China—suffered greatly for her beauty. Komachi, aware of the turmoil her looks caused in men's hearts, devised a remarkable way to atone and save her admirers from rebirth in the Realm of Hungry Spirits. To this day, two unusual statues of Jizo, the bodhisattva who guides souls through the Six Realms of Rebirth, stand testament to her efforts. These statues are preserved at Zuishin-In and Taiko-an, two temples in southeastern Kyoto.

Nearly twelve centuries ago, Ono no Komachi was renowned not only for her stunning beauty but also for her poetic talent. Her charm drew countless suitors, each vying for her attention. Overwhelmed by their advances, Komachi eventually withdrew from court life and sought refuge on her family estate east of the capital. There, she lived in seclusion for many years.

As her earthly life drew to a close, Komachi reflected on her past and the impact of her beauty.

"When I was at court," she thought with regret, "I unsettled the hearts of men. I awakened in them a yearning for love that will condemn their souls to rebirth in the Realm of Hungry Spirits. I must find a way to help them before I leave this world!"

Komachi wrestled with the problem until inspiration struck. She decided to sculpt a statue of Jizo, the compassionate bodhisattva who aids lost souls in their journey toward salvation. Halfway through her work, however, a new worry gripped her.

"Creating an image of Jizo is one thing," she mused, "but how will the bodhisattva recognize those whose suffering I have caused?"

The answer came to her in a flash of brilliance: She would place the love letters her suitors had written to her inside the statue.

"This way," she reasoned, "Jizo will be able to read their names and find them more easily in the afterlife."

Komachi filled her statue with love letters and placed it in her residence. However, she quickly realized that hundreds of letters remained. Determined to include them all, she carved a second, much larger statue. Once it was complete, she filled it with the remaining letters and installed it in a temple she had specially constructed for this purpose. Standing before the statues, Komachi offered a heartfelt prayer: "I ask you, noble Jizo, to save the souls of those whose passions I have ignited, sparing them from the Realm of Hungry Spirits. May you also guide all who have strayed from the path to rebirth in Heaven."

While Komachi's intentions were pure, the outcome was far from what she expected. Instead of renouncing their passions, the people of Kyoto misinterpreted her gesture. Word spread quickly of statues filled with love letters, and people flocked to "Komachi Temple" to seek blessings—not for spiritual liberation, but for success in love.

Even today, this tradition continues. Komachi's second statue, now housed at Taiko-an Temple, attracts visitors who pray to it in hopes of finding their soulmate. Far from quelling earthly desires, Komachi's statue has inadvertently ensured that the Realm of Hungry Spirits remains well populated for generations to come.

57 THE CURSED STONE OF FUKAKUSA GENERAL

It is said that a suitor once died while courting Ono no Komachi and became, depending on the version of the story, either an Angry Spirit who tormented couples or a ghost who opposed the poetess's entry into the Pure Land. According to some traditions, this Angry Spirit took refuge in a stone, which was later retrieved and placated by the monks of Hounji Temple. Through their prayers, the spirit transformed into a benevolent deity known as Kikuno Daimyojin, or the "Great Deity of the Chrysanthemum Plain," who grants five kinds of liberation.

Once upon a time, nearly twelve centuries ago, there lived a poetess named Ono no Komachi. So celebrated was her beauty and talent that men vied endlessly for her attention, each hoping to win her favor.

Tiring of the ceaseless courtship, Komachi left the imperial court and secluded herself on her family's estate, located to the east of the capital. But even in her self-imposed exile, one suitor managed to track her down. This was a fourth-rank general from the village of Fukakusa, known simply as "Fukakusa General." When he found her, his words were so eloquent, his devotion so profound, that Komachi agreed to marry him—on one condition.

"I will marry you," she said, "if you visit me every evening for one hundred consecutive nights, and on each visit, you must repeat your marriage proposal."

Fukakusa General, overjoyed, vowed to fulfill her request. Starting the very next evening, he crossed the mountain pass leading to Komachi's residence, paused briefly to rest on a stone at the summit, and then arrived to court her, pleading for her hand in marriage. Night after night, he repeated this ritual.

On the fateful hundredth evening, however, a fierce snowstorm swept across the mountain pass. Undeterred, the lovestruck general set out, determined to fulfill his promise. Yet as he neared the summit, the storm intensified, and the blizzard became so brutal that he was unable to proceed. With no shelter to be found, Fukakusa General froze to death beside the very stone where he had rested so many times before. His soul, filled with unfulfilled longing and bitterness, took refuge in the stone itself.

Sometime later, a happy couple walked along the same mountain path where the general had perished. Seeing their joy, the general's spirit was overcome with envy. He cursed the lovers, sowing discord in their hearts. Almost instantly, the couple quarreled and parted ways forever.

"If I cannot taste the sweetness of love," the general's spirit muttered with satisfaction, "then neither shall anyone else."

From that day forward, the Angry Spirit of Fukakusa General cursed every couple who passed by his resting place, ensuring their separation. Eventually, the villagers began to fear the stone, which they now called the Break-up Stone. Couples avoided walking past it together, wary of its power.

Centuries passed . . .

In the eighth year of Tenmei (1788), a violent earthquake struck the capital. Among the destruction it caused was a landslide that swept away the cursed stone. Not far from the site of the landslide stood Hounji Temple, which had also been severely damaged by the quake. Once the tremors subsided, the monks returned to rebuild their temple. One day, while they were hard at work, an old man appeared on the path. Without a word, he approached the monks and entered the temple courtyard.

"Do you know where the cursed stone of Fukakusa General is?" he asked. "If not, you should find it and honor it. I'm sure it would be grateful."

Before they could question him further, the old man disappeared as mysteriously as he had arrived. Intrigued, the monks searched the surrounding area and eventually found the stone. Fearing its curse, they placed it in a chest and returned to their task of rebuilding the temple.

Once the temple was restored, one monk recalled the old man's cryptic advice. "He told us to honor the stone," the monk said. "Perhaps now is the time to do so."

"How can you even consider bringing such a cursed object into the temple?" another monk protested.

"The old man also said the stone would be grateful," the first monk replied. "Perhaps if we place it under the Buddha altar, the Buddhas will calm the Angry Spirit and guide it to peace."

After much debate, the monks agreed to give the idea a chance. They placed the chest containing the cursed stone beneath the temple altar and prayed fervently to the Buddhas for the spirit's redemption.

Hearing their prayers, Fukakusa General's spirit repented for the pain he had caused over the centuries. He vowed to devote himself to bringing happiness to couples and removing obstacles from their paths. And so he does to this day. Even now, the citizens of Kyoto visit Hounji Temple to pray before the altar housing the stone of Fukakusa General, seeking liberation from whatever "bond" troubles them.

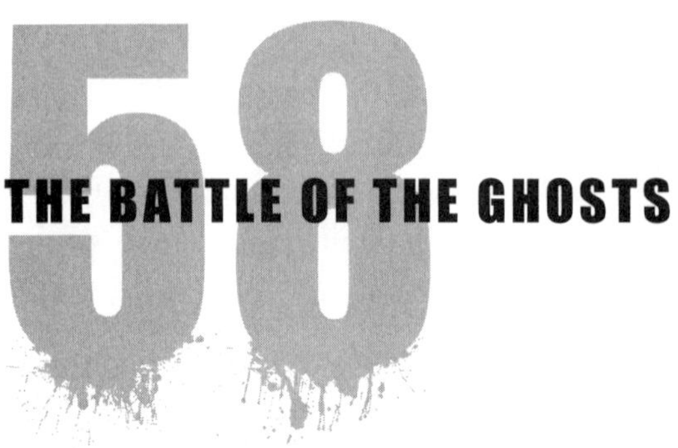

THE BATTLE OF THE GHOSTS

*Other versions of the story of the Major General from the village of Fukakusa (*Fukakusa no Shosho*) recount how he returned to Earth in the form of a ghost in order to prevent a monk from praying for Ono no Komachi's salvation. According to tradition, this confrontation took place at a temple officially named Fudarakuji, though it is more commonly known as Komachi-dera, or "Komachi Temple." Within this temple, one can see two funerary monuments—one dedicated to Komachi and the other to General Fukakusa—that suggest a peaceful resolution to the ghostly battle we are about to recount.*

Once upon a time, in an age long past, there lived a devout monk whose name has been lost to history. One summer, the monk left the capital to seek solitude in a nearby village called Yase. There, he devoted himself to prayer, his unwavering piety earning the admiration of the local villagers—particularly an elderly woman who, moved by his dedication, made it her daily habit to bring him fruit and firewood. The monk, deeply touched by her kindness, decided one day to express his gratitude.

"May I know your name?" he asked. "I would like to thank you properly."

The old woman hesitated before replying in an archaic tone, "I am no longer of this world. I am Ono no Komachi."

Rather than frightening him, her revelation filled the monk with compassion. Her ghostly presence meant that the renowned poetess had not yet been able to enter the Pure Land and had been condemned to wander the Realm of Human Beings for centuries.

"I will help you," the monk declared with heartfelt resolve. "I will pray for your salvation."

Without delay, the monk gathered his few possessions and journeyed to the nearby village of Ichihara, where Komachi had died. A temple had been constructed beside her grave. Upon arriving, the monk entered the sacred space, seated himself before the altar, and summoned the Buddhas in prayer. Just as he was about to implore them to admit Komachi into the Pure Land, a ghostly figure materialized before him. It was a woman of extraordinary beauty. The monk immediately recognized her as Ono no Komachi, who now appeared in her most radiant form. Inspired by her presence, he resumed his prayers. But before he could complete his invocation, the room was pierced by a chilling, menacing voice.

"Monk, cease your prayers!"

Startled, the monk turned to face the source of the voice. Before him stood another ghost, this one an aristocratic figure clad in the ceremonial garb of a bygone era.

"I am Fukakusa General," the ghost announced, his tone brimming with anger. "This woman forced me to propose marriage to her a hundred times. She made me drink until I was drunk, and as a result, I was denied entry to the Pure Land. She is wicked and undeserving of your prayers!"

The ghost's words, laden with bitterness, only deepened the monk's resolve. Instead of faltering, he began praying anew—this time asking the Buddhas to grant salvation not only to Komachi but also to Fukakusa General.

As his prayer concluded, the two ghosts began to fade. Their forms dissolved into the air, and the room was filled with a profound silence. Tears welled in the monk's eyes as he realized the Buddhas, in their infinite mercy, had granted his request. The two tormented spirits, their earthly grievances finally resolved, had at last been welcomed into the Pure Land.

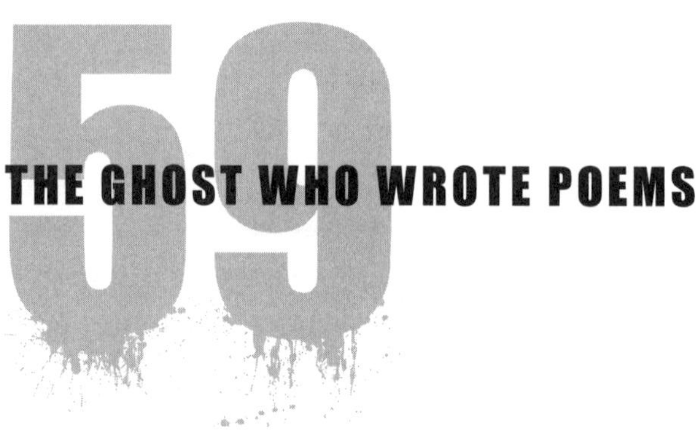

THE GHOST WHO WROTE POEMS

Officially, the temple is named Fudarakuji, but as we've just seen, it is more widely known by its affectionate nickname—Komachi-dera, or the Temple of Komachi—due to its deep connection with the legendary poetess Ono no Komachi. In addition to the stupas erected in her honor and that of her lover, visitors can also find a commemorative stele marking the very spot where her lifeless body was said to have been discovered. According to local lore, renowned poets once gathered before this monument to pay their respects and exchanged verses with the ghost of Ono no Komachi herself.

Nearly twelve centuries ago, Ono no Komachi lived—a woman of extraordinary beauty and poetic talent. Her charms drew throngs of admirers who vied endlessly for her favor. Growing weary of such relentless attention, Komachi abandoned the imperial court and sought solitude on her family's estate to the east of the capital.

Yet one suitor, undeterred, discovered her refuge. He was a general of the fourth rank from the village of Fukakusa, known simply as "Fukakusa General." He wooed Komachi with words so eloquent that she agreed to marry him—on one peculiar condition: He must visit her every night for one hundred consecutive nights and, on each occasion, repeat his marriage proposal. Fukakusa General eagerly accepted the challenge. For ninety-nine nights, he crossed a mountain pass, resting each time upon a stone before making his way to her residence. But on the final night, as he made his journey, a fierce snowstorm engulfed the pass. Unable to find shelter, he succumbed to the freezing winds and perished.

When news of his death reached her, Komachi was overcome with grief and began to lose her grip on sanity. She abandoned her family estate and retreated to a dilapidated house her father owned in Ichihara, a remote village northeast of Kyoto. There, she lived in utter poverty, her once-celebrated beauty withering as her life became a shadow of its former splendor. Anticipating her death, Komachi left behind a testament:

When I die, do not bury or cremate me.
Leave my body on the moors of Ichihara, to be
feasted upon by crows and stray dogs.
吾れ死なば / 焼くな埋むな / 野に晒せ /
痩せたる犬の / 腹肥やせ

Komachi hung this poem on a pillar in her house before passing away. Days later, villagers discovered her lifeless body. Respecting her wishes, they carried her remains to the moors and abandoned them there. News of Komachi's tragic end spread far and wide, eventually reaching a distant province where the renowned monk and poet Kukai resided. Stricken by the tale, he resolved to honor her memory.

"A great poetess has passed!" Kukai exclaimed. "I must find her remains and pray for her soul's salvation."

Undaunted by the distance, Kukai embarked on the long journey to Ichihara. Upon arrival, he questioned the villagers, who led him to the moor where Komachi's body had been discarded. There, amid the fescue grass, lay countless corpses in varying states of decay.

"Can you identify which of these is Komachi?" Kukai asked.

The villagers shook their heads. Moved by the tragic scene, Kukai grasped a handful of fescue and composed a poem:

Autumn's breath sweeps across this world.
O flowers, guide me to the resting place of Komachi!

世の中に / 秋風立ちぬ / 花すすき /
まねかばゆかん / のへも山も

No sooner had he spoken than he heard a faint whisper, as if carried on the wind. Startled, he listened intently. A woman's voice seemed to rise from a clump of fescue, reciting a poem in response:

The autumn wind burns my eyes,
yet my skull cannot tell you I am Komachi.
But the fescue sprouting from my sockets will.
秋風の / ふくにつけても / あなめあなめ /
小野とは言はし / 薄生ひけり

Realizing that the grass marked her resting place, Kukai searched the moor until he found a skull from which tufts of fescue emerged. He gathered Komachi's remains, interred them respectfully, and prayed for her spirit to ascend to the Pure Land. News of Kukai's actions spread across the empire, eventually reaching Saigyo, another monk and poet. Determined to offer his own prayers, Saigyo journeyed to Ichihara. Upon arriving, he knelt before Komachi's grave and composed his tribute:

Resting beneath the shade of fescue,
do you hear the temple bell's echo?
なき人の / いかなる草の / かけにおり /
て今うちならす / 鐘をきくらん

As Saigyo departed the village, he encountered a beautiful young peasant girl along the road. When their paths crossed, she turned to him and recited,

I hear the bell.
Beneath this vast moor's grass, I lie, listening
to its sound.

聞そとよ / 此野ゝ草の / 影にをりて /
今打ならす / かねの一こゑ

Before Saigyo could respond, the girl vanished into thin air. Trembling, he realized she was no mortal but the ghost of Ono no Komachi. Even in death, her spirit continued to weave poetry, leaving Saigyo awestruck by the enduring brilliance of her art.

60 THE DANCE OF IZUMI SHIKIBU'S GHOST

The eleventh-century poetess Izumi Shikibu, celebrated for her captivating beauty and poetic brilliance, was a woman who bewitched the hearts of countless men. For these entanglements, among other reasons, it is said that her soul remained trapped in the Realm of Human Beings after her death, inhabiting the plum tree that grows in the courtyard of Toboku-in Temple.

One serene spring day, two monks—a master and his young disciple—set out from their province and journeyed to the capital. While wandering the city, they came across Toboku-in Temple, where a resplendent plum tree stood in full bloom in the courtyard.

"What is the story behind this plum tree?" the master asked a passerby.

The man paused and replied, "This temple was built on the grounds of Izumi Shikibu's former residence. The plum tree you see was planted by her own hands and is known as 'Izumi Shikibu's Plum Tree.'"

The monks expressed their gratitude for the explanation and entered the temple courtyard. Standing beneath the plum tree, they marveled at its beauty, their thoughts lost in admiration. Suddenly, an unexpected voice startled them. Turning, they saw an old woman standing beside them.

She spoke with a calm yet enigmatic tone: "You were told this tree is called 'Izumi Shikibu's Plum Tree,' but its true names are Kobunboku, the 'Plum Tree Lover of Classical Letters,' or Oshukubai, the 'Plum Tree with Sparrows' Nests.' Izumi Shikibu herself planted it and called it Nokiba no

Ume, the 'Eaves Plum Tree.' Throughout her life, she never tired of gazing upon its blossoms. You should also know that I am not of this world; I reside within this plum tree."

With those words, the old woman disappeared as abruptly as she had appeared, leaving the monks stunned. They fled the courtyard and encountered the same man who had earlier explained the tree's origin. Breathless, they described the strange encounter.

The man listened intently, then exclaimed, "That old woman was none other than the ghost of Izumi Shikibu! You must pray for her soul and ask the Buddhas to grant her entry to the Pure Land."

Convinced of the man's wisdom, the monks returned to the temple. They sat beneath the plum tree, their voices rising in unison as they recited the Lotus Sutra. Hours passed as they prayed fervently for Izumi Shikibu's salvation.

At last, the ghost of the poetess appeared once more. This time, she took the form of a radiant young woman. She began to dance gracefully, performing an elegant courtly dance from her era. Her movements were as mesmerizing as her poetry had been. When the dance concluded, she turned and walked toward one of the temple's ancient buildings, the same one she had once called home. Just as she reached the threshold, she vanished, leaving the monks bewildered.

They awoke, as if from a shared dream, unsure of what they had truly experienced. Had they encountered the ghost of Izumi Shikibu, or was it a vision bestowed by their prayers? The mystery remains unanswered, but the monks carried the memory of that ethereal dance with them for the rest of their days.

61 THE GHOST WHO BECAME A BUDDHA

Seishin-in and Seiganji Temples share two unique distinctions: Both are nestled in the bustling heart of Shinkyogoku Shopping Arcade, and both honor the memory of the poetess Izumi Shikibu. Seishin-in is said to house her grave, where, on March 21 each year, monks hold a memorial service in her name. Seiganji, on the other hand, is believed to have drawn its name from a divine encounter involving her ghost.

Once upon a time, nearly 750 years ago, there lived a monk named Ippen.

One day, Ippen embarked on a pilgrimage to the sacred shrine of Mount Kumano. There, his fervent prayers moved the local kami so deeply that the deity descended to speak with him.

"Monk," the kami began, "you address me as the spirit of Mount Kumano, but I am, in truth, Amida Buddha—the one who descends to the Realm of Human Beings with his celestial cohorts to guide the dead to the Pure Land. Your devotion has touched me, and I entrust you with a mission: Go to the capital. Write the words 'Amida promises entry to the Pure Land to sixty thousand faithfuls' on amulets and distribute them to the people."

Ippen, humbled and inspired, vowed to fulfill this sacred task. Returning swiftly to the capital, he prepared amulets bearing the inscription and handed them out to everyone he encountered. His path eventually brought him to a temple dedicated to Amida Buddha, where he chose to stand at the entrance, offering amulets to the devotees entering to pray.

As he stood there, an old woman, frail and bent with age, approached him and said, "You are distributing amulets proclaiming that Amida will save sixty thousand worshippers. But tell me, does Amida intend to save only sixty thousand?"

"Of course not," Ippen replied earnestly. "I wrote sixty thousand because that was the number Amida revealed to me, but in truth, he will save all who call upon his name!"

"If that is so," the old woman said with conviction, "then you should proclaim it boldly. Paint the words 'Temple of the Promise Made' on the front of this temple!"

Hearing her speak with such authority, Ippen felt a jolt of realization—this was no ordinary woman but a messenger of Amida Buddha. "Who are you?" he asked, awestruck.

"I am Izumi Shikibu."

"That cannot be," Ippen exclaimed in disbelief. "Izumi Shikibu passed away over 250 years ago!"

The old woman sighed, disappointed by his doubt. "You do not believe me? My grave lies nearby. Come with me, and I will prove the truth of my words."

She turned and walked toward the graveyard of a local temple, Seishin-in. Ippen followed close behind. She stopped before a grave—her grave—and, without a word, vanished into thin air. At that moment, Ippen understood the truth: The old woman had indeed been the ghost of Izumi Shikibu. Overcome with awe, he hurried back to the temple where he had been distributing amulets. He recounted the miraculous events to the monks.

"Master Ippen," they said, deeply moved by his tale, "you must inscribe the words that Amida's messenger has requested upon our temple."

Grateful for their support, Ippen immediately set to work. With meticulous care, he painted three Chinese characters on the temple's frontispiece: Seiganji, meaning "Temple of the Promise Made."

As he completed the final stroke of the last character, the sky above the temple transformed. A luminous purple cloud descended, enveloping the temple in its divine glow. Upon this cloud stood Amida Buddha, holding a lotus blossom—symbol of his divine grace—surrounded by his celestial cohorts. Each member of the heavenly entourage exuded unparalleled beauty and serenity.

To Ippen's astonishment, one of these celestial beings bore the unmistakable features of Izumi Shikibu. The monk realized with awe that, in death, the poetess had not only entered the Pure Land but had also been elevated to the celestial ranks of Amida Buddha's divine retinue.

62 THE MONK BORN IN HIS MOTHER'S GRAVE

A recurring motif in Japanese legends revolves around women who die in childbirth, only to transform into ghosts that return to provide for their children born within their graves. In Kyoto, several tales follow this poignant pattern. One such story takes place at Ryuhonji Temple, where the graveyard houses the tomb of Nisshin (1599–1666), a monk said to have been born under these extraordinary circumstances. His unusual birth inspired Nisshin to establish a ritual to protect pregnant women, which continues to be observed on the eighth day of every month. To this day, the ritual attracts expectant mothers seeking safe deliveries.

Long ago, there lived a merchant named Emura Hisashige. The fourth year of Keicho (1599) began auspiciously for him, as his wife joyfully announced her pregnancy. Sadly, the year ended in tragedy when she fell gravely ill and passed away shortly before giving birth. Stricken with grief, Hisashige arranged an elaborate funeral service for her and had her interred in the graveyard of Ryuhonji Temple. Then he retreated into mourning. One day, a neighbor who ran a local sweets shop came to visit, attempting to lift Hisashige's spirits.

"Something strange has been happening lately," the man said. "For several nights now, a woman comes to my shop in the dead of night and buys three pennies' worth of sweets. Isn't that peculiar?"

Hisashige, distracted by his sorrow, remained silent. Disappointed, the sweets seller eventually left to share his story elsewhere, but no one in the neighborhood seemed interested.

Among Hisashige's acquaintances was another man, the caretaker of Ryuhonji Temple's graveyard. One evening, while making his rounds through the quiet, moonlit cemetery, the caretaker stopped in his tracks, startled by the sound of faint crying. He strained to listen and realized the sobs were coming from a child—and they seemed to be emanating from one of the graves.

Alarmed, the caretaker exclaimed, "I must tell the abbot!" He hurried to the temple, woke the abbot, and recounted the unsettling occurrence. Together, they returned to the graveyard and approached the source of the sound.

"I recognize this grave," the abbot said, his voice heavy with emotion. "It belongs to Hisashige's wife."

The men quickly opened the tomb and were met with a heartbreaking sight: the lifeless body of Hisashige's wife and, cradled beside her, a living baby suckling on sweets. In that moment, the abbot and the caretaker recalled the sweets seller's eerie tale and pieced together the truth: Hisashige's wife had given birth within her grave. Transformed into a ghost, she had ventured out each night to buy sweets for her child.

The abbot gently lifted the baby from the coffin. He took the boy under his care, raising and educating him as his own. When the child came of age, he became a monk, adopting the name Nisshin, and eventually succeeded the abbot as the head of Ryuhonji Temple. Deeply mindful of his own miraculous survival, Nisshin dedicated himself to serving his parishioners, particularly pregnant women. Once a month, he held elaborate religious ceremonies, invoking the Buddhas to ensure safe deliveries for expectant mothers.

Even after Nisshin's passing, his successors at Ryuhonji Temple faithfully continued his ritual, a tradition that endures to this day, bringing comfort and hope to countless pregnant women.

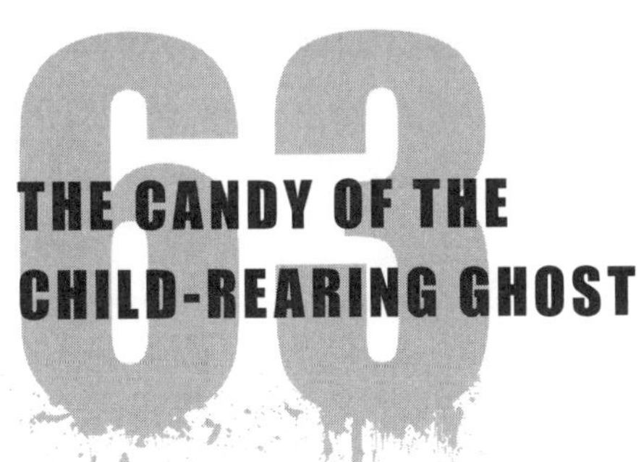

63 THE CANDY OF THE CHILD-REARING GHOST

Another poignant tale of a woman who became a ghost to feed her child born in the grave takes place near the entrance to what was once the burial grounds of Toribeno. For the past 450 years, the shop Minatoya has sold sweets made from sugar and malted barley syrup, famously known as the "Candies of the Child-Rearing Ghost." As the story goes, these candies were used by a ghostly mother to nourish the baby she had given birth to after death.

Nearly five hundred years ago, a man named Sobei ran a small shop at the entrance to Toribeno Graveyard. One day in the fourth year of Keicho (1599), Sobei opened his shop as usual, selling tea and sweets to visitors paying respects to their ancestors. After a busy day, he closed his shop and went to sleep.

Knock! Knock! Knock!

The sound startled Sobei awake in the middle of the night.

"Who's there?" he called out, puzzled.

"Please, open up and sell me some sweets," replied a faint woman's voice.

Despite the late hour, Sobei lit a candle and opened the door. Standing before him was a young woman, likely in her early twenties, looking utterly exhausted.

"I beg you, sell me a bag of sweets," she said weakly.

Moved by her pitiful state, Sobei folded some sweets into a bamboo leaf, handed them to her, and received a coin in return. The woman disappeared into the night. The next evening, the young woman returned, knocking again on his door.

"Please, I need more sweets," she pleaded.

Sobei complied, noticing that she seemed even more weary than before. This pattern repeated over the following nights. One evening, heavy rain poured down. Sobei assumed his visitor would not come, but to his surprise, the knock echoed once more. When he opened the door, there she was, soaked to the bone, standing in the downpour.

"Here are your sweets," Sobei said hurriedly. "Take cover quickly!"

She handed him a coin, took the bag, and disappeared into the storm. The next morning, as Sobei counted his earnings, he noticed he was one coin short. To his astonishment, he also found a tree leaf in his cash box. Suspicious, he muttered, "She's tricked me! Tonight, I'll get to the bottom of this."

That evening, when the woman came again, Sobei sold her the sweets and secretly followed her. Keeping his distance, he saw her walk up the street, enter Toribeno Graveyard, and approach a grave. She stood still for a moment before vanishing into thin air.

"A ghost!" Sobei gasped, trembling.

Terrified, he ran to a nearby temple and roused the monks.

"Take me to the grave," the abbot commanded after hearing Sobei's story.

Together, they approached the grave. From within, they heard the unmistakable cries of a baby. Hastily, they opened the tomb and discovered the woman's lifeless body—and beside her, a baby, very much alive, eating the sweets Sobei had sold.

"I remember this woman," the abbot exclaimed. "I conducted her funeral just days ago. She was pregnant at the time of her death. She must have given birth in the grave and returned as a ghost to feed her child. The coins she paid you with were likely those placed in her shroud for the afterlife. When she ran out of money, she must have transformed a leaf into a coin to keep buying sweets."

The abbot and Sobei took the child to the deceased woman's relatives, but they refused to care for him, fearing the stigma of raising a child born in a grave.

"What will become of him?" Sobei asked.

"I have an idea," the abbot replied. "There is a temple nearby called Kodaiji, which means 'Temple of the High Hill.' Interestingly, it is pronounced the same as the phrase *kodaiji*, meaning 'to take care of a child.' It's a sign. The monks there will surely care for him."

True to the abbot's prediction, the monks of Kodaiji welcomed the boy. They raised him with love and discipline, educating him to become a monk who spent his life praying for his mother's salvation. As for Sobei, he renamed his sweets the Candies of the Child-Rearing Ghost to commemorate the strange and touching event. His descendants have carried on the tradition, and even today, visitors can buy these sweets, each bite a testament to a mother's undying love.

64 THE STORY OF THE WARRIOR WHOSE SON WAS BORN IN HIS WIFE'S GRAVE

The tale you are about to read mirrors the one told previously, recounting how a woman gave birth to her child in the grave. However, this version presents the events from the perspective of the child's father, a man who, it is said, became a monk under the name of Kokua (1314–1405) and later served at Shohoji Temple.

Once, a long time ago, there was a lord named Hashizaki Kuniakira, who governed a large estate in Harima Province, which is now part of Hyogo Prefecture.

In the fourth year of Bunna (1355), Kuniakira received a letter from the shogun, Ashikaga Yoshimitsu, summoning him to Kyoto to discuss a matter of utmost importance. Without delay, Kuniakira prepared to leave and requested that his wife, who was several months pregnant, accompany him. Although her condition made travel difficult, the prospect of visiting Kyoto brought her great joy, and she agreed eagerly.

Accompanied by their retinue, they made their way to the capital. Upon arrival, Kuniakira immediately went to see the shogun, who tasked him with quelling a rebellion in Ise Province. Kuniakira accepted the mission without hesitation and arranged for his wife to stay in a residence within the city while he left at once, leading the shogun's forces.

While Kuniakira was away, however, his wife fell ill. Despite the best efforts of doctors, her condition worsened, and she tragically passed away before she could give birth to their child. The lord's servants arranged the funeral and buried her in Rentaino Graveyard, situated to the north of the capital. Afterward, they sent word to Kuniakira.

The news of his wife's death struck Kuniakira with deep sorrow. Though he longed to mourn and visit her grave, the urgency of his military duties prevented him from doing so. Instead, he instructed his servants to visit her grave daily, offering prayers and placing offerings in her honor. Furthermore, he commanded them to give three pennies to any beggar they encountered along the way, explaining that these acts of charity, performed in the name of his late wife, would please the Buddhas and help her journey to the Pure Land.

The servants faithfully carried out their lord's instructions. Only on two occasions did they find themselves occupied with other duties, but apart from those rare instances, they visited the grave and performed the prescribed acts of devotion.

Eventually, Kuniakira returned to Kyoto. He immediately went to his wife's grave, where he lit incense and recited prayers. As he was offering his respects, he suddenly stopped, disturbed by the sound of a child crying from the grave. Alarmed, he cried out in terror. His cries drew the attention of a man who had come to pay his respects at his own family tomb. This man, a tea merchant who ran a shop on the south side of the graveyard, approached Kuniakira.

"Something strange is afoot in this graveyard!" the merchant remarked.

"What do you mean?" Kuniakira asked, puzzled.

The merchant explained, "For some time now, I've had an unusual customer. Each night, she knocks on my door and buys three pennies' worth of mochi. With only two exceptions, she has come every night. Intrigued, I decided to follow her after one of her visits. I saw her walk up the street and enter Rentaino Graveyard. I was too frightened to continue following her, so I stopped there."

Hearing the merchant's account, Kuniakira was overtaken by a dreadful premonition. He ordered his servants to open his wife's grave, and they did so. Inside, they found the corpse of his wife, her arms still holding a living child who was eating the very mochi sold to his mother by the merchant.

At that moment, the horrible truth dawned on Kuniakira. He knelt in anguish before his wife's coffin, exclaiming, "My wife gave birth to our child in the grave and, in her ghostly form, went to buy him food!" Grief-stricken, he vowed to do everything in his power to ensure her salvation and her rebirth in the Pure Land.

In his profound sorrow and resolve, Kuniakira entrusted his son to the tea merchant, asking him to raise the child as his own. He then discarded his weapons and armor, took the name Kokua, and became a monk at Shohoji Temple. There, he spent the rest of his days praying for his wife's soul, asking the Buddhas to grant her passage to the Pure Land.

65 THE GHOST OF DAIKOKUJI TEMPLE

Daikokuji is a temple located in Fushimi Ward, dedicated to the worship of Daikoku, the Japanese deity of wealth, commerce, and exchange. At first glance, it may seem an unlikely setting for a tale of spectral motherhood, yet even here, one finds a story of a woman who became a ghost after death in order to nourish her child—born within the grave. Her name was Yashiro Mitsume, and she was the sister-in-law of Tajiri Inajiro (1850–1923), a former mayor of Tokyo. To this day, her grave and memorial tablet remain visible within the grounds of Daikokuji Temple. What makes Mitsume's story particularly striking is its chronological dissonance: Unlike most ghost-mother legends, which are typically set during the Muromachi period (1336–1573), Mitsume's tale unfolds in the nineteenth century. This detail clearly shows that the story of Mitsume is part of a long-standing tradition—proof that this narrative motif has been used and retold across generations.

Once upon a time, not so long ago, there lived a man by the name of Yashiro Ki, who worked as a steward in the residence of the lords of Satsuma, now Kagoshima Prefecture. The residence was situated in Kyoto, where the lords stayed during their visits to the capital.

Ki was married to a woman named Mitsume, who, in the twelfth year of Meiji (1879), became pregnant. As the weeks and months passed, Mitsume's pregnancy progressed smoothly without complications. However, as the time for childbirth approached, Mitsume expressed a strong desire to return to her homeland in Satsuma. She asked her husband, "I would like our child to be born in our home province of Satsuma. Will you grant me permission to return?"

Seeing no reason to refuse, Ki agreed. Mitsume prepared for the journey and, accompanied by a small group of servants, set off for Satsuma. But as they neared the city of Kobe, Mitsume suddenly fell ill. Despite the servants' best efforts to alleviate her suffering, her condition worsened, and tragically she passed away before giving birth. Devastated, the servants brought her body back to her husband in Kyoto. Unable to prevent this sorrowful fate, Ki organized a memorial service and had her buried in the graveyard of Daikokuji Temple.

Not far from this temple, there was a small sweets shop run by an elderly man. One night, he was suddenly awakened by a knock at his door. He rose, opened the door, and found a woman dressed entirely in white standing before him.

"Please forgive my disturbance at this late hour," she said softly. "Would you kindly sell me some sweets?"

Though somewhat surprised, the old man agreed and sold her the sweets. Once the transaction was complete, he closed the door and returned to bed. The next night, the woman appeared again, and on every subsequent night, she came without fail. The shopkeeper began to grow suspicious of this strange nocturnal visitor.

"If she comes again tonight, I will follow her and discover the reason for her odd behavior," he resolved.

That night, as expected, the woman arrived, requesting her usual sweets. After selling them to her, the shopkeeper quietly locked the shop and followed her discreetly. The woman walked through the darkened streets and, to the old man's astonishment, entered the graveyard of Daikokuji Temple.

"What is she doing in the graveyard at this hour?" the shopkeeper wondered, his curiosity growing as he watched her walk among the graves. Suddenly, the woman stopped in front of one particular tombstone and, as if by magic, disappeared from sight. The old man, trembling, approached the grave to read the inscription: Mitsume, wife of Lord Yashiro Ki.

At that moment, the shopkeeper was struck by a horrific realization: Mitsume had died, along with her unborn child. Yet, driven by an unrelenting maternal instinct, she had returned as a ghost to fetch food for her baby. Overcome with sympathy for Mitsume's tragic fate, the shopkeeper decided to honor her memory. From that day forward, he sold his sweets under a new name: "Sweets That Fed a Ghost's Son."

66 THE PINE TREE THAT STOPS CHILDREN FROM CRYING AT NIGHT

In some stories, women who gave birth in their graves become ghosts that seek out food for their newborns. This was the case in the last four tales. In other stories, women become ghosts, rise from their graves with their child, and try to entrust the baby to someone. The story from Honryuji Temple offers a perfect example of this type of ghost. It tells how a ghostly woman entrusted her child—born in the grave—to a monk at the temple, and how he managed to lull the baby to sleep by carrying it in his arms and walking around the pine tree that grew in the courtyard. For a very long time, women from the neighborhood followed this precedent: With their children in their arms, they would walk around the "Pine Tree That Stops Children from Crying at Night" before putting them to bed.

Once, a very long time ago, there lived a monk named Nittai, who served as the abbot of Honryuji Temple.

One evening, in the fourth year of Daiei (1532), Nittai decided to pray in the temple's Buddha hall. As he crossed the courtyard, he noticed a woman. She was strikingly beautiful, her long black hair flowing over her shoulders, though her skin was unnaturally pale. She held a baby tightly in her arms. Despite her serene appearance, her expression was laden with sorrow. Nittai, intent on his prayers, refrained from addressing her and continued to the Buddha hall.

The next evening, as he once again made his way to the Buddha hall, the same woman appeared. She walked slowly, cradling her child, her face streaked with tears. Moved by her evident despair, Nittai called out to her, "Why are you so sad? Why do you cry so bitterly?"

The woman turned her mournful gaze to him. "Good monk," she began, "I am no longer among the living. I passed away a week ago. After my death, this child, my son, was born within my grave. I became a ghost to search for someone to care for him, but alas, I have found no one willing to take him. That is why I weep."

Nittai was stunned but resolute. "I will raise your child," he declared. "Entrust him to me, and I will educate him and guide him to become a monk. Your burden will be lifted, and your soul can find peace in the Pure Land."

Hearing these words, the woman wept even harder, her tears flowing like a river.

"Do you truly mean this?" she asked, her voice trembling.

To prove his sincerity, Nittai reached out and took the child in his arms. At that moment, the woman's sorrowful face softened into one of serenity. With a final, peaceful expression, she vanished into thin air, her spirit finally freed to enter the Pure Land.

The baby, now motherless, began to cry inconsolably. Nittai, unsure of how to comfort him, gently rocked the child and, almost absentmindedly, walked around a pine tree standing near the Buddha hall. As if by some miracle, the baby stopped crying and fell into a deep sleep just as Nittai completed his circuit around the tree.

From that day forward, whenever the child cried, Nittai would cradle him and walk around the pine tree. Without fail, the crying ceased, and the child fell peacefully asleep. It wasn't long before the mothers of the area, noticing Nittai's peculiar success, began to imitate him. They too discovered that circling the pine tree could calm their children and lull them to sleep. Convinced of the tree's extraordinary powers, the locals named it Yonakidome no Matsu, or "the Pine Tree That Stops Children from Crying at Night." The tradition of walking around the tree became a cherished custom among the temple's visitors.

As for the child saved by Nittai, he grew up studying Buddhism, eventually taking the name Nisshu. In time, he succeeded Nittai as the abbot of Honryuji Temple, continuing the legacy of compassion that had begun under the branches of the miraculous pine tree.

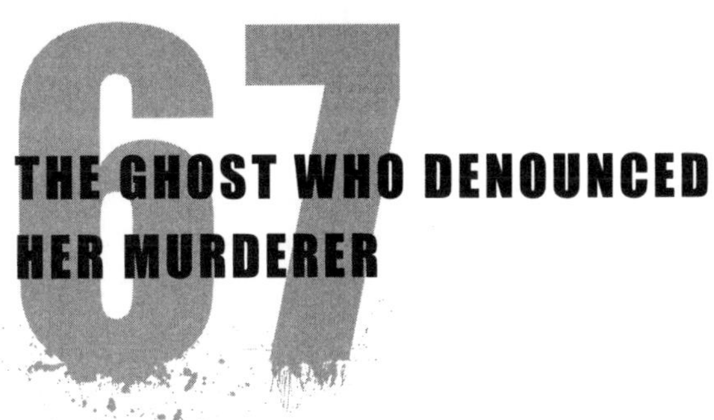

67 THE GHOST WHO DENOUNCED HER MURDERER

Many Japanese legends recount the tragic fates of women who were either beaten to death or driven to suicide and who, as ghosts, lingered while awaiting guidance to the Pure Land. These tales, deeply rooted in Edo-period societal struggles, echo the plight of women during that era. At Gyoganji Temple, located in Kyoto, a painting is displayed each year from August 21 to 23. It depicts the ghost of a woman murdered by her employer. Affixed to the painting is a mirror said to have belonged to the unfortunate woman and to have played a pivotal role in her story.

Long ago, there lived a pawnbroker named Hachizaemon. On New Year's Day in the thirteenth year of Bunka (1816), Hachizaemon became a father. Seeking a nurse for his newborn, he employed a young girl named Ofumi, just fifteen years old, whose parents were humble farmers in the neighboring province of Omi (modern-day Shiga Prefecture).

Ofumi moved into Hachizaemon's household and devoted herself to caring for his son. Among her daily routines, she would carry the child in her arms and take him for walks, often stopping at Gyoganji Temple. The temple, dedicated to the compassionate goddess Kannon, was a gathering place for pilgrims who chanted invocations while striking a small gong:

Now that I can admire the flowers in the garden of
    Gyoganji Temple,
My faith, like these flowers, blooms anew.

Ofumi, charmed by the rhythmic invocation, began using it as a lullaby for the baby. However, when Hachizaemon overheard her singing this prayer, he became enraged.

"I forbid you to sing that to my son! And you are never to visit Gyoganji Temple again!" he shouted before striking her.

Terrified, Ofumi promised to obey. She refrained from singing the prayer at home but could not resist returning to the temple, where the child continued to hear the melodic chants of the pilgrims. Several months later, Hachizaemon's son surprised his parents by uttering his first words. Delighted, his father leaned in to listen.

"Now that I can admire the flowers . . ."

Upon hearing his son repeat the invocation to Kannon, Hachizaemon flew into a violent rage. He beat Ofumi mercilessly, dragged her to the storeroom, and locked her inside.

"You'll spend the night here! That will teach you a lesson!" he shouted before bolting the door and returning to the warmth of his home.

The following morning, Hachizaemon returned to the storeroom. Inside, he found Ofumi's lifeless body; she had frozen to death during the frigid night. Panicked, he carried her body to the garden and buried her in a shallow grave. To conceal his crime, he wrote a letter to Ofumi's parents, claiming their daughter had eloped with a lover.

A few days later, Ofumi's parents arrived at Hachizaemon's house, deeply apologetic for their daughter's supposed misconduct. Hachizaemon coldly confirmed their suspicions, and they left in shame. On their way home, they passed Gyoganji Temple and decided to pray to Kannon for their daughter's guidance. Exhausted by grief and travel, they fell asleep at the feet of the goddess's statue. Both had the same dream. In the dream, Ofumi appeared before them.

"Father! Mother!" she cried. "I did not run away! Hachizaemon murdered me and buried my body in his garden!"

Startled awake, the parents recounted their identical dreams, stunned by the revelation. As they processed what they had seen, they noticed a mirror lying beside them—a mirror they instantly recognized as their daughter's.

"This is no dream," said the father. "She left this mirror as proof of her visit!"

"She has returned from the dead to accuse her murderer," added the mother, tears streaming down her face.

Armed with this evidence, Ofumi's parents reported Hachizaemon's crime to the authorities. The police conducted a search of his property and unearthed Ofumi's body from the garden. Hachizaemon was arrested, imprisoned, and later executed for his heinous act. Before returning to their home province, Ofumi's parents visited Gyoganji Temple one last time to express their gratitude to Kannon. They commissioned an ex-voto painting of their daughter as she had appeared to them in the dream and placed it, along with her mirror, in the temple. Then, with heavy hearts, they departed Kyoto and never returned.

THE GHOST OF THE GEISHA

From time to time, Bunda-in Temple displays its treasures. Among them is a painting titled Young Girl in White Kimono, *created by a twentieth-century artist named Amano Shoshi. Though seemingly unremarkable at first glance, the artwork in fact portrays a geisha from Gion just moments before she took her own life. Ultimately, this piece serves as a stark reminder that behind the elegant façade of the "flower districts" lay a reality that was often as harsh as it was sordid—a world that witnessed many tragedies, leading numerous women to "transform" into ghosts.*

Once upon a time, a century ago, there lived a painter named Amano Shoshi, who frequented the geisha districts of Kyoto.

One day, in the tenth year of Taisho (1921), Shoshi visited the Gion district and stayed at Tsujikome, a teahouse near the crossroads of Kawabata and Shijo Streets. At dawn, he was roused from his sleep by the commotion of hurried footsteps and urgent voices in the corridors. Intrigued, Shoshi dressed quickly and went to investigate. The household was abuzz, all rushing toward the canal that bordered the teahouse. Following the crowd, Shoshi soon discovered the cause of the uproar: A young geisha from the Tsujikome house had taken her own life, hanging herself from one of the poplar trees lining the canal. The area was already teeming with onlookers, their voices a cacophony of speculation and gossip.

"That was the geisha they accused of all kinds of misdeeds!"

"Yes, she always swore she was innocent, saying she'd never done anything wrong."

"In the end," another chimed in, "she must have killed herself to prove her innocence."

Someone, exasperated by the chatter and inaction, finally declared, "I'm going to call the police!"

Meanwhile, Shoshi, deeply moved, hurried back to his room to retrieve his sketchbook. Returning to the scene, he began to draw the deceased while awaiting the authorities. This sketch later inspired a painting: a woman in a white kimono, her figure ethereal, seemingly dissolving into mist—a vision akin to a ghost. Once the painting was complete, Shoshi gifted it to the patroness of the teahouse before departing.

The patroness of Tsujikome House, a devout woman, was accustomed to praying at Bunda-in, a sub-temple of Tofukuji Temple. She took it upon herself to pray for the salvation of the geisha's soul. The night after her visit, the resident monk of Bunda-in experienced a peculiar dream. In it, a beautiful young woman appeared suddenly in his room. Approaching his couch, she softly commanded, "You must go to Tsujikome House."

The monk awoke the next morning, the vividness of the dream lingering in his mind. Compelled by its urgency, he made his way to Tsujikome. Upon arrival, he noticed an altar adorned with offerings. Curious, he inquired about it, and the patroness explained her intentions to honor the young geisha's memory. Eventually, the patroness said, "Let me show you what this poor girl looked like. An artist I know painted her portrait!"

She then unfurled the painting by Amano Shoshi. The moment the monk's eyes fell upon the image, he gasped in recognition. The woman in the portrait was the very figure who had visited him in his dream!

"I understand now!" the monk exclaimed. "She appeared to me so that I might bring this painting to my temple and pray for her salvation."

Moved by his revelation, the patroness entrusted the painting to the monk, who carried it back to Bunda-in. To this day, the painting remains there, and until recently, it was displayed annually during the Festival of the Dead in August, serving as a poignant reminder of the geisha's sorrowful tale.

69 THE MAN WHO FELL IN LOVE WITH A GHOST

Among the myriad tales passed down through the ages, some recount the tragic fates of women who linger in the Realm of Human Beings after death, unable to relinquish their yearning for love. One such spectral figure was said to haunt the streets of Kyoto, preying on her victims in the vicinity of Manjuji Temple. While the temple itself has since moved to another part of the city, the street in front of its original location still bears the name Manjuji-dori, or "Manjuji Temple Street," in memory of these eerie events.

Nearly five centuries ago, there lived a man named Ogiwara Shinnojo in the Gojo-kyogoku district of the capital. A widower, Shinnojo led a solitary life, occupying his days with the study of sutras and the composition of poetry.

One evening, on the fifteenth day of the seventh month, Shinnojo ventured outside and encountered a vision of beauty: a young woman with a delicate countenance and long black hair, accompanied by a little girl holding a lantern adorned with peony motifs.

"Excuse me, sir," the young woman said, noticing his gaze. "The streets of the capital are perilous after dark. Would you kindly escort me home?"

"Of course," replied Shinnojo gallantly. "Or, if you prefer, you are welcome to stay the night at my house."

The young woman graciously accepted his offer. That night, they spent hours in lively conversation, exchanging verses of poetry. As dawn broke, the young woman departed, promising to return the next evening—and she did. Each night thereafter, she arrived at Shinnojo's home, and their bond deepened.

Curiosity soon consumed Shinnojo's neighbor, who wondered about the mysterious woman visiting the reclusive widower. One evening, after she arrived, the neighbor peered through a crack in the wall. What he saw chilled him to the bone: Shinnojo sat across from a skeleton dressed in the white kimono of the dead, conversing as if with a living person! The next morning, the neighbor confronted Shinnojo with what he had seen.

"That's impossible!" protested Shinnojo. "She cannot be dead. She even gave me her address—near Manjuji Temple!"

"If that's true, then you should confirm it," urged the neighbor.

Determined to prove him wrong, Shinnojo went to the area near Manjuji Temple, asking locals about the woman. None knew her. Exhausted, he sought respite in the temple and wandered into the pavilion of the dead. There, he noticed a coffin surrounded by offerings. A funerary tablet identified the deceased as a young woman. Among the objects nearby were a lantern adorned with peony motifs and a doll resembling the child who had accompanied his nocturnal visitor.

"My neighbor was right," Shinnojo murmured in disbelief.

Horrified, he returned home and placed a protective amulet on his door to ward off spirits. The ghost ceased her visits. Over time, Shinnojo began to forget the ordeal. One evening, at the invitation of a friend, he indulged in a drink. On his way home, he passed Manjuji Temple. Memories of the enigmatic woman surfaced, and he felt a pang of longing for the evenings they had shared. At that moment, the ghost appeared at the temple gates.

"I promised to visit you every night, but your amulet kept me away," she said. "I am so glad to see you again. Please come into my home!"

Overwhelmed by his emotions, Shinnojo replied, "I care not who you are. I will never leave you again." Taking her hand, he allowed himself to be led into the temple.

Shinnojo's companion, however, saw the ghost's true form: a skeleton animated by an otherworldly force. Terrified, he fled to gather help. Returning with neighbors, they stormed the pavilion of the dead. Inside, they found Shinnojo's lifeless body in the open coffin, entwined in the arms of the deceased woman. His once-vibrant form was now withered, though his face bore a serene smile.

The two bodies were buried together in Toribeno Graveyard. That night, the locals saw their spirits walking hand in hand down the street, led by the spectral child carrying the lantern with peony motifs. Frightened, the townsfolk waited until morning to return to the gravesite. There, they placed offerings and prayed fervently to the Buddhas. Their devotion ensured that the two lovers could find peace in the Pure Land.

PART FIVE

GHOSTS AND SPIRIT HEALERS

Life, death, and the possibility of becoming a ghost are unyielding laws of nature. Yet some extraordinary individuals have found ways to bend these rules. In this part, we encounter fascinating characters who bring the dead back to life, breathe life into inanimate objects or fragments of corpses, journey to the underworld, or transform themselves into ghosts to protect Kyoto from supernatural threats.

70

THE MONK WHO BROUGHT HIS DEAD FATHER BACK TO LIFE

It is believed that the deceased either enter the Pure Land, are reborn into the Six Realms, or remain as ghosts in the Realm of Human Beings. However, Japanese legends recount tales of individuals who, through extraordinary means, managed to transcend this cycle of life and death. Among them was the monk Jozo (891–964), who is said to have brought his late father back to life through the sheer force of his prayers. This miraculous event took place on Kyoto's First Avenue Bridge, which later came to be known as Modori-bashi, or "Bridge of Return."

More than a thousand years ago, Jozo, a monk devoted to spiritual practice, began his training at Enryakuji Temple. Later, seeking to enhance his mystical powers, he retreated to a remote mountain, where he lived in seclusion and undertook rigorous ascetic exercises.

Our story begins after Jozo had spent several years in isolation atop the mountain. One day, he was suddenly struck by an overwhelming premonition. A sense of dread compelled him to return to his parents immediately. Without hesitation, he left the mountain and journeyed back to the capital. After several days of travel, he arrived, only to encounter a funeral procession crossing the First Avenue Bridge.

"Who lies in that coffin?" Jozo asked one of the mourners, a strange unease stirring within him.

"It is Lord Miyoshi no Kiyoyuki," came the reply. "He passed away suddenly four days ago. We are taking him to Rentaino Graveyard."

"But he is my father!" Jozo exclaimed in shock. "I have spent the last six years in the mountains, unable to see him. Now, even in death, I wish to see his face one last time."

Moved by his grief, the mourners paused and allowed Jozo to approach the coffin. They opened the lid, revealing his father's lifeless body. Jozo gazed down, his father's features pale and unrecognizable, drained of all vitality.

"O Buddhas!" Jozo cried out. "I have devoted my days to prayer, reciting the Lotus Sutra, and performing good deeds. We live in an age where virtue is rewarded—so hear my plea! Even if it costs my life or brings divine punishment, I beg you to return my father to the living. Allow me to see him alive once more! If you do not answer my prayer, how can future generations find solace in the chanting of the Lotus Sutra?"

The mourners watched as Jozo raised his rosary and directed his fervent prayers to the heavens. His voice was filled with desperation and faith. Moments later, a miracle occurred. From within the coffin came the sound of breathing, followed by a loud gasp. The astonished onlookers witnessed Jozo open the lid, pull his father out, and embrace him tightly.

Jozo's father, now alive, recounted his extraordinary experience. "I found myself at the court of judgment in Hell, standing before Great King Enma, who was about to pass his verdict. Suddenly, a powerful voice echoed through the court, declaring, 'This man's son has done enough good deeds to redeem his sins! Send him back to the Realm of Human Beings!' Obeying this command, Great King Enma ordered his servants to return me to life. And so, here I am!"

Overcome with emotion, Jozo realized that his prayers had been answered by the Buddhas. Tears streamed down his face as he rejoiced with his father. The two spent the night talking, and at dawn, they discarded their mourning garments and returned home together.

News of this miraculous event quickly spread throughout Kyoto. From that day forward, the First Avenue Bridge was called the Bridge of Return. People began crossing it whenever they wished for some form of return—such as safely coming home from war. Conversely, the bridge was avoided during weddings, funerals, or moving house to prevent any unintended "returns."

71 THE BRIDGE WHERE A THOUSAND DEAD WERE BROUGHT BACK TO LIFE

Kannonji Temple stands just beside the "Bridge of Return." We've already spoken of this temple and seen how its gates were said to contain the souls of prisoners killed in the dungeons of Fushimi-Momoyama Castle. The temple is also known for its statue of the merciful goddess Kannon, who is said to have brought back to life a thousand dead whose bodies had been abandoned beneath the infamous Bridge of Return. It was because of this miracle that the temple became more widely known in Kyoto by the nickname Sennindo, or "Hall of a Thousand People."

In the first year of Meitoku (1390), a devastating epidemic swept through Kyoto, claiming countless lives. The death toll was so high that there was no time to bury the deceased properly. Instead, their bodies were unceremoniously cast into the rivers that crisscrossed the city.

One day, a young man named Yamane Shigeshi left his home and crossed the First Avenue Bridge. As he glanced at the river below, expecting to see its familiar flow, he was overcome with horror. What lay beneath him was not a river but a grotesque mass of corpses piled so thickly that the water was no longer visible.

"I must do something for these poor souls!" exclaimed Shigeshi, shaken by the grim sight.

Desperate to help, the young man remembered the legend of the Bridge of Return. It was said that long ago, a monk had prayed fervently at this very spot and brought his deceased father back to life. Inspired by this story, Shigeshi resolved to act. He scanned his surroundings and noticed a small temple near the bridge. Known as Kannondo, it was dedicated to the worship of the compassionate goddess Kannon. Without hesitation, Shigeshi rushed to the temple, entered its prayer hall, and knelt before the statue of the goddess.

"O Kannon, merciful goddess!" he implored. "I beg you to come to the aid of the countless dead abandoned beneath the Bridge of Return!"

Barely had he finished his prayer when panicked cries and eerie howls erupted from beneath the bridge. Startled, Shigeshi hurried back to the scene. There, he witnessed an extraordinary sight: The lifeless bodies discarded under the Bridge of Return were coming back to life, one after another!

Later, Shigeshi and the people of Kyoto learned that the goddess had not only resurrected the dead but had also vanquished the epidemic. Overwhelmed with gratitude, the survivors offered fervent thanks to Kannon. In homage to the lives saved that day, they renamed the temple Sennindo, the "Hall of a Thousand People."

THE PLUM TREE THAT FLEW TO REJOIN ITS MASTER

In the courtyard of Kandaijin Jinja, or "Minister Sugawara Shrine," stands a renowned plum tree known as Tobi-ume, or the "Flying Plum Tree." Each February, Kyoto's inhabitants gather to marvel at its blossoms, said to grow on the very spot where another plum tree once stood—a tree that, according to legend, flew across Japan to be reunited with its master, the exiled poet Sugawara no Michizane. This enchanting tale illustrates how, in Japanese folklore, the magic of words could breathe life into the inanimate, weaving miracles as potent as prayers.

Long ago, there lived an aristocratic poet named Sugawara no Michizane. This celebrated figure adored plum trees, and his affection for them was so profound that he immortalized them in verse. When he became a master of Chinese characters, he composed poetry extolling the plum tree's beauty. Later, as an official in the imperial administration, he planted a splendid red plum tree in the courtyard of his home and found great joy in watching its blossoms herald spring.

Over the years, Michizane's command of language deepened, and he harnessed the power of words not only to entertain foreign ambassadors but also to communicate with the gods. It is said that on one occasion, he wrote a plea to the heavens for rain. As soon as he finished reading his letter aloud, rain cascaded from the skies, quenching the parched earth for three days and nights.

Michizane's talents earned him significant political influence, but his success aroused envy among rivals. Falsely accused of a crime, he was stripped of his titles and exiled to Dazaifu on the distant island of Kyushu. Though he protested his innocence, his pleas fell on deaf ears. Resigned to his fate, Michizane bid farewell to his wife, his children, and, at last, the cherished red plum tree in his garden. Standing before the tree, he was struck by inspiration and composed a poignant farewell:

O plum blossoms! When spring comes and the east
  wind blows,
send me your fragrance all the way!
Even if your master is no longer here,
don't forget to bloom when spring comes!
東風吹かば / にほひをこせよ / 梅の花 /
  主なしとて / 春を忘るな

With those words, Michizane turned his back on his home and began his journey into exile. What followed was nothing short of extraordinary. Overcome by the beauty of Michizane's poem and the sheer magic of his words, the red plum tree sprang to life. Stirring from its rooted slumber, it looked around in dismay. Realizing that its beloved master had departed, the tree lifted itself from the earth and soared through the skies, flying to Dazaifu to rejoin him. When Michizane saw the plum tree standing before him, he was astonished.

"What are you doing here?" he exclaimed.

If flowers continue to revive my memories,
how will I ever forget the past?
古里の / はなのものいふ / 世なりせば、 /
  むかしの / 事をとはまし

Moved by his words, the tree felt remorse. Saddened by its master's melancholy, it responded with a poem of its own:

In the mansion where you once dwelled in
    the capital,
the fences lie untended, and deer roam freely.
The sun sets in sorrow over this abandoned home,
a place bereft of its master.
先久於故宅、癈離於久年、
    麋鹿在住所、無主独碧天

Michizane, deeply touched, softened. “If that is so,” he replied, “then you may stay with me.”

And so, the Flying Plum Tree remained by Michizane’s side. When the poet passed away, the tree settled beside his grave, ensuring it was forever sheltered by its shade. Centuries have since passed, but the Flying Plum Tree continues its vigil. Today, it stands proudly in front of Dazaifu Tenmangu, the shrine built atop Michizane’s grave, its blossoms a timeless testament to loyalty and love.

73

THE MONK SAIGYO AND THE SPIRIT OF THE CHERRY TREE

Another master of words was the monk Saigyo (1118–1190). According to tradition, Saigyo gave life to a cherry tree through the power of his poetry and even encountered the incarnate spirit of that tree. This legendary tree, known as Saigyo's Cherry Tree, still stands today in the courtyard of Shojiji Temple.

Long ago, nearly a thousand years past, a monk named Saigyo roamed the provinces of the empire before finally settling at Shojiji, a temple west of Kyoto. In the courtyard of this temple, he planted a cherry tree and took immense pleasure in watching it bloom each spring. The tree blossomed with extraordinary beauty, producing flowers so radiant that they filled Saigyo's heart with joy.

However, the fame of the tree's blossoms spread far and wide. When the cherry tree was in full bloom, crowds from the capital flocked to the temple gates, demanding to admire its beauty. Saigyo, who had retreated from city life in search of peace and solitude, grew increasingly unhappy. In his frustration, he began to resent the tree for its splendid display.

One day, Saigyo approached the cherry tree and, overcome with emotion, composed a poem filled with reproach:

> They come in droves, those crowds from the capital, drawn to see
> your blossoms. Ah, beautiful flowers, it is you who are to blame!

花見んと / 群れつつ人の / 来るのみぞ、 /
あたら桜の / とがにはありける

That night, Saigyo had a most peculiar dream. An old man appeared before him and spoke.

"I stand before you in the guise of an old man," the apparition began, "but you should know that I am, in truth, the incarnate spirit of your cherry tree. While I appreciate your poetic gifts, I must say that I do not care for the poem you addressed to me. How can you blame me for blooming? I am simply fulfilling the role that the heavens have assigned to me in this world!"

Humbled, Saigyo apologized and expressed his delight at meeting the spirit of his cherished cherry tree. The two then engaged in a lively discussion about poetry and famous sites known for their cherry blossoms throughout the provinces. As dawn broke, the old man vanished, and Saigyo awoke to find the ground around him covered in cherry blossom petals. Perhaps, he thought, his dream had not been a dream after all.

74

SAIGYO CREATES A MAN FROM CORPSE PARTS

The monk Saigyo, renowned for instilling life in a cherry tree with his poetry, is also the subject of a darker legend—one in which he delves into far more extreme experimentation by animating a man assembled from parts of corpses.

Long ago, over a thousand years past, there lived a monk named Saigyo who resided at a temple atop Mount Koya.

During his time there, he formed a deep friendship with an elderly ascetic. Many evenings, under the luminous glow of the moon, they would wander the mountains together, discussing nature's wonders: flowers, birds, the wind, and the moon. One evening, however, the ascetic announced that he would soon leave. Saigyo was despondent, realizing he would lose his sole companion for these serene nighttime walks.

In his sadness, Saigyo recalled a peculiar tale shared by his friend Fujiwara no Saneyoshi.

"Once," Saneyoshi had said, "an *oni*—a supernatural being—visited me and boasted about creating a woman from parts scavenged from corpses in the capital's burial grounds. The oni described its method in meticulous detail."

This memory sparked an idea in Saigyo. "If an oni could do such a thing, then so can I," he mused. "I shall create my own companion!"

Determined, Saigyo descended to the plain at the foot of Mount Koya, a place where villagers abandoned their dead. Among the decaying remains, he gathered bones and began assembling a human form. Piece by piece, he strung the bones together and constructed a body. Though his creation resembled a man, it was hideous to behold. Its skin was ghastly, its voice had a discordant rasp like a poorly tuned instrument, and it lacked the essential essence of humanity—a heart.

"A man is defined by his heart," Saigyo told the grotesque figure. "Without one, you can never truly be my companion. But what am I to do with you now? I cannot destroy you—that would be a grave sin. I have no choice but to abandon you deep in the forests of Mount Koya."

With that, Saigyo left his creation behind and journeyed to the capital, seeking advice. He first visited Saneyoshi's residence but learned that his friend was away. Undeterred, Saigyo sought out Chancellor Minamoto no Moronaka, a man rumored to have successfully created a human being who now served in high office within the imperial administration.

When Saigyo recounted his failed experiment, the chancellor listened attentively before offering his insights.

"Tell me," Moronaka said, "how did you go about creating this being?"

Saigyo described his process in detail: "I began by coating the bones with an arsenic-based ointment and covering them with strawberry leaves. I then bound the bones with wisteria roots and washed the structure with cool water. Next, I burned *shikakai* pods (*Senegalia rugata*) and rose of Sharon leaves (*Hibiscus syriacus*), using their ashes to treat the skull where hair grows. I laid the body on a mat and waited for two weeks. Finally, I burned incense and recited the Spell of Return to Life."

Moronaka nodded thoughtfully. "I see where you went wrong," he replied. "You burned incense and recited the spell too soon. Incense repels malevolent forces but also summons the Buddhas, who despise such forbidden rites of resurrection. Moreover, when I succeeded in creating a man, I had a peculiar dream that same night. An elderly figure appeared before me, approached my bedside, and declared, 'I am the guardian of death. By what right do you dare grant life? If you share your secret, your descendants shall bear the weight of my curse.'"

These words sent a chill down Saigyo's spine. He deeply regretted his attempt to create life and resolved never to try again. From that day forward, he kept his secret to himself, ensuring it would never pass to another.

75 THE SEAL OF THE KING OF HELL

The historical figure Abe no Seimei (921–1005) gained renown for his mastery of rituals, during which he invoked Taizan Fukun, the Chinese god of life and death, to either heal his clients or extend their lifespans. In Seimei's era, Taizan Fukun was closely associated with Enma, the Buddhist King of Hell. It is therefore unsurprising that legend transformed this connection into a tale about Seimei meeting King Enma during one of his supposed deaths. After a remarkable series of events—recounted here—Seimei was granted King Enma's seal and sent back to the Realm of Human Beings. This seal, said to have originated in the underworld, still exists today and is preserved at Shinnyodo Temple. The monks there use it to create safe-conduct passes, possession of which is believed to guarantee immediate rebirth in Heaven.

Over a thousand years ago, a master of yin and yang named Abe no Seimei lived and practiced his mystical arts.

Seimei was a devout worshipper of Fudo Myoo, the "Immovable King of Light," a deity enshrined at Shinnyodo Temple. He frequently visited the temple to pay his respects to the deity's statue and to seek guidance in his spiritual endeavors.

One fateful day, Seimei fell gravely ill. Despite his mastery of spells and incantations, nothing could cure him, and he succumbed to his illness, passing into the next world. Upon arrival, he was immediately seized by demonic figures and dragged to the court of Hell to stand judgment before Enma, the Great King of Hell.

As Enma prepared to deliver his verdict, a swirling cloud appeared in the center of the courtroom. From within this luminous mist emerged a radiant figure: Fudo Myoo himself, the Immovable King of Light!

"What brings you to my domain?" demanded Enma, his voice heavy with irritation. "I am overwhelmed with souls to judge and have no time for such interruptions!"

"I am here to plead for Master Seimei," replied Fudo Myoo, his presence glowing with divine authority. "He is a devout follower who prays to me with unwavering faith. Moreover, he has performed countless meritorious deeds in service to others. I firmly believe that if you grant him a reprieve and allow him to return to the world of the living, he will accomplish even greater acts of virtue."

Enma considered the deity's words and finally spoke: "If what you say is true, I shall send this Seimei back to the Realm of Human Beings. Furthermore, I shall entrust him with a task of the utmost importance. I will give him my seal, the same seal I use to authorize the passage of souls into the Pure Land. With this seal, Seimei shall issue permits granting direct entry to the Pure Land, bypassing judgment. Those who bear these permits when they arrive at my court shall be sent straight to eternal bliss."

Having decreed this, the Great King of Hell commanded his attendants to escort Seimei back to the Realm of Human Beings.

At that very moment, Seimei awoke in his room. To his amazement, he found himself completely healed. "It was just a dream," he murmured, still dazed. But as he shifted on his futon, his hand brushed against something solid wrapped in cloth. Curious, he unfolded the bundle and revealed a seal—King Enma's seal, exactly as it had appeared in his vision.

"It wasn't a dream," exclaimed the yin-yang master. "I truly met King Enma in Hell, and he has entrusted me with a sacred mission!"

Seimei wasted no time and hurried to Shinnyodo Temple. There, he recounted his extraordinary journey to the monks and presented them with the seal.

"I entrust this divine seal to you," he declared. "Use it to craft permits for entry into the Pure Land and distribute them to the faithful."

The monks solemnly vowed to honor his request. From that day forward, they began creating safe-conduct passes and distributing them to their congregation. The practice has endured through the centuries, and even today, the monks of Shinnyodo Temple continue to make these sacred permits, ensuring the faithful a guaranteed path to enlightenment and eternal peace.

76 THE WARRIOR WHO BECAME THE INSTRUMENT OF THE KING OF HELL

Great King Enma presides over the Court of Justice in Hell, where he judges the dead and determines their next rebirth. As his duties keep him extremely busy, he occasionally entrusts mortals with special missions to reduce the number of souls appearing in his court. This was the case with Abe no Seimei, to whom he gave a seal for issuing safe-conducts allowing rebirth in the Pure Land without facing judgment. Another such case involved a warrior, Minamoto no Tametomo (1139–1170), who "purified" Hungry Ghosts and thieves that plagued the area around Injoji Temple (Senbon Enmado). This temple, known for its grand statue of the King of Hell and its traditional religious theater, hosts performances of the Senbon Enmado Kyogen. The performances begin with Enmacho [King Enma's Court of Justice], depicting the court of Hell, and conclude with Senningiri [The Salvation of a Thousand Souls], recounting Tametomo's battle against thieves and Hungry Ghosts.

Over a thousand years ago, there lived a monk named Jogaku.

In the first year of Kannin (1017), Jogaku traveled to Kyoto and strolled along the main avenue, Suzaku-oji. Although formally named Red Phoenix Avenue, locals called it Senbon ("Thousand Stupas") because it led to the Rentaino Burial Ground.

As Jogaku walked, he reached the burial ground and noticed a temple in ruins near its entrance. Moved by the sight, he approached a neighbor and asked about the temple.

"Long ago," the neighbor explained, "an aristocrat built this temple to ensure monks could administer last rites for the dead brought to Rentaino. But now the temple is abandoned."

Tears filled Jogaku's eyes. "No one prays for the salvation of the dead anymore!" he lamented.

Overcome with emotion, he decided to rebuild the temple himself. However, he failed to inquire why the monks had abandoned it. Jogaku restored the temple and installed a grand statue of the King of Hell inside. He then took up residence, but on the first night, strange noises woke him. Looking outside, he saw a horrifying sight: a thousand thieves and Hungry Ghosts swarming the burial ground.

The thieves stripped the corpses of their clothing, while the Hungry Ghosts devoured their flesh. Terrified, Jogaku feared they would attack him upon discovering the temple's revival. However, the intruders departed without noticing him.

The next morning, Jogaku hurried to the palace of Chancellor Fujiwara no Michinaga and recounted his ordeal. Moved by the monk's dedication, the chancellor said, "I will assign a guard to your temple!"

When Jogaku expressed doubt about one man's ability to fend off so many enemies, the chancellor reassured him. "This will not be just any man. I will send Minamoto no Tametomo!"

Accompanied by Tametomo, Jogaku returned to the temple. That night, the thieves and Hungry Ghosts reappeared. To Jogaku's horror, they turned toward the temple after finishing their gruesome work.

"Lord Tametomo!" he cried in panic. "They are coming!"

"Do not worry," the warrior replied calmly. "They do not deserve my arrows. A stick will suffice."

Tametomo grabbed a pilgrim's staff and paused to pray before the King of Hell's statue.

"O King Enma, my cause is just. Grant me victory!"

With that, he charged outside and began striking the intruders. To his astonishment, each blow caused the thieves and Hungry Ghosts to weep, abandon their wicked ways, and repent. Tametomo's staff became an instrument of redemption, and he purified hundreds that night.

Jogaku, watching from the temple, realized the King of Hell had empowered Tametomo to guide sinners back to righteousness. Inspired, Jogaku devised a new ritual involving gentle strikes with a staff to symbolically cleanse participants of their sins. This method proved so effective that his successors continued the practice, now known as the "salvation of a thousand souls."

Even today, Senbon Enmado Temple upholds this tradition, commemorating the miraculous deeds of Minamoto no Tametomo and the enduring justice of King Enma.

77

TAKAMURA AND THE GHOST OF HIS HALF-SISTER

Twelfth-century collections of tales such as Konjaku Monogatarishu *often mention a nobleman named Ono no Takamura (802–852) and explain that he served the imperial court by day and descended to hell by night to help King Enma judge the dead. Seventeenth-century travel guides from Kyoto add that Takamura reached the realm of the dead by descending into the well at Rokudo Chinnoji Temple. In earlier times, this temple stood at the entrance to Toribeno, the eastern burial ground, and thus symbolically marked the boundary between the world of the living and that of the dead. Its well, which still exists and is accessible at certain times of the year, appears ideally suited for crossing from one realm to the other. As for the reasons that supposedly led Takamura to concern himself with the fate of the dead, several theories exist. Some say he was moved to do so after the death of his mother; others claim it was after the death of his half-sister. The latter version, which I present here, has been adapted into a novel entitled* The Tale of Takamura.

A long time ago, Ono no Takamura was a young scholar. One year, he was tasked with teaching Chinese literature to his half-sister, Hiuko. As they studied together and exchanged poems, their bond deepened, and they fell in love. Secretly, Takamura began visiting Hiuko's room at night, always leaving before dawn. Inevitably, Hiuko became pregnant.

When her mother discovered the affair, she was enraged and locked Hiuko in the storeroom.

"Your father may forgive you," she declared, "but I will not!"

Desperate to help his half-sister, Takamura sent a servant with food, but Hiuko, disheartened that he had not come himself, refused to eat. Four days later, Takamura managed to sneak into the house. He made a small hole in the storeroom wall and peered inside. Hiuko lay weakly on the floor.

"How are you?" he asked.

She replied with a mournful poem:

Though my body will fade to ash,
my soul will remain by your side, like a dream.
消えはてて / 身こそは灰に / なりはてめ /
　　夢の魂 / 君にあひそへ

Takamura, stricken with fear, pleaded with her to hold on, but she fell silent.

"Hiuko is dying!" he cried. "Someone, open the door!"

The servants rushed to unlock the storeroom, but it was too late—Hiuko was dead. Takamura wept inconsolably, remaining by her side for hours. As night fell, Takamura suddenly felt a presence in the room. A gentle rustling sound came from behind him, followed by the light pressure of a hand on his shoulder.

"Hiuko has returned from the dead!" he thought, his heart racing. "If only I could hold her once more!"

He reached out to embrace the figure, but his arms met only air. Overcome with emotion, he composed a poem:

Now we are carried away by tears.
We have been separated by the inevitability of
　　death.
Was there truly a moment when we were together?
泣き流す / 涙の上に / ありしにも /
　　さらぬわかれに / あはにむすべる

Before the echo of his words faded, Hiuko's voice filled the room, reciting her own poem in reply:

The little time we spent together was as fleeting as
 a bubble.
What a pity it dissolved!
常に寄る / しばしばかりは / 泡なれば /
 ついに溶けなん / ことぞ悲しき

With that, her ghost vanished. Yet Hiuko's spirit returned each night to speak with Takamura, disappearing at dawn. For twenty-one days, she appeared without fail; after twenty-eight days, her visits became less frequent. Three years after her death, she ceased appearing altogether.

Heartbroken, Takamura never married. Instead, he dedicated himself to understanding the fate of the dead. Wondering how he might aid them, he made his way to Rokudo Chinnoji, the temple that marked the entrance to the Toribeno burial grounds. There, in a quiet corner of the temple grounds, he noticed a well rising from the earth.

"Wells plunge deep into the ground," he mused. "Perhaps they lead to Hell . . ."

Moved by an impulse he could neither explain nor resist, Takamura grasped a branch of the Koya pine growing beside the well and let himself slide down into its depths. He descended all the way to the bottom—and just as he had suspected, he found himself at the threshold of Hell. Without hesitation, he stepped inside and made his way to the court of Hell, presided over by King Enma. As soon as he caught sight of the sovereign, Takamura called out, "I wish to assist you in judging the souls of the dead!"

To the court's surprise, Enma did not grow angry. On the contrary, he welcomed the proposal with great delight and appointed Takamura as an assessor at the court of Hell! Takamura had found a way to help the departed—and to ease his own sorrow.

78 THE BELL THAT CAN BE HEARD TO THE DEPTHS OF HELL

Rokudo Chinnoji Temple is renowned not only for its "Well Leading to the Realm of the Dead" (Meido-gayoi no ido)*, but also for its bell tower. Within its precincts hangs a bell that, ever since the events we are about to recount, is said to resonate across all Six Realms of Rebirth. Because of this extraordinary attribute, it has become customary for the people of Kyoto to visit Rokudo Chinnoji in the days leading up to the Obon festival—a time dedicated to honoring the spirits of the deceased—and to ring this so-called "welcoming bell"* (mukae-gane) *in order to invite their departed ancestors to return to the world of the living.*

Long ago, there lived an aristocrat named Ono no Takamura. This man was no ordinary noble, for during the day, he served at the imperial palace, but by night, he sat in the court of Hell, dispensing justice alongside its ruler, Great King Enma. To travel to Hell, Takamura used a special well located at the entrance to Toribeno, the burial ground east of the capital. Clinging to a branch of the pine tree that grew beside the well, he would slide down and arrive in Hell.

After frequenting Toribeno so often, Takamura decided to build a temple at the graveyard's entrance. He summoned a group of carpenters and a master bell founder to explain his vision for the project. The craftsmen set to work immediately.

One day, the master bell founder approached Takamura with a unique proposal:

"I understand that you wish to build a remarkable temple. I propose crafting a bell that will strike the hours on its own."

"Is such a thing even possible?" asked Takamura.

"Yes," replied the craftsman. "The bell must be buried for three years. After that, when it is unearthed and hung, it will ring by itself."

Delighted, Takamura commissioned the bell immediately. Once completed, it was buried in the courtyard of the temple under construction. Time passed, and when the temple was finished, Takamura installed monks there to pray for the salvation of the dead. He also instructed them never to dig up the bell until the three years had passed. The monks agreed to his request. Alas, curiosity got the better of the abbot. Before the three years were up, he ordered the monks to dig up the bell and hang it in the bell tower. They obeyed.

"Excellent!" exclaimed the abbot. "Now let us wait and see how the bell rings by itself!"

The monks waited, but the hour came and went, and the bell remained silent. Learning of this, Takamura was furious and chastised the abbot for his impatience. However, a few days later, Takamura returned from a night spent judging souls in Hell and, to everyone's surprise, thanked the abbot.

The astonished abbot asked, "Why are you thanking me?"

"Last night, while in Hell's court, I heard the sound of the bell from our temple! Its ringing echoes all the way to the depths of the underworld!"

"What does that mean?" asked the abbot, still puzzled.

Takamura explained, "During the eighth month's Festival of the Dead, the faithful can ring this bell to call upon their ancestors. Its sound will guide the spirits back to the Realm of Human Beings."

The abbot finally understood the bell's unique importance. He shared this revelation with the temple's followers. From that time onward, during the Festival of the Dead, people would visit the temple to ring the bell, inviting their ancestors to return and share in their world once more.

79 THE MONK WHO CURED THE KING OF HELL

According to legend, Ono no Takamura sculpted numerous statues of Jizo, the Buddhist deity who tirelessly traverses the Six Realms of Rebirth to rescue the dead and guide them to the Pure Land. One such statue, crafted by Manmai, is preserved at Yata-dera Temple. When the capital was relocated to present-day Kyoto in 794, an annex of Manmai's temple was built, and a new statue of Jizo was carved by Takamura and installed there. This particular depiction of Jizo is unique, as it shows the bodhisattva surrounded by the flames of hell—a feature tied to the following story.

Long ago, there lived an aristocrat named Ono no Takamura, renowned for his unusual life. By day, Takamura served at the imperial palace. By night, he descended into hell, where he dispensed justice alongside Enma, the Great King of Hell. To reach the underworld, Takamura used a well at a temple near the entrance to Toribeno, the eastern burial ground of the capital. Grasping the branch of a pine tree growing beside the well, he would slide down into Hell. Each morning, he returned to the Realm of Human Beings by emerging from a well at another temple near Adashino, the western burial ground.

One evening, as Takamura arrived in Hell, he found King Enma in great distress.

"Your Majesty, what troubles you?" Takamura inquired.

"The sins of humankind weigh heavily on me," Enma replied, clutching his head. "They are so numerous and grievous that they overwhelm me, leaving me desolate and plagued with ceaseless headaches. Lord Takamura, do you know of any remedy for my suffering?"

"As a matter of fact, I do," Takamura said without hesitation. "You should become a bodhisattva—a being detached from worldly passions. I know a monk who can guide you on this path. His name is Manmai, and he resides at Yata-dera Temple in Yamato Province."

"Then fetch him without delay and bring him to me!" Enma exclaimed, hope rekindled.

Takamura returned to the realm of the living and sought out the monk Manmai. He explained Enma's plight and pleaded for his help.

"I am old, and my legs no longer carry me well," the monk replied. "If you bear me on your back, I will go with you."

Tall and strong, Takamura agreed without hesitation. He carried Manmai to the well leading to Hell, descended with him, and presented him to King Enma.

"Venerable monk, please ease my torment!" Enma implored.

Manmai recited a prayer, and as soon as he uttered the final word, Enma's headaches vanished as if by magic.

"Monk, you have healed me!" the King of Hell cried with joy. "Ask for any boon, and I shall grant it."

"I wish to visit your kingdom," Manmai replied.

With Enma's permission, Manmai explored Hell. In the deepest depths, he witnessed a horrifying scene: a massive cauldron filled with boiling oil into which the damned, bound hand and foot, were hurled after falling for two thousand years. Demonic jailers with fiery manes, long horns, and brightly colored skin—red, green, or blue—inflicted relentless torture.

Amid the flames beneath the cauldron, Manmai was startled to see a monk wielding a cane, pulling the damned from the boiling oil one by one. Realizing he was being watched, the monk turned to Manmai and spoke: "Visitor to hell, I am Jizo. I descended into this inferno to rescue the damned and guide them to Heaven, but I am overwhelmed. Their numbers are too great, and I cannot save them all. Return to the Realm of Human Beings, create a statue in my likeness, and encourage the people to pray to me. If they do, I will save them from rebirth in hell."

Deeply moved, Manmai promised to fulfill Jizo's request. He asked Takamura to escort him back to the human world. Once home, Manmai sculpted a statue of Jizo and urged his followers to pray to it.

When the capital was relocated to present-day Kyoto in 794, an annex of Manmai's temple was built, and a new statue of Jizo was installed there. To commemorate the extraordinary circumstances of the original statue's creation, the sculptor depicted Jizo surrounded by the flames of Hell. This unique statue endures to this day and remains a source of devotion for the people of Kyoto.

80 THE SIX-ARMED JIZO OF CHIEKO-IN TEMPLE

Among the many statues of Jizo believed to have been crafted by Ono no Takamura, one stands out for its unique feature: The bodhisattva is depicted not with two, but with six arms, symbolizing his ability to rescue the dead from each of the Six Realms of Rebirth. This extraordinary statue is housed in Chieko-in Temple and is displayed to the public only once a year, on August 24, the day dedicated to Jizo's veneration.

Long ago, there lived an aristocrat named Ono no Takamura.

One day, in his forty-ninth year, Takamura was struck down by a severe fever. He passed away and found himself in the Netherworld. Upon his arrival, demons seized him and took him to the Court of Justice of Hell. There, he was told to wait his turn to be judged.

While waiting, Takamura observed everything happening around him. He saw demons leading the deceased, one by one, to stand before a great mirror. This mirror reflected their sins, and Enma, the king and judge of Hell, used it to tally their misdeeds before passing judgment. Few souls were fortunate enough to be sent to the Pure Land. Most were condemned to be reborn in one of the Six Realms of Rebirth.

As Takamura watched, he noticed something extraordinary—a monk standing among the dead. But this monk was no ordinary soul; he was full of vigor and moved with determination. Each time King Enma condemned a soul, the monk intervened, pulling the condemned toward him and declaring, "You will not have this one! I will guide him to the Pure Land!"

Despite his efforts, the monk could only save one soul at a time, while countless others were condemned to the Six Realms. The monk's struggle seemed hopeless, yet he persevered, tirelessly trying to save as many as he could.

Moved by the scene, Takamura realized who the monk was—Jizo, the bodhisattva who tirelessly works to save all beings from suffering. Sensing Takamura's compassionate gaze, Jizo turned to him and said, "Judging by the tears in your eyes, you care deeply for the fate of the deceased. If that is so, help me! I do not have six arms, and I cannot act in all Six Realms of Rebirth simultaneously."

Takamura replied, "I would gladly help, but I am dead!"

No sooner had he spoken these words than Takamura vanished from the court of Hell and reappeared, alive and fully healed, in the world of the living.

Overwhelmed by the memory of what he had witnessed, Takamura secluded himself in his home. For seven days, he remained locked in his room, sculpting a statue of Jizo. When he emerged, he revealed a remarkable creation: Jizo depicted with six arms, symbolizing his ability to intervene in all Six Realms of Rebirth.

Takamura then built a temple in the heart of the capital, placed the statue within it, and urged the people to pray to it, saying, "If you pray to this statue, Jizo will come to your aid, no matter which realm of rebirth you may fall into, and he will guide you to the Pure Land!"

The people were deeply moved by Takamura's words and gave their thanks. From that time onward, they began fervently praying to the six-armed Jizo, entrusting him with their salvation after death. This tradition continues today.

81 HOW MURASAKI SHIKIBU WAS SAVED FROM ETERNAL DAMNATION

Ono no Takamura's grave—or rather, the grave traditionally considered to be his—is located in the northern part of Kyoto, in what was once Rentaino's burial ground. It stands beside another grave which, according to tradition, belongs to Murasaki Shikibu, the renowned author of The Tale of Genji. *Legend has it that Murasaki Shikibu was buried next to Takamura so he could use his influence at the court of Hell to plead her case before King Enma, ultimately securing her rebirth in the Buddhist Heaven of the Pure Land.*

Once upon a time, there lived a noblewoman named Lady Kaga.

One night, Lady Kaga had an extraordinary dream. She dreamt of a shadow that appeared suddenly in her room, taking on human form and approaching her bed.

"Who are you? What do you want from me?" she asked, her voice trembling.

"I am the ghost of Murasaki Shikibu," replied the apparition.

"Murasaki Shikibu? The author of *The Tale of Genji?*"

"Yes. I wrote a fictional work, and because of it, King Enma has accused me of lying and condemned me to the torments of Hell. I have been suffering unimaginable agony ever since! I beg you to gather a group of poets and have them compose works that each incorporate the title of a chapter from my novel, along with the words "In the name of the great

Buddha." Doing so will increase my store of good deeds and grant me the chance to escape Hell!"

After delivering her plea, the ghost vanished, and Lady Kaga awoke. Convinced she had been visited by the spirit of Murasaki Shikibu, she wasted no time. She assembled a group of poets and relayed the ghost's request. She also prayed fervently to the Buddhas, imploring their intervention to free the author of *The Tale of Genji* from her suffering. Alas, her efforts were in vain.

Proof of this came later from a monk named Shokaku. While traveling through the province of Omi, Shokaku visited Mii-dera Temple, where Murasaki Shikibu is said to have secluded herself to write her masterpiece. There, he encountered a beautiful young woman who, to his astonishment, revealed herself to be the ghost of Murasaki Shikibu. She recounted her plight and begged the monk to hold a religious service in her honor.

Shokaku agreed and prayed fervently to the Buddhas on her behalf. His efforts succeeded in alleviating some of her suffering, but he was unable to secure her passage to the Pure Land.

The admirers of *The Tale of Genji* were deeply distressed. They too held religious ceremonies in Murasaki Shikibu's memory, but their attempts also failed to save her.

"What more can we do?" lamented one admirer after yet another unsuccessful service. "We've tried everything, and yet we cannot free her!"

"I know a way to save Murasaki Shikibu," came a voice from the back of the assembly.

Everyone turned to see who had spoken. Could this anonymous admirer succeed where the empire's greatest scholars and monks had failed?

"We should move Ono no Takamura's grave next to Murasaki Shikibu's," explained the man. "When he was alive, Takamura worked at the imperial palace during the day and at the Court of Justice of Hell at night. He could plead her case before King Enma and secure her release into the Pure Land."

The assembly found the man's idea ingenious. That very night, they crept into the graveyard, dismantled Takamura's tomb, and rebuilt it beside Murasaki Shikibu's. After that, Murasaki Shikibu's ghost was never seen again. Her admirers concluded that Takamura had successfully argued her case in the underworld, winning her salvation and granting her peace in the Pure Land.

82

JIZO AND THE PRISONERS SENTENCED TO DEATH

We have already mentioned the name of Jizo (the Japanese name for Ksitigarbha) on numerous occasions and seen how this bodhisattva tirelessly travels through the Six Realms to rescue souls and guide them to the Pure Land. For this reason, Jizo is immensely popular. Statues of him can be found in temples and at nearly every crossroads in Kyoto. Some of these statues are attributed to famous historical figures, such as Ono no Komachi or her grandfather, Ono no Takamura, as we have seen in previous tales. Another such statue is believed to have been carved from a piece of rock by an eleventh-century aristocrat named Taira no Shigeyuki. People pray to this statue in a very peculiar manner—by pouring oil over it. This practice has earned the statue its nickname, Aburakake Jizo, or "Oil-sprayed Jizo." The unique ritual and the nickname of the statue are directly tied to the story of its creation.

Once upon a time, nearly six hundred years ago, there lived a deeply pious aristocrat named Taira no Shigeyuki.

One day, Shigeyuki went for a walk in the countryside west of the capital. As he strolled, he happened upon the field where executions were carried out. He watched as prisoners sentenced to death were led to the site. There, the executioners made the condemned kneel in the middle of the field before cutting off their heads.

"Poor souls!" exclaimed Shigeyuki at the sight of this horrifying spectacle. "They are executed without the chance to beseech the Buddhas for help! Under such conditions, how will they ever escape the eternal cycle of rebirth and find their way to the Pure Land?"

This thought weighed heavily on Shigeyuki's mind, tormenting him for days. Finally, he resolved to find a way to help those condemned to death. While surveying the execution ground, he noticed a large rock standing nearby. An idea struck him: He would carve an image of Jizo into the stone so that the condemned could gaze upon it as they faced their final moments.

Shigeyuki immediately set his plan into motion. His act of compassion touched everyone who heard of it—even the executioners. From that day onward, the executioners developed the habit of positioning the prisoners so they faced the statue at the moment of their death, giving them the chance to pray to Jizo and ask for his guidance to the Pure Land. To further ensure Jizo's attention, the executioners adopted another practice: They dipped the blades of their swords in oil and shook the oil over the statue's head before carrying out the sentence.

"Do not fear," they would say to the prisoners. "Gaze upon Jizo as we perform this grim task. Do not fear, for by doing so, you will not become a wandering ghost, doomed to haunt this field and terrify the living."

The villagers, who closely observed these executions, noted with relief that no wandering spirits of the executed appeared in the days that followed. Convinced of the statue's power, they began to pray to the Oil-Sprayed Jizo as well, pouring oil over its head as an offering to ensure their prayers would be answered.

Over time, this practice became a deeply rooted tradition. The statue, which still stands today, glistens with the accumulated layers of oil poured over it by generations of devotees.

JIZO SAVES A WICKED MAN

Jizo is venerated not only at crossroads but also in temples, such as the renowned Mibu-dera Temple. This temple is famous for its statue of Jizo and its traditional theater, Mibu Dainenbutsu Kyogen, created by the monk Engaku in the early fourteenth century. The repertoire includes thirty plays, some featuring Jizo himself. One such play, Sai no Kawara *[The Riverbed of the Netherworld], recounts how Jizo ventures into Hell to save a wicked man.*

Once, long ago, there lived a particularly wicked man in Kyoto. When this man died, no one grieved his passing. On the contrary, many were relieved, hoping he would be condemned to the tortures of Hell as retribution for his earthly misdeeds.

Upon his death, the wicked man crossed the River of Three Crossings, which separates the world of the living from the world of the dead. As soon as he reached the opposite bank, he was brought before Great King Enma's Court of Justice. There, standing before the Mirror That Reflects Sins, his wicked deeds were laid bare. Without hesitation, King Enma sentenced him to the lowest depths of hell.

"Jailers!" thundered the Great King. "Take this man away and punish him severely for his misdeeds in life!"

Demonic jailers immediately seized the condemned man and dragged him to the deepest hell. There, they tied him to a fiery pillar. A red demon grabbed a pair of pliers and cruelly tore out the man's tongue.

Next, a yellow demon wielded a massive club, smashing the man into a shapeless, bloodied heap. After this gruesome ordeal, the demons threw his remains into a cauldron of boiling water. But the torment did not end there. The cauldron, enchanted with dark magic, reconstituted the man's body only for the demons to repeat the process endlessly. They smashed him, boiled him, and devoured him, a cycle of suffering meant to last for millions of years.

As the demons were carrying out their dreadful work, a sudden presence startled them: Jizo, the compassionate bodhisattva of the Six Realms of Rebirth, appeared before them.

"What are you doing here?" asked Jizo, his calm demeanor contrasting sharply with the infernal surroundings.

"We've just finished eating a man!" the demons boasted gleefully, tossing the man's bones back into the cauldron. "We'll reassemble him soon, smash him again, and eat him over and over. Reconstructing him is a skill you surely don't possess!"

"Who knows?" Jizo replied serenely. "Would you allow me to try? If I succeed, will you let me take him to the Pure Land?"

At this, the demons burst into mocking laughter. Certain that Jizo could not perform such a miracle, they agreed. Jizo approached the cauldron and waved his pilgrim's staff over it. In an instant, a miraculous transformation took place: The man's body was fully restored. With compassion and urgency, Jizo helped the man out of the cauldron. Before the bewildered demons could react, Jizo swiftly escorted the man out of Hell and guided him to the Pure Land, thus saving his soul from eternal torment.

84 A SUMO CONTEST IN HELL

Another play from the Mibu Kyogen's repertoire, titled Gaki zumo *[The Sumo Contest of the Hungry Ghosts], recounts the surprising method Jizo used to save three souls condemned to rebirth in Hell.*

One day, Jizo, curious about how King Enma judged the dead, decided to see for himself. Taking up his pilgrim's staff, he descended into Hell. Upon arrival, he was met by demonic jailers, hideous and terrifying creatures beyond description.

"What brings you here?" they asked.

"I am curious," replied Jizo. "I wish to observe how your master, Great King Enma, judges the dead."

"If that is your desire," said the jailers, "we shall escort you to the court of Hell."

The jailers led Jizo to the court of Hell, where King Enma welcomed him warmly. Learning of Jizo's purpose, the king invited him to sit beside him to witness the proceedings.

"Normally," Enma explained, "I place the deceased before the Mirror that Reflects Sins, count the crimes displayed on its surface, and determine their rebirth—either in the Pure Land or one of the Six Realms of Rebirth. However, since you honor me with your presence, I shall try something different today!"

He instructed the jailers to bring forth the next condemned souls. They presented three trembling individuals before the king.

"Listen, dead ones!" proclaimed Enma in a booming voice. "Today, your fate will be decided by a sumo contest! If you lose, you will be condemned to Hell. But if you win, I shall entrust you to Jizo, who will lead you to the Pure Land."

One of the dead was shoved into the arena to face a monstrous, red-skinned jailer with horns protruding from his forehead. At Enma's signal, the demon charged and effortlessly flung the man out of the ring. The same fate befell the other two souls, each defeated by their demonic opponents.

"That's three for Hell!" Enma declared with satisfaction.

Jizo, distressed at the thought of the souls' eternal suffering, interceded. "Would you grant them a second chance?" he asked.

Convinced that the outcome would not change, Enma agreed. Jizo descended into the arena and touched the foreheads of the three dead, reciting a heartfelt prayer. "They are ready," he announced when he finished.

The first soul entered the ring again, facing the same demonic jailer. At Enma's signal, the demon charged—only to be thrown out of the arena by the previously helpless soul! The remaining two also triumphed against their opponents, stunning the onlookers. Unhappy with this unexpected turn of events, Enma bellowed, "Let us see if Jizo's prayers can protect you from me! All three of you, attack me together! If you manage to throw me out of the arena, I shall entrust you to Jizo."

Descending into the ring himself, Enma squared off against the three souls. Despite their newfound strength, the King of Hell effortlessly defeated them, casting them out of the arena. Jizo, unwilling to give up, stepped forward.

"What if you were to decide their fate by facing me in the ring?" he proposed.

Confident in his strength, Enma readily agreed.

The match began with an intense grapple between the King of Hell and the tireless bodhisattva. After a fierce and prolonged struggle, Jizo managed to push Enma out of the arena, securing victory.

"Hurry!" Jizo shouted to the three souls. "Follow me before King Enma devises another trial for you!"

The three dead quickly obeyed, and together they escaped Hell. Thus, it is said, Jizo saved three condemned souls and led them to the Pure Land.

85 THE ABBOT WHO BECAME A TENGU

The stories presented earlier in this part have depicted men or deities who aided the dead in reaching the Pure Land. The next three stories, however, focus on men who, upon dying, renounced paradise and became protective divinities. The first of these tales brings us once again to Enryakuji Temple. According to tradition, Enryakuji was built atop Mount Hiei to guard the northeastern direction—known as the "Demons' Gate"—and to prevent ghosts and monsters from invading Kyoto. It is also said that Ryogen (912–985), the temple's eighteenth abbot, devised a way to reinforce this spiritual barrier by having his tomb placed in the temple's northeastern corner and by transforming himself into a flying creature. His tomb still stands today and is considered a sacred site—one that, according to legend, should be approached only with the utmost caution.

Once upon a time, a very long time ago, there lived a man named Ryogen, who served as the abbot of Enryakuji Temple. This temple was situated northeast of Kyoto, a cardinal direction known as the Demons' Gate. According to beliefs of the time, ghosts, vengeful spirits, and yokai emerged from this direction. The temple had been strategically built on this spot so that its monks could, through prayers and magical rituals, prevent these malevolent forces from entering the capital.

Throughout his life, Ryogen dedicated himself to protecting the capital from monsters and ghosts. As his death approached, he gathered his most loyal disciples and declared, "Our temple guards the Demons' Gate of the capital. It serves as a rampart against the onslaught of supernatural creatures. Should this rampart falter, the capital will be doomed, overrun by monsters and ghosts. To ensure this never happens, the Demons' Gate of our temple must also be protected. This is my final wish: When I die, bury me in the northeast corner of the temple grounds, at the very location of the Demons' Gate. From my grave, I will ensure that the temple's defenses remain unbroken. However, under no circumstances must anyone approach my grave!"

Hearing these words, the monks wept bitterly. For good reason: Ryogen was renouncing the Pure Land to remain in the Realm of Human Beings and guard the Demons' Gate of their temple. Though consumed with grief, the monks vowed to honor their abbot's last wishes. Satisfied, Ryogen retired to his cell and passed away on the third day of the first month of the third year of Eikan (985). At the moment of his death, a strange purple cloud formed above the temple, enveloping its buildings. The cloud was so vast that even the residents of the capital could see it. It was the sign of Amida's arrival, accompanied by celestial hosts. Yet rather than rejoice, Ryogen's disciples were filled with sorrow—for they knew their master would refuse the invitation and remain on Earth.

After his passing, Ryogen was posthumously named Ganzan Daishi, or "Grand Master of the Third Day of the Month of New Year." True to his vow, he was buried in the northeast corner of Enryakuji Temple. Soon after, the monks began to hear peculiar rumblings emanating from Ryogen's grave. At first, they were terrified. Over time, they came to understand these sounds as warnings of impending catastrophes, encouraging them to take shelter.

Later, monks and pilgrims witnessed a winged creature—a tengu—flying over Ryogen's grave. To them, there was no doubt: This supernatural being was the reborn form of their late abbot. This realization brought tears to their eyes, for Ryogen had renounced the Pure Land and accepted rebirth in the Realm of Beasts. He had become a monster to protect the capital from other monsters and ghosts. Only then did the monks fully grasp why Ryogen had forbidden them from approaching his grave: It was the site of epic battles between him and the supernatural creatures threatening their temple's Demons' Gate.

Despite his warnings, some monks and pilgrims ventured too close to Ryogen's grave. These unwary souls found themselves paralyzed, unable to move or speak. To this day, approaching Ryogen's grave is considered an act requiring great caution.

86

THE ONE-EYED AND ONE-LEGGED GHOST

It is said that another abbot of Enryakuji Temple, Jinzen (942–990), also renounced entry into the Pure Land to remain in the human realm and guide his fellow monks. According to legend, Jinzen implored the Buddhas to allow him to return as a ghost. Believing he needed only the bare essentials to fulfill his mission, he reappeared in the mortal world as a ghost with just one leg and one eye. Until recently, a painting depicting his spectral form was displayed on a tablet in Sojibo, the temple where Jinzen resided during his lifetime.

More than a thousand years ago, there lived a monk named Jinzen. In the first year of Kanna (985), Jinzen was appointed head of Enryakuji Temple. During his four short years as abbot, he enforced strict discipline, ensuring that the monks pursued their studies with unwavering dedication and upheld dignity at all times. His commitment to their spiritual growth weighed on him even as death approached.

"What will happen after I die?" Jinzen wondered. "Who will guide the monks and keep them on the righteous path?"

These concerns haunted him until his last moments, which came on the seventeenth day of the second month in the second year of Eiso (990). When he breathed his last, Amida Buddha and his celestial retinue appeared, descending on a radiant white cloud. Amida carried a lotus flower—a symbol of enlightenment—while his attendants played heavenly music, their melodies beyond mortal description.

"Jinzen," Amida called. "The time has come for you to join us in the Pure Land. Come, ascend with us."

Ordinarily, one would leap at such an offer, but Jinzen declined to everyone's astonishment.

"Master of the Western Pure Land," he replied, "I am deeply honored, but I cannot go. My duty to watch over the monks of Enryakuji Temple is not yet complete. I must ensure they remain steadfast on their path."

Amida and his retinue, though disappointed, admired his resolve and returned to the heavens. Left alone, Jinzen reflected on his situation. He had chosen to stay on earth, but there was one problem: He no longer had a body. "I don't need much," he thought. "Just one leg to move around the temple, one eye to observe the monks, and two arms to carry a pilgrim's staff and a bell."

No sooner had he spoken these words than he was reborn as a ghostly figure: a one-legged, one-eyed monk with a staff in one hand and a bell in the other. Without delay, Jinzen began his nightly patrols of the temple, inspecting every hall and chanting as he went: "Monks! Never forget who you are! Monks! Never forget who you are!"

One evening, Jinzen found a monk sleeping with his feet pointed toward a statue of Ryogen, the revered former abbot of the temple.

"This monk does not understand the honor he disregards by turning his feet toward such a venerable figure!" Jinzen exclaimed.

Quietly, the ghost repositioned the monk so his head faced the statue. When the monk awoke and saw how he had been moved, he realized his error and resolved never to repeat it. From that day on, he became an exemplary monk.

Elsewhere, Jinzen's ghost caught a monk neglecting his spiritual exercises and another dozing during a religious service. On both occasions, Jinzen shook his bell furiously. The errant monks found themselves paralyzed, unable to move or speak, until dawn. Their peers, upon discovering them, expelled them from the temple for their misconduct.

Every night, Jinzen continued his rounds, and soon the monks grew fearful of the One-Eyed and One-Legged Propagator of the Law. All except one—a particularly wayward monk who believed he could escape Jinzen's vigilance by sinning outside the temple.

This monk often sneaked into town, spending his evenings in taverns and drinking sake with young women. One night, as he raised a cup to toast his companions, he froze in terror. Sitting beside him was Jinzen's ghost, watching him with a stern and reproachful gaze.

"Help!" the monk cried, fleeing the tavern in panic.

Word of the incident spread, and the monks, inspired by fear and respect, committed themselves to their studies with renewed fervor. Even the less diligent among them redoubled their efforts, while the devoted monks strove harder than ever. To ensure that Jinzen's vigilance was never forgotten, the monks commissioned a painting of his ghostly form. They hung it at the entrance of Sojibo, Jinzen's former quarters. To this day, the monks of Enryakuji Temple bow deeply before the painting each time they pass, a lasting tribute to the one-legged and one-eyed guardian who kept them on the righteous path.

87 TEMPLES WITH BLOOD-STAINED CEILINGS

The temples Yogen-in, Genko-an, Koshoji, Hosen-in, Shodenji, Jinnoji, Tenkyu-in, Eijunji, and Zuiun-in share a common feature: They were all located along the outer boundaries of Kyoto during the seventeenth century. These nine temples are also known for their "blood ceilings" (chitenjo)*. A visit to the first two in particular makes the name immediately clear: The ceilings visibly bear the imprints of bodies, arms, and legs. These wooden boards were originally floorboards soaked with the blood of samurai who died during the fall of Fushimi Castle (1600) and were later repurposed as temple ceilings. This act was intended to honor the warriors, prevent them from becoming Wrathful Spirits, and invite them to serve as guardians of Kyoto.*

Over four centuries ago, there lived a warlord named Tokugawa Ieyasu, who dreamed of unifying Japan under his rule.

One summer day in the fifth year of Keicho (1600), Ieyasu left his Fushimi-Momoyama Castle in the care of his loyal vassal, Torii Mototada, as he marched off to wage war in the provinces. However, while Ieyasu was away, his rival Ishida Mitsunari launched an attack on the castle. The defenders, led by Torii Mototada, held out valiantly for nearly two weeks. But when ninjas infiltrated the castle and set it ablaze, they knew the battle was lost. Refusing to surrender, 384 warriors performed seppuku, the ritual suicide of samurai, spilling rivers of blood across the castle's wooden floors.

When Ieyasu returned, he was met with a gruesome sight—corpses lay scattered, and the blood of the fallen had permanently stained the floors, etching ghostly silhouettes into the wood. Yet what troubled Ieyasu most was not the physical devastation but the spiritual danger.

"Their tragic deaths might prevent them from finding peace," Ieyasu declared, deeply concerned. "If left unaddressed, their spirits could become ghosts or, worse, Angry Spirits!"

One of his advisors suggested a traditional solution: "In such cases, we build a temple to honor the deceased, appoint monks, and have them pray for the spirits to enter the Pure Land."

"That's true," agreed another. "But how can we possibly build 384 temples? We don't have the resources, especially with so many temples already damaged by the wars!"

A third advisor added, "And even if we had the wood for construction, we lack the manpower to both rebuild and protect the capital!"

Faced with these three challenges—the appeasement of 384 souls, the repair of damaged temples, and the defense of Kyoto—Ieyasu pondered the dilemma. Then, in a stroke of ingenuity, he exclaimed, "I have it! We will use the blood-stained floors of my castle to repair the ceilings of the war-damaged temples! This way, we solve the problem of the temples. By installing these floors, imbued with the essence of our fallen warriors, in sacred spaces, we can also pacify their spirits and enlist their aid in protecting Kyoto from the afterlife!"

His advisors were astounded.

"But how will you choose the temples, my lord?" one of them asked.

"I will donate the floors to the monks of nine temples surrounding the capital," Ieyasu explained. "In return, the monks must not only pray to prevent the spirits of our fallen soldiers from becoming Angry Spirits, but also petition the fallen soldiers to guard Kyoto from the beyond!"

Thus, Ieyasu's bold plan addressed all three concerns. The blood-stained floors became sacred "blood ceilings," and the defenders of Fushimi-Momoyama Castle were transformed into the immortal protectors of Kyoto.

To this day, visitors to these nine temples can look up at the ceilings and see the outlines of hands, feet, and bodies etched into the wood—a poignant reminder of the warriors' sacrifice and the enduring connection between the living and the dead.

EPILOGUE

In the introduction, I mentioned the entertainment known as Hundred Stories, where participants would gather in a room, share one hundred fantastic tales, and anticipate that—upon the conclusion of the final story—a supernatural being might appear. In 1666, the writer Asai Ryoi (1612–1691) drew inspiration from such gatherings. He published a book titled *Otogiboko* [Hand Puppets for Children] that, however, contains less than one hundred stories. He justified this decision with the following explanation: "A proverb says that one should not speak of demons at night because they might truly appear . . . For this reason, I will lay down my brush and cease writing before reaching the dreaded one-hundredth story."*

Taking heed of this wise advice, I too, like Asai Ryoi in his time, will stop well before reaching the hundredth story.

* Asai Ryoi (浅井了意), *Otogiboko*, 伽婢子 [Hand Puppets for Children] (Tokyo: Iwanami Shoten, Shin Nihon Koten Bungaku Taikei, 2001), 25:333–334.

SOURCES

1. KANCHO'S SPECTACULAR ENTRY INTO THE PURE LAND: Yamamoto Daijun (山本泰順), *Rakuyo meishoshu,* 洛陽名所集 [Collection of Famous Sites in Rakuyo] (Tokyo: Koseisha, Shinshu Kyoto sosho, 1967), 1:308–9; travel guide to Kyoto published in 1658.

   Akisato Rito (秋里籬島), *Miyako meisho zu-e,* 都名所図会 [Illustrations of Famous Places in the Capital] (Tokyo: Koseisha, Shinshu Kyoto sosho, 1968), 11:204–9; travel guide to Kyoto and its surroundings published in 1780.

2. BONFIRES TO SEE OFF THE SOULS OF DEAD ANCESTORS: Kurokawa Michisuke (黒川道祐), *Yoshufushi,* 雍州府志 [Chronicles of Yamashiro Province] (Tokyo: Koseisha, Shinshu Kyoto sosho, 1968), 3:204–6; travel guide to Kyoto published in 1686.
3. THE DANCE OF THE DEAD: Koma Toshio (駒敏郎), *Omi no Densetsu,* 近江の伝説 [Legends of Omi Province] (Tokyo: Kadokawa shoten, 1977), 154–56.
4. THE STONE THAT BLOCKS THE ENTRANCE TO THE NETHERWORLD: Koma Toshio (駒敏郎), *Omi no Densetsu,* 近江の伝説 [Legends of Omi Province] (Tokyo: Kadokawa shoten, 1977), 83.
5. THE MONK POSSESSED BY HUNGRY GHOSTS: Anonymous, *Uji shui monogatari,* 宇治拾遺物語 [A Collection of Tales from Uji] (Tokyo: Shogakukan, 1996), 64–67; collection of tales written around the beginning of the thirteenth century.
6. THE POET WHO BECAME A SPARROW: Hakue (白慧), *Sanshu meiseki shi,* 山州名跡志 [Famous Places of Yamashiro Province] (Tokyo: Koseisha, Shinshu Kyoto sosho, 1968), 19:272; travel guide to Kyoto published in 1711.
7. THE MAN WHO BECAME AN OX: Akisato Rito (秋里籬島), *Miyako meisho zu-e,* 都名所図会 [Illustrations of Famous Places in the Capital] (Tokyo: Koseisha, Shinshu Kyoto sosho, 1968), 204; travel guide to Kyoto and its surroundings published in 1780.

8. THE BUDDHIST PAINTING ON A COWHIDE: Fujiwara no Akikane (藤原顕仲), *Kojidan*, 古事談 [Reflections on Ancient Matters] (Tokyo: Kokushikenkyukai, 1914), 104–5; collection of Buddhist stories written between 1212 and 1215.
9. THE RED SHADOW ON THE TEMPLE WALL: Inoue Yoritoshi (井上頼寿), *Kyo no nanafushigi*, 京の七不思議 [Seven Wonders of Kyoto] (Kyoto: Kyoto kiroku sosho, 1944), 7.
10. THE CAT AND THE PAINTING OF THE BUDDHA ENTERING NIRVANA: Ota Nanpo (太田南畝), *Jinjutsu kiko*, 壬戌紀行 [Travel Diary of the Year 1802] (Kyoto: Hosokan, Shiryo Kyoto Kenbunki, 1991), 1:412; travel diary written in 1802.

    Inoue Yoritoshi (井上頼寿), *Kyoto minzokushi*, 京都民俗志 [Ethnological Study of Kyoto] (Tokyo: Heibonsha, 1968), 205; study of Kyoto legends published in 1933.
11. THE MONK WHO BECAME A MONSTER: Gento (玄棟), *Sangoku denki*, 三国伝記 [Buddhism Stories of the Three Countries] (Tokyo: Bussho hakkokai, Heibonsha, 1912), 148:419–20; collection of Buddhist tales set in India, China, and Japan, written in 1407.
12. THE CURSE OF THE GOLDEN FLOWERS: Asai Ryoi (浅井了意), *Dekisai kyo miyage*, 出来斎京土産 [Dekisai's Souvenirs of Kyoto] (Tokyo: Koseisha, Shinshu Kyoto sosho, 1967), 4:150; travel guide to Kyoto published in 1677.

    Yamamoto Daijun (山本泰順), *Rakuyo meishoshu*, 洛陽名所集 [Collection of Famous Sites in Rakuyo] (Tokyo: Koseisha, Shinshu Kyoto sosho, 1967), 256; travel guide to Kyoto published in 1658.
13. THE SHAME OF THE CHERRY TREE: Hakue (白慧), *Sanshu meiseki shi*, 山州名跡志 [Famous Places of Yamashiro Province] (Tokyo: Koseisha, Shinshu Kyoto sosho, 1968), 19:5; travel guide to Kyoto published in 1711.

    Takemura Toshinori (竹村俊則), *Showa Kyoto meisho zu-e*, 昭和京都名所図会 [Illustrated Guide to Famous Places in Kyoto from the Showa Era] (Osaka: Shinshindo, 1986), 6:98–99.
14. THE STORY OF ORYU, THE WILLOW SPIRIT: Tamai Seibundo Hensanbu (玉井清文堂編輯部), *Sanjusangendo munagi no yurai – keikobon*, 卅三間堂棟由来・稽古本 [The Story of the Foundation of Sanjusangendo Temple – Rehearsal Manual] (Tokyo: Tamai seibundo, 1930), 143–51; play written in 1825.
15. THE FORMER SKULL OF EMPEROR GOSHIRAKAWA: Nakagawa Kiun (中川喜雲), *Kyo-warabe*, 京童 [Kyoto's Children] (Tokyo: Koseisha, Shinshu Kyoto sosho 1, 1968), 25–26; travel guide to Kyoto and its surroundings published in 1658.
16. THE NAIL-PULLING JIZO: Kyoto Shinbun Sha (京都新聞社), *Kyoto densetsu sanpo* 京都・伝説散歩 [A Stroll in Kyoto's Legends] (Kyoto, Kyoto shinbun sha, 1971), 142–43.

17. MASTER KUYA AND THE THIEVES: Yoshishige Yasutane (慶滋保胤), *Honcho Koso Den*, 本朝高僧伝 [Biographies of Japanese Monks Who Achieved Rebirth in the Pure Land of Amitābha] (Tokyo: Bussho hakkokai, Heibonsha, 1916), 107:9–10; edited in 1702 by the Rinzai monk Mangen Shiban.
18. THE GIRL AND THE BUCKET OF WATER POURED ON JIZO'S STATUE: Tsumurau Soan (津村淙庵), *Tankai*, 譚海 [Sea of Stories] (Kyoto: Hosokan, Shiryo Kyoto Kenbunki 4, 1991), 423; collection of tales written in 1780.
19. THE STONE ON WHICH STOOD A WRATHFUL SPIRIT: Anonymous, *Suika Tenjin ryaku engi* 水火天神略縁起 [Abridged Story of the Founding of Suika Tenjin Shrine] (Kyoto, 1696); story of the founding of Suika Tenmangu Shrine written in 1696.
20. THE CURSE OF THE NURSEMAID: Tanaka Ryokko (田中緑紅), *Senryo no tsuji*, 千両の辻 [Senryo Crossroads] (Kyoto: Ryokko zensho, 1958), 48–51.
21. THE FLYING HEAD OF A GREAT WARRIOR: Akisato Rito (秋里籬島), *Miyako meisho zu-e shui*, 都名所図会拾遺 [More Famous Places in the Capital] (Tokyo: Koseisha, Shinshu Kyoto sosho, 1968), 12:64–65; travel guide to Kyoto and its surroundings published in 1786.

    Takemura Toshinori (竹村俊則), *Showa Kyoto meisho zu-e*, 昭和京都名所図会 [Illustrated Guide to Famous Places in Kyoto from the Showa Era] (Osaka: Shinshindo, 1986), 5:346–47.
22. THE GHOST OF THE WISTERIA PAVILION: Akisato Rito (秋里籬島), *Miyako meisho zu-e shui*, 都名所図会拾遺 [More Famous Places in the Capital] (Tokyo: Koseisha, Shinshu Kyoto sosho, 1968), 12:128–31; travel guide to Kyoto and its surroundings published in 1786.
23. THE STATUE THAT EATS PEOPLE: Oshima Takeyoshi (大島武好), *Yamashiro Meishoshi*, 山城名勝志 [Record of Famous Places in Yamashiro] (Tokyo: Koseisha, Shinshu Kyoto sosho 8, 1968), 149–50; travel guide to Kyoto published in 1705.

    Takemura Toshinori (竹村俊則), *Showa Kyoto meisho zu-e*, 昭和京都名所図会 [Illustrated Guide to Famous Places in Kyoto from the Showa Era] (Osaka: Shinshindo, 1986), 2:195.

    Takemura Toshinori (竹村俊則), *Kyo no Ojizosan*, 京のお地蔵さん [Kyoto's Statues of Jizo] (Kyoto: Kyoto shinbun shuppan center, 2005), 24–25.

    Kyoto Shinbun Sha (京都新聞社), *Kyoto densetsu sanpo* 京都・伝説散歩 [A Stroll in Kyoto's Legends] (Kyoto, Kyoto shinbun sha, 1971), 62–63.
24. THE ANGRY SPIRIT AND PRINCE GENJI'S MISTRESS: Murasaki Shikibu (紫式部), *Genji Monogatari*, 源氏物語 [The Tale of Genji] (Tokyo: Shogakkan, Shinpen Nihon koten bungaku zenshu, 1994), 20:135–96; classic work of Japanese literature written by the lady-in-waiting Murasaki Shikibu in the early eleventh century.

Takemura Toshinori (竹村俊則), *Kyo no Ojizosan*, 京のお地蔵さん [Kyoto's Statues of Jizo] (Kyoto: Kyoto shinbun shuppan center, 2005), 5:344.

25. THE CURSED FIELD OF THE LADY OF GION: Tanaka Ryokko (田中緑紅), *Maruyama Koen*, 円山公園 [Maruyama Park] (Kyoto: Kyo wo kataru kai, 1972), 42–50.

Takemura Toshinori (竹村俊則), *Kyoto densetsu no tabi*, 京都伝説の旅 [Journey Through the Legends of Kyoto] (Osaka: Shinshindo, 1972), 97–107.

26. THE CURSE OF MASTER KUKAI'S CALLIGRAPHY: Anonymous, *Konjaku monogatari*, 今昔物語 [Anthology of Tales Old and New] (Tokyo, Shogakukan, Shinpen Nihon koten bungaku zenshu, 1999), 35:62–69.

Oe no Masafusa (大江匡房), *Honcho shinsenden*, 本朝神仙伝 [Transmission of Divine Japanese Immortals] (Tokyo: Kondo shuppan, Shiseki shuran, 1921), 19:chap. 8, 2–3; biographies compiled around 1098.

27. BENKEI'S STONE: Hakue (白慧), *Sanshu meiseki shi*, 山州名跡志 [Famous Places of Yamashiro Province] (Tokyo: Koseisha, Shinshu Kyoto sosho, 1968), 154;

Inoue, *Kyoto minzokushi*, 117; travel guide to Kyoto published in 1711.

28. THE GATES THAT WEEP AT NIGHT: Kyoto Shinbun Sha (京都新聞社), *Kyoto densetsu sanpo* 京都・伝説散歩 [A Stroll in Kyoto's Legends] (Kyoto, Kyoto shinbun sha, 1971), 178–79.

Takemura Toshinori (竹村俊則), *Showa Kyoto meisho zu-e*, 昭和京都名所図会 [Illustrated Guide to Famous Places in Kyoto from the Showa Era] (Osaka: Shinshindo, 1986), 5:227–28.

29. THE GHOST IN THE BELL OF HOKOJI TEMPLE: Inoue Yoritoshi (井上頼寿), *Kyo no nanafushigi*, 京の七不思議 [Seven Wonders of Kyoto] (Kyoto: Kyoto kiroku sosho, 1944), 5.

Takemura Toshinori (竹村俊則), *Showa Kyoto meisho zu-e*, 昭和京都名所図会 [Illustrated Guide to Famous Places in Kyoto from the Showa Era] (Osaka: Shinshindo, 1986), 1:114–17.

30. THE TWO GRAVES OF GENERAL AKECHI: Kyoto Shinbun Sha (京都新聞社), *Kyoto densetsu sanpo* 京都・伝説散歩 [A Stroll in Kyoto's Legends] (Kyoto, Kyoto shinbun sha, 1971), 202–3.

31. THE LANTERN OF THE TEA MASTER: Inoue Yoritoshi (井上頼寿), *Kyo no nanafushigi*, 京の七不思議 [Seven Wonders of Kyoto] (Kyoto: Kyoto kiroku sosho, 1944), 26–27.

32. THE STATUE WITH GROWING HAIR: Miyazawa Segen (宮沢説賢), *Danzei shonin ryakuden*, 弾誓上人略伝 [Abridged Biography of Priest Danzei] (Nagano: Miyasaka insatsusho, 1936), 26–28.

Takemura Toshinori (竹村俊則), *Showa Kyoto meisho zu-e*, 昭和京都名所図会 [Illustrated Guide to Famous Places in Kyoto from the Showa Era] (Osaka: Shinshindo, 1986), 3:146–48.

33. BANZEI, THE LIVING DOLL: Kyoto Shinbun Sha (京都新聞社), *Kyoto no tori-nadera aruki*, 京の通称寺散歩 [A Stroll in Kyoto's Temples That Have a Nickname] (Kyoto: Kyoto shinbun sha, 1985), 16.

34. KYOTO'S ALARM BELL: Anonymous, *Heike Monogatari*, 平家物語 [The Tale of the Heike] (Tokyo: Shogakkan, Shinpen Nihon Koten Bungaku Zenshu 45, 1994), 351–53; epic account compiled prior to 1330 of the struggle between the Taira clan and Minamoto clan at the end of the twelfth century.

Usui Kosaburo (碓井小三郎), *Kyoto bomokushi*, 京都坊目誌 [Kyoto Ward Register] (Tokyo: Koseisha, Shinshu Kyoto sosho, 1968), 15:557–59; compiled in 1916.

35. SHOKI, "THE DEMON SWALLOWER": Izhizuka Hokaishi (石塚豊芥子), *Gaidan Bunbun Shuyo*, 街談文々集要 [Collection of Street Talks] (Tokyo: San-ichi-shobo, 1993), 45–46; collection of events recorded during the twenty-six-year period of the Bunka and Bunsei eras (1804 to 1830).

36. THE CURSE OF THE GHOST STATUE: Tsutsumi Kunihiko (堤邦彦), *Nihon yureiga kiko*, 日本幽霊画紀行 [Discovering Japanese Ghost Paintings] (Tokyo: Miyai Shoten, 2020), 8–9.

37. THE GHOST OF THE WATERFRONT MANSION: Anonymous, *Konjaku monogatari*, 今昔物語 [Anthology of Tales Old and New] (Tokyo, Shogakukan, Shinpen Nihon koten bungaku zenshu, 1999), 38:26–27.

Oe no Masafusa, 大江匡房, *Godansho* 江談抄 [Oe Conversations] (Tokyo: Kokushikenkyukai, 1914), 357.

38. THE BELL OF THE CURSED TEMPLE: Akisato Rito (秋里籬島), *Miyako meisho zu-e*, 都名所図会 [Illustrations of Famous Places in the Capital] (Tokyo: Koseisha, Shinshu Kyoto sosho, 1968), 54–55; travel guide to Kyoto and its surroundings published in 1780.

39. THE HORSE-RIDING GHOST: Kurokawa Michisuke (黒川道祐), *Yoshufushi*, 雍州府志 [Chronicles of Yamashiro Province] (Tokyo: Koseisha, Shinshu Kyoto sosho, 1968), 91; travel guide to Kyoto published in 1686.

40. THE GHOST AND THE CHERRY BLOSSOMS: Anonymous, *Oshio*, 小塩 [Mountains of Salt], in Sanari Kentaro (佐成謙太郎), *Yokyokutaiken*, 謡曲大観 [Great Anthology of Noh Plays] (Tokyo: Meiji Shoin, 1931), 5:3455–70; Noh play written in the first half of the fifteenth century.

Anonymous, *Chigusa Nikki*, 千種日記 [Diary of Sunny Days] (Kyoto: Hosokan, Shiryo Kyoto Kenbunki, 1991), 1:136–37; travel diary written in 1683.

41. NARIHIRA'S GHOST AND THE ENAMORED VILLAGER: Kyoto Shinbun Sha (京都新聞社), *Otokuni Yamashiro no Densetsu*, 乙訓・山城の伝説 [Legends of Otokuni and Yamashiro] (Kyoto: Kyoto Shinbun Sha, 1977), 18–19.

42. THE GHOST'S GIFT: Akisato Rito (秋里籬島), *Miyako meisho zu-e shui*, 都名所図会拾遺 [More Famous Places in the Capital] (Tokyo: Koseisha, Shinshu Kyoto sosho, 1968), 75; travel guide to Kyoto and its surroundings published in 1786.

43. THE POET'S GHOST AND THE ITINERANT MONK: Zeami (世阿弥), *Tadanori*, 忠度 [Tadanori], in Sanari Kentaro (佐成謙太郎), *Yokyokutaiken*, 謡曲大観 [Great Anthology of Noh Plays] (Tokyo: Meiji Shoin, 1931), 3:1903–21; Noh play written in the fifteenth century.

44. THE ANGRY SPIRIT OF UJI BRIDGE: Asai Ryoi (浅井了意), *Otogiboko*, 伽婢子 [Hand Puppets for Children] (Tokyo: Iwanami Shoten, Shin Nihon Koten Bungaku Taikei, 2001), 25:286–89; collection of horror tales published in 1666.

45. THE WOMAN WHO LOST HER HUSBAND TWICE: Kitamura Kigin (北村季吟), *Tsuginefu*, 菟芸泥赴 [Rabbit Skills and Mud Journey] (Tokyo: Koseisha, Shinshu Kyoto sosho, 1968), 5:203–4; travel guide to Kyoto published in 1684.

46. PENNY BRIDGE GHOSTS: Kyoto Shinbun Sha (京都新聞社), *Otokuni Yamashiro no Densetsu*, 乙訓・山城の伝説 [Legends of Otokuni and Yamashiro] (Kyoto: Kyoto Shinbun Sha, 1977), 44–45.

Kyoto Shinbun Sha, *Kyo no Ohashi kobashi*, 京の大橋こばし [Big and Little Bridges of Kyoto] (Kyoto: Kyoto Shinbun Sha, 1982), 74–77.

47. THE GHOST OF THE DISSECTED CORPSE: Akama Shizuko (赤間倭子), *Toba Fushimi Senso no Nazo: Shinsengumi Taishi to Ireihi—Naze, Senryomatsu no Chi ni Ireihi to Shinsengumi Taiki ga Tatte iru no ka*, 鳥羽伏見戦争の謎 新選組隊士と慰霊碑 なぜ、千両松の地に慰霊碑と新選組隊旗が建っているのか [The Mystery of the Battle of Toba-Fushimi: Shinsengumi Soldiers and the Memorial Monument—Why Are the Memorial and the Shinsengumi Flag Erected at Senryomatsu?], in *Rekishi Kenkyu*, 歴史研究 [Study of History] (Tokyo, Ebisukosho, April 1987), 21–23.

48. THE PARADE OF GHOST SOLDIERS: Tanaka Ryokko, *Kyo no kaidan to nanafushigi*, 京の怪談と七不思議 [Kyoto's Ghost Stories and Seven Wonders] (Kyoto, Kyo wo kataru kai, 1959), 7–9.

49. THE GHOST SHIP SAILING ON A SEA OF MIST: Koma Toshio (駒敏郎), *Omi no Densetsu*, 近江の伝説 [Legends of Omi Province] (Tokyo: Kadokawa shoten, 1977), 159–62.

50. THE GHOST OF THE FUNERARY TABLET: Koma Toshio (駒敏郎), *Omi no Densetsu*, 近江の伝説 [Legends of Omi Province] (Tokyo: Kadokawa shoten, 1977), 152–54.

51. THE GHOST WHO BRINGS GOOD NEWS: Samukawa Tokikiyo, 寒川辰清, *Omi no kuni yochishiryaku*, 近江国輿地志略 [Geographical records of Omi Province] (Tokyo, Dainihon chishi taikei hakkokai, 1916), 3:188; description of Omi province (Shiga prefecture) written in 1730.

52. THE GHOST WHO SOUNDED THE ALARM: Koma Toshio (駒敏郎), *Omi no Densetsu*, 近江の伝説 [Legends of Omi Province] (Tokyo: Kadokawa shoten, 1977), 148–50.

53. THE EMPRESS WHO WANTED HER MORTAL REMAINS ABANDONED IN A BURIAL GROUND: Akisato Rito (秋里籬島), *Miyako meisho zu-e*, 都名所図会 [Illustrations of Famous Places in the Capital] (Tokyo: Koseisha, Shinshu Kyoto sosho, 1968), 222; travel guide to Kyoto and its surroundings published in 1780.

Tosanjin (桃山人), *Tosanjin yawa*, 桃山人夜話 [Night Stories of Tosanjin] (Tokyo: Kadokawa shoten, 2006), 28; collection of tales published in 1841.

54. THE DEAD WOMAN WHO DIDN'T WANT TO GO TO THE BURIAL GROUND: Anonymous, *Uji shui monogatari*, 宇治拾遺物語 [A Collection of Tales from Uji] (Tokyo: Shogakukan, 1996), 128–31; collection of tales written around the beginning of the thirteenth century.

Kitamura Kigin (北村季吟), *Tsuginefu*, 菟芸泥赴 [Rabbit Skills and Mud Journey] (Tokyo: Koseisha, Shinshu Kyoto sosho, 1968), 89–90; travel guide to Kyoto published in 1684.

55. THE GHOST WOMAN AND THE TAXI DRIVER: Anonymous, *Kuruma kara jokyaku kieta—Patoka mo kaidan-meita todokede ni asedaku*, 車から乗客消えたパトカーも"怪談"めいた届出に汗だく [Passenger Vanished from the Car—Even the Patrol Car Was Flustered by the Ghostly Report], in *Asahi Shinbun*, 朝日新聞 [Asahi Journal] (October 7, 1969, Kyoto city edition), 16.

56. STATUES FILLED WITH LOVE LETTERS: Hakue (白慧), *Sanshu meiseki shi*, 山州名跡志 [Famous Places of Yamashiro Province] (Tokyo: Koseisha, Shinshu Kyoto sosho, 1968), 71; travel guide to Kyoto published in 1711.

Akisato Rito (秋里籬島), *Miyako meisho zu-e*, 都名所図会 [Illustrations of Famous Places in the Capital] (Tokyo: Koseisha, Shinshu Kyoto sosho, 1968), 151.

57. THE CURSED STONE OF FUKAKUSA GENERAL: Inoue Yoritoshi (井上頼寿), *Kyoto minzokushi*, 京都民俗志 [Ethnological Study of Kyoto] (Tokyo: Heibonsha, 1968), 138; study of Kyoto legends published in 1933.

58. THE BATTLE OF THE GHOSTS: Kan-Ami (観阿弥), *Kayoi Komachi*, 通小町 [The Courtship of Komachi], in Sanari Kentaro (佐成謙太郎), *Yokyokutaiken*, 謡曲大観 [Great Anthology of Noh Plays] (Tokyo: Meiji Shoin, 1931), 2:761–74; Noh play written in the fourteenth century.

59. THE GHOST WHO WROTE POEMS: Kitamura Kigin (北村季吟), *Keishi junkenki*, 京師順見記 [Diary of My Visits to Kyoto's Masters] (Kyoto: Hosokan, Shiryo Kyoto ken-i bunki, 1991), 2:136–38; diary written around the year 1684.
60. THE DANCE OF IZUMI SHIKIBU'S GHOST: Zeami (世阿弥), *Toboku*, 東北 [Toboku Temple], in Sanari Kentaro (佐成謙太郎), *Yokyokutaiken*, 謡曲大観 [Great Anthology of Noh Plays] (Tokyo: Meiji Shoin, 1931), 4:2189–203; Noh play written in the fourteenth century.
61. THE GHOST WHO BECAME A BUDDHA: Anonymous, *Rakuyo Seiganji engi*, 洛陽誓願寺縁起 [The Story of the Founding of Seiganji Temple in the Capital] (Tokyo: Bussho kankokai hensan, 1913), 117:364–68; founding story written in 1751.
62. THE MONK BORN IN HIS MOTHER'S GRAVE: Tanaka Ryokko, *Kyo no kaidan to nanafushigi*, 京の怪談と七不思議 [Kyoto's Ghost Stories and Seven Wonders] (Kyoto, Kyo wo kataru kai, 1959), 132–34.
63. THE CANDY OF THE CHILD-REARING GHOST: Tanaka Ryokko, *Kyo no kaidan to nanafushigi*, 京の怪談と七不思議 [Kyoto's Ghost Stories and Seven Wonders] (Kyoto, Kyo wo kataru kai, 1959), 36–38.

    Takemura Toshinori (竹村俊則), *Showa Kyoto meisho zu-e*, 昭和京都名所図会 [Illustrated Guide to Famous Places in Kyoto from the Showa Era] (Osaka: Shinshindo, 1986), 2:283.
64. THE STORY OF THE WARRIOR WHOSE SON WAS BORN IN HIS WIFE'S GRAVE: Anonymous, *Kiizodanshu*, 奇異雑談集 [Collection of Various Strange Tales] (Tokyo: Iwanami bunko, Edo kaidan shu, 1989), 1:242–45; collection of tales compiled in 1687.
65. THE GHOST OF DAIKOKUJI TEMPLE: Tsutsumi Kunihiko (堤邦彦), *Kyoto kaidan junrei*, 京都怪談巡礼 [Pilgrimage in Kyoto's Spooky Places] (Kyoto: Kodansha, 2019), 184–85.
66. THE PINE TREE THAT STOPS CHILDREN FROM CRYING AT NIGHT: Inoue Yoritoshi (井上頼寿), *Kyoto minzokushi*, 京都民俗志 [Ethnological Study of Kyoto] (Tokyo: Heibonsha, 1968), 138; study of Kyoto legends published in 1933.
67. THE GHOST WHO DENOUNCED HER MURDERER: Tanaka Ryokko, *Kyo no kaidan to nanafushigi*, 京の怪談と七不思議 [Kyoto's Ghost Stories and Seven Wonders] (Kyoto, Kyo wo kataru kai, 1959), 16–19.

    Takemura Toshinori (竹村俊則), *Showa Kyoto meisho zu-e*, 昭和京都名所図会 [Illustrated Guide to Famous Places in Kyoto from the Showa Era] (Osaka: Shinshindo, 1986), 5:258–59.
68. THE GHOST OF THE GEISHA: Tanaka Ryokko, *Kyo no kaidan to nanafushigi*, 京の怪談と七不思議 [Kyoto's Ghost Stories and Seven Wonders] (Kyoto, Kyo wo kataru kai, 1959), 26–28.

69. THE MAN WHO FELL IN LOVE WITH A GHOST: Asai Ryoi (浅井了意), *Otogiboko*, 伽婢子 [Hand Puppets for Children] (Tokyo: Iwanami Shoten, Shin Nihon Koten Bungaku Taikei, 2001), 75:76–85.
70. THE MONK WHO BROUGHT HIS DEAD FATHER BACK TO LIFE: Gento (玄棟), *Sangoku denki*, 三国伝記 [Buddhism Stories of the Three Countries] (Tokyo: Bussho hakkokai, Heibonsha, 1912), 148:144–46; collection of Buddhist tales set in India, China, and Japan, written in 1407.
71. THE BRIDGE WHERE A THOUSAND DEAD WERE BROUGHT BACK TO LIFE: Akisato Rito (秋里籬島), *Miyako meisho zu-e shui*, 都名所図会拾遺 [More Famous Places in the Capital] (Tokyo: Koseisha, Shinshu Kyoto sosho, 1968), 34; travel guide to Kyoto and its surroundings published in 1786.
72. THE PLUM TREE THAT FLEW TO REJOIN ITS MASTER: Anonymous, *Tenjin-ki*, 天神記 [The Story of Tenjin] (Tokyo: Shinto Koten Kenkyusho, Shinto Taikei–jinja-hen, 1992), 11:103–30; biography of Sugawara no Michizane written in 1194.
73. THE MONK SAIGYO AND THE SPIRIT OF THE CHERRY TREE: Zeami (世阿弥), *Saigyo Zakura*, 西行桜 [Saigyo Cherry Tree], in Sanari Kentaro (佐成謙太郎), *Yokyokutaiken*, 謡曲大観 [Great Anthology of Noh Plays] (Tokyo: Meiji Shoin, 1931), 2:1167–81; Noh play written in the fourteenth century.

    Akisato Rito (秋里籬島), *Miyako meisho zu-e*, 都名所図会 [Illustrations of Famous Places in the Capital] (Tokyo: Koseisha, Shinshu Kyoto sosho, 1968), 219; travel guide to Kyoto and its surroundings published in 1780.
74. SAIGYO CREATES A MAN FROM CORPSE PARTS: Anonymous, *Senjusho*, 撰集抄 [Tales from Renunciation] (Tokyo: Iwanami shoten, 1970), 157–59; collection of Buddhist tales from the early Kamakura period (1185–1333).
75. THE SEAL OF THE KING OF HELL: Anonymous, *Yamashiro meisho tera yashiro monogatari*, 山城名所寺社物語 [Tales of the Temples and Shrines of Yamashiro Province] (Tokyo: Koseisha, Shinshu Kyoto sosho, 1967), 2:429; travel guide to Kyoto and its surroundings published in 1757.
76. THE WARRIOR WHO BECAME THE INSTRUMENT OF THE KING OF HELL: Senbon Enmado Dainenbutsu Kyogen Hozonkai (千本ゑんま堂大念仏狂言保存会), *Senbon Enmado kyogen*, 千本ゑんま堂狂言 [Senbon Enmado Plays] (Kyoto: Injoji, n.d.), 19.
77. TAKAMURA AND THE GHOST OF HIS HALF-SISTER: Anonymous, *Takamura monogatari*, 篁物語 [The Tale of Takamura], in Ishihara Shohei (石原昭平), dir., *Takamura monogatari Shinko*, 篁物語新講 [A New Commentary on the Tale of Takemura] (Tokyo: Musashino shoten, 1977), 3–77; tale written in the tenth century.

78. THE BELL THAT CAN BE HEARD TO THE DEPTHS OF HELL: Anonymous, *Konjaku monogatari*, 今昔物語 [Anthology of Tales Old and New] (Tokyo, Shogakukan, Shinpen Nihon koten bungaku zenshu, 1999), 38:540–41.
79. THE MONK WHO CURED THE KING OF HELL: Asai Ryoi (浅井了意), *Dekisai kyo miyage*, 出来斎京土産 [Dekisai's Souvenirs of Kyoto] (Tokyo: Koseisha, Shinshu Kyoto sosho, 1967), 17–18; travel guide to Kyoto published in 1677.
80. THE SIX-ARMED JIZO OF CHIEKO-IN TEMPLE: Tanaka Ryokko (田中緑紅), *Senryo no tsuji*, 千両の辻 [Senryo Crossroads] (Kyoto: Ryokko zensho, 1958), 32–35.
81. HOW MURASAKI SHIKIBU WAS SAVED FROM ETERNAL DAMNATION: Fujiwara no Nobuzane (藤原信実), *Ima monogatari*, 今物語 [Stories of Present Times] (Tokyo: Yuhodo bunko, 1922), 479–80; collection of tales compiled around the year 1240.

    Anonymous, *Genji kuyo*, 源氏供養 [A Mass for Prince Genji], in Sanari Kentaro (佐成謙太郎), *Yokyokutaiken*, 謡曲大観 [Great Anthology of Noh Plays] (Tokyo: Meiji Shoin, 1931), 2:1025–41; Noh play written around the year 1488.
82. JIZO AND THE PRISONERS SENTENCED TO DEATH: Takahashi Seii, *Kyoto-fu chishi: Kii gunmura-shi*, 京都府地誌：紀伊郡村誌 [History of the Villages of Kii District, Prefecture of Kyoto] (Kyoto: Rinzen Shoten, 1972), 166–67; history of the Kii district published in 1915.
83. JIZO SAVES A WICKED MAN: Tanaka Ryokko (田中緑紅), *Mibu Dainenbutsu*, 壬生大念仏 [Mibu Plays] (Kyoto: Mibu-dera jimusho, 1943), 26–27.
84. A SUMO CONTEST IN HELL: Tanaka Ryokko (田中緑紅), *Mibu Dainenbutsu*, 壬生大念仏 [Mibu Plays] (Kyoto: Mibu-dera jimusho, 1943), 17–18.
85. THE ABBOT WHO BECAME A TENGU: Miyoshi no Tameyasu (三善為康), *Shui-ojo-den*, 拾遺往生伝 [Continued Collected Biographies of Rebirth] (Tokyo: Bussho kankokai hensan, 1913), 117:108–10; biographies compiled in 1102.

    Anonymous, *Toeizan Kan-ei-ji Ganzan Daishi Engi*, 東叡山寛永寺元三大師縁起 [Legend of the Great Monk Ganzan of Toeizan Kaneiji Temple] (Tokyo: Hakubunkan, Kozojitsuden, 1906), 10:904–5; biography of Ryogen written in 1680.
86. THE ONE-EYED AND ONE-LEGGED GHOST: Koma Toshio (駒敏郎), *Omi no Densetsu*, 近江の伝説 [Legends of Omi Province] (Tokyo: Kadokawa shoten, 1977), 146–48.
87. TEMPLES WITH BLOOD-STAINED CEILINGS: Inoue Yoritoshi (井上頼寿), *Kyo no nanafushigi*, 京の七不思議 [Seven Wonders of Kyoto] (Kyoto: Kyoto kiroku sosho, 1944), 9.

ABOUT THE AUTHOR

ÉRIC FAURE is a specialist in Japanese legends and has been living in Kyoto for over thirty years. With a doctoral thesis on the motifs found in Japanese legends, he has published numerous works on the subject. The idea for this collection of legends came from his daughter, who frequently asked him to recount the stories he had uncovered during his fieldwork.

Cover art: "うらめしさう urameshisaw -resentment" by Ranryoutei Shibai 蘭陵亭子梅